LEONORA C

(born 1917) was the daughter
an Irish mother. Her childh
mansion, and she was educat
to Florence to be "finished"
1936, and a disquetingly fera
found in her story, *The Debutante*. Now her ramny
her desire to paint, and she went to an influential school the same year as the first Surrealist exhibition in London. This electrified her, and soon afterwards she met Max Ernst, a leader of the movement. She was nineteen, he was forty-six and married. They eloped, first to Paris, then to the South of France: her painful difficulties with Ernst's wife are brilliantly transmuted in the story *Little Francis*. There, both painted, exhibiting in Paris, while she started writing. In 1939 Ernst was arrested as an enemy alien, but she procured his release. But when, the following year, he was imprisoned again Leonora descended into the madness recorded in *Down Below*. Subjected to horrifying treatment in a Madrid asylum, she was rescued by her nanny who arrived in a submarine. Leonora met her first husband, a Mexican diplomat, in Lisbon, and went with him to New York. Separated amicably, she then married Imre Weisz, a Hungarian photographer, and settled in Mexico City. They had two sons, and she continued her work as a surrealist painter and writer, as well as writing and designing for the theatre. Disillusioned by the savage reaction to student unrest in 1968 she left Mexico with her sons, but though she returned she was horrified by the later handling of the 1985 earthquake and moved to New York.

Leonora Carrington now divides her time between Chicago and Mexico City. She maintains her interest in all forms of arcane knowledge, and is a disciple of the Tibetan lamas. The richness and depth of her imagination have led to her recognition as one of the liveliest talents in Surrealism.

Virago also publishes *The House of Fear: Notes from Down Below*.

VIRAGO
MODERN
CLASSIC
NUMBER
326

Leonora Carrington

THE SEVENTH HORSE

AND OTHER STORIES

Translations by Kathrine Talbot and Anthony Kerrigen

WITH A NEW INTRODUCTION BY
MARINA WARNER

Published by VIRAGO PRESS Limited 1989
20-23 Mandela Street, Camden Town, London NW1 0HQ

First published by E.P. Dutton 1988
Copyright © 1988 Leonora Carrington
Translation Copyright © 1988 Leonora Carrington
Notes and Compilation Copyright © E.P. Dutton
Line Art Copyright © Leonora Carrington
Introduction Copyright © Marina Warner 1989

This edition published in association with E.P. Dutton

The stories "The Sisters", "White Rabbits", "Waiting", "The Seventh Horse", and "The Neutral Man" were published in French or in French translation in slightly different form, in the volume *La Débutante* © 1978 by Editions Flammarion.

The novel version of *The Stone Door* was first published, in French translation, as *La Porte de pierre* © 1976 by Editions Flammarion.

The play *Judith* was written for Leonora Cardiff in Mexico City in 1961, copyright © Leonora Carrington 1989.

Publisher's Note: These stories are works of fiction. Names, characters, places, and incidents either are the product of the author's imagination or are used fictionally, and any resemblance to actual persons, living or dead, events, or locales is entirely coincidental.

All rights reserved

British Library Cataloguing in Publication Data
Carrington, Leonora
 The seventh horse. (Virago modern classic)
 I. Title
 823'.912 [F]

ISBN 1-85381-049-5

Printed by Cox and Wyman Ltd,
Reading, Berkshire

Contents

Introduction

I THE SEVENTH HORSE

As They Rode Along the Edge, 3
The Skeleton's Holiday, 16
Pigeon, Fly! 19
The Three Hunters, 30
Monsieur Cyril de Guindre, 34
The Sisters, 42
Cast Down by Sadness, 50
White Rabbits, 56
Waiting, 61
The Seventh Horse, 66

II THE STONE DOOR

The Stone Door, 75

III THE NEUTRAL MAN

The neutral Man, 145
A Mexican Fairy tale, 151
Et in bellicus lunarum medicalis, 159
My Flannel Knickers, 165
The Invention of Mole, A Play, 169
The Happy Corpe Story, 176
How to Start a Pharmaceuticals Business, 181
My Mother Is a Cow, 187
"Judith.", 193
A Note on the Texts, 205

Introduction

Leonora Carrington wrote the first group of stories collected here in a stone Provençal farmhouse which still stands, on a hill above the deep valley of the Ardèche, east of the great gorges and natural arches carved by the spate of the river. Behind the house a fragmentary carving of a horse lies on the broken wall; another white horse's head bares teeth on the balustrade of the terrace. Inside, the owners told me — though they would not let me in — there are cupboards and doors also painted by her. The inner walls of the courtyard are decorated in relief and painted too, though the pigments have faded and the concrete and plaster are eroding. The outside rampart wall, facing the unpaved incline to the house, was sculpted by Max Ernst with towering fantastic creatures: a willowy young woman, with a pigeon's face and a fish on top of her head, holds a curled cat-like totem in her left hand; beside her, a huge hieratic beaked monster raises his arms, while a smaller winged demon issues dancing from the wall beneath him. The beaked

INTRODUCTION

giant is easy to recognize as Max Ernst's alter ego, Loplop, Prince of Birds, and his partner as the mythologized figure of the surreal muse, incarnate at that time for Ernst in Leonora Carrington; the horse is a recurrent figure of release and power in Carrington's imagery.

The three years they lived together in Saint Martin d'Ardèche was a time of inspiration for both of them, and, after Max Ernst finally separated from his wife Marie-Berthe Aurenche, a period of happiness on the whole for Leonora. The novella 'Little Francis', published in *The House of Fear*, the companion volume to this collection, was inspired by earlier torments. When she met Max Ernst in London, in 1937, she was studying at the Amédée Ozenfant Academy in London, though her painting and drawing, even at the early age of nineteen, already departed from the Purist discipline of her teacher and her fellow students. She was already exploring her inner world, the "hypnagogic vision" where consciousness and the unconscious merge, and she recognized, at the first Surrealist show in London, immediate kinship with the movement. She exhibited twice with the group, in Paris in 1937 and in Amsterdam in 1938, and though most of the paintings have since been lost, their titles ("What shall we do tomorrow, Aunt Amelia?" and "The Silent Assassin") reveal their kinship with the complex of autobiography, invention, playfulness and mystery, of the comic and the gruesome in the stories she began writing at the same time, under the enthusiastic gaze of Ernst and his circle.

She chose to write in French — the language she shared in common with Max Ernst and with many of their friends. The first results were published in two tiny volumes, illustrated by Ernst's collages, now reissued in *The House of Fear*. But many other short stories had not yet been published, and were scattered when the fall of France drove Leonora Carrington and Max Ernst, as well as many French nationals among the Surrealists — Marcel Duchamp, André Breton — to flee the invaders and their sympathizers. The stories appear here for the first time in English.

INTRODUCTION

Carrington tells a tale in a unique tone of voice, that deadpan innocence of the masters of the macabre. The simplicity of her syntax, and the cool sequential structure of her narratives ("She sucked, sucked for long minutes . . . She threw back her head and crowed like a cock. Afterwards she hid the corpse in the drawer of a chest.") owes something to her adoption of French, a language she had studied only at home with a French governess and in English convent schools. But unfamiliarity does not cramp her style; rather it sharpens the flavour of ingenuous knowingness which so enchanted the Surrealists. Like Gisèle Prassinos, a child poet whom the Surrealists idolized — rather to her bewilderment — or Violette Nozières, who murdered her aunt because she wanted to go to a party and had been forbidden to, or the convulsionary women of St Médard in the eighteenth century and the hysterics Charcot had photographed in attitudes of despair and desire, Leonora Carrington was cast by André Breton, Paul Eluard and others in the circle around Max Ernst as a kind of hierodule — a holy and erotic nymph who uniquely knew by instinct certain delinquent mysteries which old men — or older men — could not reach without her help.

Such a calling was not considerate, and the stories of 1937–40 reflect its exactions. Yet it was also a calling that appealed to Leonora Carrington, who was the daughter of a Lancashire textile tycoon and was suffocated by a childhood in the nursery under Nanny's rules, and later by the regulations of nuns in various convent schools. Like a Henry James heroine, she had been "finished" at Miss Penrose's Academy in Florence, where she at least came to know and love the Italian painters of the *trecento* and *quattrocento*, and had "come out" in the débutante season, been given a showy ball at the Ritz by her mother and father and presented at court, to King George V. She was destined for a life of prosperous tedium.

A squib like "The Three Hunters" satirizes the pursuits of her class, most particularly her father and brothers, who were keen sportsmen; a story like "The Neutral Man" the stifling social round. But by contrast, stories also reflect the pleasure

INTRODUCTION

— even the intense pleasure — Carrington found in her changed surroundings. The peculiar austerities of the English propertied class, the filthy tepid food and the cold draughty rooms, the distant and yet crushing family relationships were behind her: beneath a shivery, Poe-like surface, the stories vibrate with Carrington's deep relish for warmth and colour, abundant and delicious herbs and foods, spectacular and unbridled clothes; they show her revelling in wildness, in smells — cinnamon and musk — in the release of the imagination, and the discovery of physical sensation. Virginia Fur, a quintessential Carrington heroine, discovers passion with Igname the boar:

> Virginia . . . spat hard into the fire, a curse on the words of love. She was afraid of Igname's beauty . . . With a savage cry . . . she jumped around Igname, tearing her hair out by the roots; Igname stood up and together they danced a dance of ecstasy. The cats caterwauled and stuck their claws into Igname and Virginia, who disappeared under a mountain of cats . . .

The nuns who expelled Carrington from school probably judged right: they saw something in her, something she identifies as the element of Fire in "The Stone Door", and they recognized that their kind of holy water would not douse it.

But the overweeningness of Ernst's ego (according to Peggy Guggenheim's memoirs, he got cross when someone suggested Napoleon was the greater genius), combined with the cruelty of Surrealist principles, infuse many scenes with a kind of terror that rises above the usual range of the macabre tale. Célestin of Airlines-Drues in "Pigeon, Fly!" wears the striped socks and cloak of feathers in which Carrington dressed Ernst in the portrait she painted of him. Here he is a frightening, not a comic vampire. He asks the narrator to paint a picture of his dead wife — who turns out to be herself. Art becomes a sentence of death, or at least a prophecy of a fatal conclusion in this story; like Helen, who wove the story of Troy and her part in its destruction into the tapestry she was making during the siege, Leonora's artist protagonist finds her own fate in the

INTRODUCTION

canvas. "Waiting", with its opening sentence describing the fight of two old women, "like angry black lobsters", and its concluding glimpse of carnal knowledge — "I cut his toenails myself . . ." — catches the lingering anguish of jealousy very vividly from the point of view of a young woman who was made to stand by while Ernst carried out what Leonora calls elsewhere his "genital responsibilities".

Although they collaborated on the transformation of the house in Saint Martin d'Ardèche, Ernst did not encourage Leonora's art as much as her writing. It is easy to imagine, and perhaps not unjust, that he could annexe her stories more fruitfully, and certainly the works of this period incorporate many Carrington motifs — horse-headed figures, journeys through craggy and forested landscapes out of the fairytale reading of her youth, mane-headed young women, emaciated ghouls.[1] The Irish faery lore and Edwardian nursery moralities which formed the staple of her childhood education meshed with the Surrealist web of sinister romancing and occult games, and her writings were eagerly read. She collaborated on a picaresque novel, *L'homme qui a perdu son squelette*, with Duchamp, Eluard, Ernst, Prassinos and others, under the editorship of Hans Arp: she contributed the chapter "The Skeleton on Holiday", published here.[2]

Max Ernst, however, also expected his *femme enfant* to be a *femme de ménage*, and to provide for the guests who flowed in from Paris and London and other points and stayed to talk and play, dress up, quarrel, tease one another, explore and feast and drink — the house had its own vineyard. There is a series of photographs, taken by Lee Miller when she came to stay with Roland Penrose, which show Leonora in the kitchen, wearing a lace blouse and a long skirt that Leonor Fini, one of Max Ernst's "pets" — as Peggy Guggenheim later sharply put it — had bought for Leonora in the Puces in Paris. Later, on the same contact sheet, Ernst cradles his child-bride — she was forty years his junior — beaming to himself. What emerges from Leonora's look, from the vigour of her head's tilt and the steady expression of her eyes, is that she was holding her own,

INTRODUCTION

but that it was hard, for she was being wrapped up in so much, posed in borrowed clothes, given a new language, cast to perform the role of the marvellous erotic and farouche child. Leonor Fini painted her on several occasions at this time as a kind of Pre-Raphaelite Joan of Arc, in black armour, engaged in enigmatic rites.

The charades, the fancy dress, the interplay of roles, both adoptive and prescribed, influence the fantastic metamorphoses in the stories: Arabelle Pegase with her "dress made entirely of the heads of cats" represents another aspect of the immortal Fear whose house Carrington visited in an early tale. Carrington is often Gothic in her humour, but the horror has its face towards real, endured experience. In this, she brings to mind Mary Shelley, who also fantasized improbable things and managed to survive Romanticism. Similarly, Carrington managed to live through Surrealism.

Leonora Carrington herself never bothered about the whereabouts of the early stories collected here, indeed, she had completely forgotten that she had written them when the manuscripts surfaced again recently — some, for instance, among the papers of Jimmy Ernst at his death in New York in 1986. He had been sent ahead to safety in New York in June 1938, and was there to meet his famous father when Max Ernst landed in the summer of 1940 in the company of Peggy Guggenheim, the gallant, open-handed and often giddy-headed enthusiast who helped so many artists by buying their works or otherwise extending them her patronage. Jimmy Ernst, an artist himself, was Max's only child and the son of his first marriage to Lou Straus, who was Jewish (unlike Ernst). She did not leave France in time; she was deported from a Paris detention camp to Auschwitz on one of the last trains, on 30 June 1944.[3]

"Down Below", Leonora Carrington's autobiographical account of the crisis she suffered when France fell, describes her derangement after Max Ernst's arrest, the scattering of her friends and the panic of defeat. She gave the house and all its contents into the safe keeping of one of the villagers before leaving herself for Spain; when Max Ernst, before his final escape from France, found his way back to Saint Martin, he was denied access to the property and could not even rescue their pictures. For a while, Leonora Carrington went mad; she was institutionalized in Spain and harshly treated, as "Down Below" describes; from there she made her way to Lisbon, where she married Renato Leduc, a Mexican diplomat whom she had met in Picasso's studio in Paris — he was a bullfighting crony of the artist's. Peggy Guggenheim meanwhile had come to the rescue of many of the Surrealists who were stranded in Marseilles,[4] including Max Ernst, with whom she fell painfully in love. With her former husband Laurence Vail, his wife the writer Kay Boyle, half a dozen children from various marriages and one or two lovers of both kinds in tow (including Ernst, by now) the *ménage à treize* arrived in Lisbon to take the Clipper, the first of the transatlantic passenger planes. There Ernst again met Leonora, who recalls that after her recent ordeals she found herself free at last from the spell Loplop's ravishing charms had once held for her. Peggy Guggenheim observes, in her memoirs:

> She had written about her adventures and they were really terrifying. God knows how she ever got out of the place [the asylum] but after she did, she met the Mexican in Lisbon and he looked after her. He was like a father to her. Max was always like a baby and couldn't be anyone's father. I think she felt she needed a father more than anything else, so as to give her some stability and prevent her from going mad again.[5]

Leonora feels that Peggy Guggenheim has been much maligned in reputation, that she was remarkably noble and generous; in Lisbon, although Max Ernst's clear continuing attachment to Leonora caused Peggy Guggenheim much pain, she offered to pay for her passage to New York on the plane with them. Leonora refused, and when the Guggenheim household left, on 13 July 1941, "we passed over the American boat that was carrying Leonora and her husband to New York".[6]

Their interwoven lives continued in the city: the Surrealists in exile produced papers, journals (*VVV* and *View*) and, with Peggy Guggenheim's help, exhibitions. Leonora Carrington published drawings, paintings and stories (for instance "The Seventh Horse" and "Waiting", in this collection); she illustrated "*L'Ame Sœur — (L'androgyne)*" ["The Soul Sister — The Androgyne"] in a Bretonian alphabet, with a delicate evocation of the cats, horses and tempestuous embraces that recur in her stories;[7] she answered the questionnaires Breton loved devizing, giving the Unicorn as her favourite mythological figure, followed by the Werewolf, the Vampire, the Succubus-Incubus. She placed Narcissus last, and — even more significantly — Galatea, Pygmalion's creation, last but one.[8]

In 1941, with Renato Leduc — "a nice man", she says now, "neglectful, but nice" — Leonora Carrington left New York for Mexico, where she was to remain for the next forty years almost without interruption until her move back to New York in 1985. "The Stone Door", and the stories in the second half of this volume, were all written there, some of them in Spanish.

André Breton had visited Mexico in 1938 and declared, on his return, "*La Mexique est surréaliste en elle-même*", with its mythic past, cult of the dead, art of the fantastic and astonishing landscapes. Many of the group fled there during the War, creating another constellation of artists and writers in exile, including Benjamin Péret, who was married to the artist Remedios Varo. Above all other friends she made in Mexico, Carrington became closest to Remedios Varo, and the two artists' imagery shows the profound and intimate exchanges that took place between them as they evolved together a mystical image of female creativity.[9] Varo's unexpected death at the age of fifty-four in 1963 was the hardest loss Leonora Carrington has suffered, and she still speaks of it with intense distress.

The era of New Age spirituality makes it hard to invoke the journeys of the mind Carrington undertook, with Varo also questing at her side. The commercialized hokum of West Coast mysticism since the sixties — the crystals and amulets and synthetic quoting from the world's adepts — and the widespread decadence of mythological borrowing (mostly from Jung

INTRODUCTION

and Joseph Campbell) make it difficult to find a vocabulary for Carrington's clusters and webs of symbols that does not sound like a circular from the Personal Growth Movement. Like André Breton, who elevated the idea of random chance into a principle of art, Carrington is fascinated by divination, magic, horoscopes, and sorcery of all kinds. Although the metaphysical search in Carrington is undertaken in earnest, it is never carried out with solemnity. Although at one time she was deeply involved in alchemy, she brings to its tabulations the light fantastic touch of a fairytale wizard rather than the bombast of a guru. She is never shallow; although she believes that there is something to find — the Philosophic Stone — she does not believe that she has special powers to reach it, nor that she ever will. Aware of the depths, she often laughs at her ambitions too, as in the short and melancholoy plea for awareness of the female principle, "My Mother is a Cow".

"The Stone Door", the centrepiece of this book, is an alchemical and zodiacal fable, but it is also a love story, in which Carrington is the little girl who appears in the dreams of the Hungarian orphan and is united with him after he has passed into Mesopotamia — the poetic land that stands here for Mexico. In 1946, at the time she was writing "The Stone Door", Leonora Carrington married Imre (Csizi) Weisz, a newspaper photographer who had left Hungary with Robert Capa, scraped a living in Paris with him, and then left to take part in the Spanish Civil War. On their return, as Capa became more and more successful, Weisz came to run his studio in Paris; the war swept him up, along with so many others, and deposited him in the comparative haven of Mexico City, where the government offered citizenship to political refugees.

"The Stone Door" transforms her husband's story, his poverty and his wanderings, into a parable about a young seeker — Zacharias — who absorbs into himself the wisdom of Jewish cabbalistic mysticism, symbolized by the mummy of the old king which first shrinks, then, soaked in water, swells again. He first cuts from the skin a pair of trousers for a giant, then uses them as a sail on his goat-ship to sail across the subterranean sea to join with the White Child, who is also Fire, fusing in herself the red and white of the alchemical process. The novella dares to shift tone constantly: from liturgical invocation to nursery-rhyme ironies, from autobiographical narrative to allegorical fable, in the daffy but pointed Irish tradition that begins with *Gulliver's Travels* and continues with the eldritch fun of James Stephens at the turn of the century. Jane Miller reviewed "The Stone Door" in the *Times Literary Supplement* when it was first published in English, in 1977: "In spite of all its waywardness and intimations of profundity," she wrote, "the novel is finally a good deal more like a prettily embroidered sampler than some gravely worked cabbalistic banner, for its eclectic, not to say magpie, snatching at bright detail and unexplained incident is controlled by a tastefulness and sense of design which are old-fashioned and charming rather than portentous".[10]

Leonora Carrington was possessed by the need to paint in Mexico, and after the war she worked above all as a visual artist, setting down on wood panels or on canvas her waking dreams. Her imagery, wherever gathered, becomes personal: the bark which appears at the close of "The Stone Door" reappears in different shape many times in her art. It symbolizes her transition from nymph to mother, in such paintings as "*L'amor che move'l sole e le altre stelle*", dated two days before the birth of her first child, Gabriel, and again in the magical painted "*bateau-berceau*", the rocking cradle a Mexican sculptor, Jose Hórna, made with her for the baby.[11] Other motifs, like heaped banquets of exotic and paradoxical ingredients, recur in her imagery and in her life; she continued to follow the inspiration of the Surrealists in this respect: that life itself was far more marvellous than art, and art need only try to fix life for a moment. Her inventions in the kitchen became famous; in Breton's *Anthologie de l'humour noir*, in which Carrington keeps company with Swift and Jarry, Breton recalls a rather special hare with oysters Carrington once prepared.[12] She also writes often about dream spreads, commenting for instance on a siren in "The Temptation of St Anthony", painted in 1946:

> The bald-headed girl in the red dress combines female charm and the delights of the table — you will notice that she is engaged in making an unctuous broth of (let us say) lobsters, mushrooms, fat turtle, spring chicken, ripe tomatoes, gorgonzola cheese, milk chocolate, onions and tinned peaches. The mixture of these ingredients has overflowed and taken on a greenish and sickly hue to the fevered vision of St. Anthony, whose daily meal consists of withered grass and tepid water with an occasional locust by way of an orgy.[13]

At the time, Leonora Carrington was living mainly on ice-cream, "which was the cheapest thing you could get", so the saint's imaginings have a certain urgency (those tinned peaches tell of wartime very clearly). She was paid $200 for the picture, which was "a considerable fortune at that time".

In the Carrington universe, there are no hierarchical differences between the cooking pot and the alchemist's alembic, between the knitting of a jumper and the weaving of the soul from "cosmic wool", between beasts and people — though animals impress her more than humans, on the whole. ("Dogs are such saints", she will say. "They make a point of understanding us, they sacrifice their intelligence to ours.") One activity or being is as serious as the other, all are sublime, yet all are of this world too, and therefore fundamentally comic. She has said that "dailiness" is very important to her, and that the making of art is like "making strawberry jam — really carefully and well".

The wheel, the island, bounded and circular and enclosing forms at once safe and confining, return again and again in her stories and her images, and within their constrictions energies spark and fly as in a magnetic field — the energies of questors, of wild and maned or feathered creatures who bring forth out of themselves, springing surprises, changing face, transmuting matter. Carrington is an instinctive follower of Pythagoras, who taught that all matter is related and even the humblest forms are owed respect. Stones are no more inert than fire; only another element, equally capable of transformation. Edward

INTRODUCTION

James, the Surrealist patron whose rich collection of Carringtons was recently sold when his Sussex house, Monkton, was put up for auction, wrote of Leonora's images that they were "not merely painted, they are brewed".[14] It is an apt choice of word, and describes her writings too: these small and concentrated potions in which the oddest elements from metaphysics and fantasy, daily routine and material life are simmered together and mischievously served up. Her witchcraft, which had so enchanted the Surrealists (Breton, typically, discussing Michelet's *"La Sorcière"*, praised the author particularly for pointing out that witches were often young and beautiful!) entered another phase in the surroundings of *lo real maravilloso americano*, as the Cuban Alejo Carpentier has called the culture of Latin America — the marvellous American reality. Alongside the painters Rufino Tamayo, Frida Kahlo, Gunther Gerczso and Remedios Varo, Leonora Carrington came to seem a medium of the Latin American imagination: in the early days of theatre in Mexico City, she wrote plays — *Pénélope*,[15] *Judith*, *The Story of the Last Egg* — and designed masks and costumes for these and other plays; she was commissioned to celebrate the people of Chiapas, descendants of the Aztecs, in a mural for the Museum of Anthropology.[16] She continued to defy traditions, too, opening her house to meetings during the student action of the sixties and participating in the beginnings of the women's movement. When the government opened fire on demonstrators in 1968, killing over six hundred of them, Leonora left Mexico with her two sons. They returned, but she has never recovered from the disillusion of those days.

In her story about the Aztecs' invention of *mole*, the savoury chocolate sauce of Mexican cuisine, they boil the Archbishop, a typical Carrington figure of insufferable pomposity; in her play *Judith*, written for her friend Leonora Cardiff in 1961 and published here for the first time, the biblical heroine cuts off the head of another grotesque tyrant, "Issachar her great bearded father", who has brutally ordered Judith's suitor Esrom, "Rape her tonight, you fool, and carry her off." In the earlier writing of Leonora Carrington the figure of the all-

INTRODUCTION

powerful father fascinates, and the authoritative male — the malignant Célestin of Airlines-Drues, the shadowy Fernando of *Waiting* — is capable of anything, and binds his child-bride to the fate he chooses for her. But in these later, often harshly comic stories, the protagonist clears the path on which she makes her way. Leonora Carrington recently told me that the story of Jacob wrestling with the angel is her favourite from the Bible. There is a ladder there, in the background of the biblical account, waiting to be climbed to heaven, but for the moment the here and now demands struggle. "We have to hang on", she says. "Even if the angel cries, 'Let me go, let me go.' We don't listen. No. We have to hang on." Through the journeys and the struggles which these stories transcribe and transform, Leonora Carrington has held on to a fierce angel, sometimes laughing wickedly, sometimes fighting mad.

Marina Warner, London, 1989

All quotations of Leonora Carrington are from conversations over 1986–88, for which I should like to express my thanks. My gratitude too to Paul de Angelis, Leonora Carrington's American editor, who provided me with much helpful information; to Janice Helland, whose forthcoming article 'Surrealism and Esoteric Feminism in the Art of Leonora Carrington' will be published soon in the *Canadian Art Review*; to the work of Gloria Feman Orenstein; and to Whitney Chadwick.

1. See Angelica Rudenstine, *The Peggy Guggenheim Collection, Venice* (New York, 1985), pp. 306–18, for a discussion of the cross-fertilization of ideas in some of Ernst's great paintings, like 'The Robing of the Bride' 1940.
2. Plastique, Nos 4–5. (Paris–New York, 1939).
3. Jimmy Ernst, *A Not-So-Still Life* (New York, 1984) gives a telling account of being the son of Max Ernst.
4. See catalogue, *La Planète affolée. Surréalisme, dispersion et influences 1938–1947*, Musée de Marseille, 1986. (Paris, 1986).
5. Peggy Guggenheim, *Out of This Century: Confessions of an Art Addict*, (New York, 1946), p.239.

INTRODUCTION

6. ibid., p.254.
7. André Breton (ed.), *First Papers of Surrealism. Coordinating Council of French Relief Societies* (New York, 1942).
8. *VVV*, 1, June 1942 (New York).
9. See Janet A. Kaplan, *Unexpected Journeys: The Art and Life of Remedios Varo* (London, 1988).
10. Jane Miller, 'A surreal sampler', *Times Literary Supplement*, (London, 1977).
11. Catalogue, *Los Surrealistos en Mexico*. Museo de arte nacional. (Mexico City, 1986).
12. André Breton (ed.), *Anthologie de l'humour noir* (Paris, 1950), pp.333–37.
13. Catalogue, *The Temptation of St. Anthony. Bel Ami International Competition and Exhibition of New Paintings by Eleven American and European Artists 1946–7* (Washington DC, 1947).
14. Edward James, Introduction to *Leonora Carrington: A retrospective exhibition*, Center for Inter American Relations, New York, 1976.
15. Leonora Carrington, *Pénélope*, in *Cahiers Renaud Barrault. Deuxième trimestre*, 1969; pp.70 ff.

See also Marina Warner's Introduction to Leonora Carrington's *The House of Fear*, Virago, London, 1989.

I
THE
SEVENTH
HORSE

As They Rode Along the Edge

As they rode along the edge, the brambles drew back their thorns like cats retracting their claws.

This was something to see: fifty black cats and as many yellow ones, and then her, and one couldn't really be altogether sure that she was a human being. Her smell alone threw doubt on it—a mixture of spices and game, the stables, fur and grasses.

Riding a wheel, she took the worst roads, between precipices, across trees. Someone who's never travelled on a wheel would think it difficult, but she was used to it.

Her name was Virginia Fur, she had a mane of hair yards long and enormous hands with dirty nails; yet the citizens of the mountain respected her and she too always showed a deference for their customs. True, the people up there were plants, animals, birds; otherwise things wouldn't have been the same. Of course, she had to put up with being insulted by the cats at times, but she insulted them back just as loudly and in the same language. She, Virginia Fur, lived in a village long abandoned by human beings. Her house had holes all over, holes she'd pierced for the fig tree that grew in the kitchen.

Apart from the garage for the wheel, all the rooms were occupied by cats; there were fourteen in all.

Every night she went out on her wheel to hunt; whatever their respect, the mountain beasts didn't let themselves be killed as easily as all that, so several days per week she was forced to live on lost sheepdog, and occasionally mutton or child, though this last was rare since no one ever came there.

It was one night in autumn when she found to her surprise that she was being followed by footsteps heavier than those of an animal; the footsteps came rapidly.

The sickening smell of a human entered her nostrils; she pushed her wheel as hard as she could, to no avail. She stopped when her pursuer was beside her.

"I am Saint Alexander," he said. "Get down, Virginia Fur, I want to talk to you."

Who could this individual be who dared address her so familiarly? An individual, furthermore, of a rare filthiness, there in his monk's habit. The cats kept a contemptuous distance.

"I want to ask you to enter the Church," he went on. "I hope to win your soul."

"My soul?" replied Virginia. "I sold it a long time ago for a kilo of truffles. Go ask Igname the Boar for it."

He considered this across the whole length of his greenish face. Finally he said with a cunning smile, "I have a pretty little church not far from here. It's a marvel of location, and what comfort! My friend! Every night there are apparitions, and you really have to see the graveyard, really, it's a dream! There's a view of the surrounding mountains for a hundred miles and more. Come with me, Virginia." He continued in a tender voice. "I promise you, on the head of little baby Jesus, that you'll have a beautiful spot in my graveyard, right next to the statue of the Holy Virgin. (And believe me that's the very best place.) I'll conduct your funeral rites myself. Imagine, funeral rites celebrated by the great Saint Alexander!"

The cats growled impatiently, but Virginia was thinking it over. She'd heard there was good dinnerware in churches, some of it made of gold, and the rest would always have its uses. She alerted the cats in their language, and told the saint, "Sir, what you're telling me interests me to a certain degree, but it is against my principles to interrupt the hunt. If I come with you, I shall have to dine with you, and so shall the hundred cats of course."

He looked at the cats with a certain amount of apprehension, then nodded his head in agreement.

"To bring you to the path of True Light," he murmured, "I shall arrange a miracle. But understand that I am poor, very, very poor. I eat only once a week, and this solitary meal is sheep's droppings."

The cats set off without enthusiasm.

About a hundred yards from the Church of Saint Alexander there was what he called "my garden of the little Flowers of Mortification." This consisted of a number of lugubrious instruments half buried in the earth: chairs made of wire ("I sit in them when they're white-hot and stay there until they cool off"); enormous, smiling mouths with pointed, poisonous teeth; underwear of reinforced concrete full of scorpions and adders; cushions made of millions of black mice biting one another—when the blessed buttocks were elsewhere.

Saint Alexander showed off his garden one object at a time, with a certain pride. "Little Theresa never thought of underwear of reinforced concrete," he said. "In fact I can't at the moment think of anybody who had the idea. But then, we can't all be geniuses."

The entrance of the church was lined with statues of Saint Alexander at various periods of his life. There were some of Jesus Christ too, but much smaller. The interior of the church was very comfortable: velvet cushions in ash pink, bibles of real silver, and *My Unblemished Life, or The Rosaries of the Soul of Saint Alexander* by himself, this in a binding of peacock blue jewels. Amber bas-reliefs on the walls gave intimate details of the life of the saint in childhood.

"Gather yourselves," said Saint Alexander, and the hundred cats sat down on a hundred ash pink cushions.

Virginia remained standing and examined the church with interest. She sniffed the altar, which exuded a vaguely familiar smell, though she couldn't remember where she had smelled it.

Saint Alexander mounted the pulpit and explained that he was going to perform a miracle: everyone hoped he was talking about food.

He took a bottle of water and sprinkled drops everywhere.

> *Snow of purity*

he began in a very low voice,

> *Pillar of virtue*
> *Sun of beauty*
> *Perfume . . .*

He continued in this vein until a cloud flowed from the altar, a cloud like sour milk. Soon the cloud took the shape of a fat lamb with baneful eyes. Immediately Saint Alexander cried out, more and more loudly, and the lamb floated up to the ceiling.

"Lamb of God, dearly beloved Jesus, pray for the poor sinners," cried the saint. But his voice had reached its maximum strength and broke. The lamb, which had become enormous, burst and fell to the ground in four pieces. At this moment the cats, who had watched the miracle without moving, threw themselves on the lamb in one great bound. It was their first meal of the day.

They soon finished off the lamb. Saint Alexander was lost in a cloud of dust, all that was left of the odour of sanctity. A weak, remote voice hissed, "Jesus has spilled his blood, Jesus is dead, Saint Alexander will avenge himself."

Virginia took this opportunity to fill her bag with holy plates, and left the church with the hundred cats behind her.

The wheel crossed the woods at a hissing speed. Bats and moths were imprisoned in Virginia's hair; she gestured to the beasts with her strange hands that the hunt was over; she opened her mouth and a blind nightingale flew in: she swallowed it and sang in the nightingale's voice: "Little Jesus is dead, and we've had a fine dinner."

A wild boar lived near Virginia's house. This boar had a single eye in the middle of his forehead, surrounded by black curls. His hindquarters were covered with a thick russet fur, and his back with very tough bristles. Virginia was acquainted with this animal and did not kill it, since it knew where the truffles were hiding.

The boar was called Igname, and he was very pleased with his beauty. He enjoyed decorating himself with fruits, leaves, plants. He made himself necklaces of little animals and insects, which he killed solely to make himself look elegant, since he ate nothing but truffles.

Every evening when the moon was shining, he went to the lake to admire himself in the water. It was here, one evening, while bathing in the moonlight, that Igname decided to take Virginia as his mistress. He admired most her fruity smell and her long hair, always full of nocturnal animals. He decided she was very beautiful and probably a virgin. Igname rolled in the mud luxuriously, thinking of Virginia's charms.

"She has every reason for taking me. Am I not the finest animal in all the forest?"

When he had finished his moon- and mudbath, he got up to find the most sumptuous outfit in which to ask Virginia for her love.

No animal or bird ever looked so splendid as did Igname in his attire of love. Attached to his curly head was a young nightjar. This bird with its hairy beak and surprised eyes beat its wings and looked constantly for prey among the creatures that come out only at the full moon. A wig of squirrels' tails and fruit hung around Igname's ears, pierced for the occasion by two little pikes he had found dead on the lakeshore. His hoofs were dyed red by the blood of a rabbit he had crushed while galloping, and his active body was enveloped by a purple cape which had mysteriously emerged out of the forest. (He hid his russet buttocks, as he did not want to show all his beauty at one go.)

He walked slowly and with great dignity. The grasshoppers fell silent with admiration. As he was passing under an oak tree, Igname saw a rosary hanging down among the leaves. He knew there must be a body attached to this rosary, and he heard a shrill and mocking laugh from above.

Any other time, thought Igname, and he'd be laughing on the other side of his face, and he continued on his way without turning his head.

Igname arrived at Virginia's house. She was sitting on her heels in front of a stewpot which trembled on the fire, making little musical noises. The cats were sitting motionless in every corner of the kitchen, staring at the stewpot.

When Virginia saw Igname she jumped on the table.

"You look impressive coming out of the forest," she breathed, dazzled by his beauty.

Igname's eye became pale and brilliant; the nightjar sent up its thin cry, almost too high to be heard by the ear. Igname advanced and sat down beside the fire on his russet backside.

"Do you recognize my garments of love?" said Igname gravely. "Do you know, Virginia, that I am wearing them for you? Do you realize that the nightjar's claws are thrust deep into my skull? It's for you, I love you. I double up with laughter when I see the night, for my body is exploding with love. Answer me, Virginia, will this night belong to us?"

He faltered, since he had prepared his speech only to this point. Virginia, trembling, spat hard into the fire, a curse on the words of love. She was afraid of Igname's beauty. Then she spat into the stewpot and put her lips into the boiling liquid and swallowed a big mouthful. With a savage cry she brought her head back out of the pot; she jumped around Igname, tearing her hair out by the roots; Igname stood up, and together they danced a dance of ecstasy. The cats caterwauled and stuck their claws into one another's necks, then threw themselves in a mass onto Igname and Virginia, who disappeared under a mountain of cats. Where they made love.

Hunters came seldom to the mountains, but one morning Virginia Fur saw two humans with guns. She hid herself in a bramble bush, and the human beings passed near without noticing her smell. She was terrified by their ugliness and clumsy movements. Abusing them under her breath, she returned home to warn Igname. He wasn't there.

She went out again on her wheel, accompanied by the hundred cats.

In the forest Virginia learned that there had been several deaths. Flocks of birds and groups of wild beasts were having funeral feasts. Full of anguish, they filled their stomachs and cursed the hunters.

Virginia went looking for her lover, but found neither track nor scent of him.

Towards dawn she heard from a badger that Igname was dead: he had been murdered along with a thousand birds, forty hares, and as many deer.

The badger, sitting on a tree trunk, told the story:

"The hunters, who you noticed, passed close to the Church of Saint Alexander. The saint was sitting in his concrete underwear. He saw them coming, he was praying aloud. The hunters asked him news of game.

"I am the Protector of the Little Animals of God," he answered. "But inside my church is a box of alms for the poor. If you put something in it, it's just possible the good Lord will show you the lake where every evening a big wild boar can be found."

After having a good look to see how much the hunters had put into the box, Saint Alexander led them to the lake.

Igname was looking deeply at himself in the water. The hunters fired, and the dogs finished him off. They put Igname into a big sack and said, "This one will do for the bistro in Glane, we'll get at least a hundred francs."

Virginia returned home, followed by the cats. There, in the kitchen, she gave birth to seven little boars. Out of sentiment she kept the one most like Igname, and boiled the others for herself and the cats, as a funeral feast.

The wheel, the cats, and Virginia merged with the trees and the wind. Their shadows, black and disquieting, passed with extraordinary speed across the slope of the mountains. They were shouting something; the nightbirds replied: "Wheeee-eeech? Saint Francis? That bore again! Let's kill him! Isn't he dead yet? Enough of his damned stupidities. It isn't him? Who then? Ah, Saint Alexander, ayyyyy! Kill him too, he's a saint." And they flew along with the shadows, crying, "Killll himmmm! Killll himmmm!"

Soon the earth moved with all the beasts out of their holes crying, "Killll himmmm!"

Ninety thousand horses bounded and broke from their stables to gallop along, beating the earth with their hoofs and neighing, "Killll himmmm, death to foul Alexander!"

Two ladies dressed in black were walking in the snow. One of them talked a lot, the other appeared to have had enough of walking, but wore the icy look of a dutiful lady. The other one, with her pinched, dry face, talked in a crystal clear voice, one of those voices that are so tiresome when one wants to go to sleep in a railway compartment.

"My husband," she was saying, "loves me very much, you know. My husband is so well-known. He's such a child, my husband. My husband has his flings, but I leave him totally free, my dear little husband. And yet I am very ill, I shall die soon, in a month I shall be dead."

"No, no," the other said, her attention elsewhere. "Aren't the mountains ravishing in the snow?"

The talkative lady gave a laugh. "Yes, aren't they? But all I see are the poor people who suffer in these isolated little villages. I feel my heart fill to bursting with love and pity." She struck her flat chest, and the dutiful lady thought, "There isn't room for a heart, her bust's too tight."

The path climbed suddenly, and at the end of a long lane they saw a convent.

"What a beautiful place to die. I feel so pure with the Sisters of Jesus's Little Smile of Anguish. I know that there, with my prayers, I shall get back the soul of my darling little husband."

Two men came down the path. They were carrying the corpse of a beautiful boar.

"I shall buy the boar and give it to the good sisters," the lady said. "I am very generous, you know. My little husband often scolded me, said I throw money out the window. But won't they be happy, the good sisters?" She gave the hunters some money and they said they'd take the boar to the convent. "I myself eat very little, you know, I am too ill. I am very near to death, very near."

"We're approaching the convent," said the other, with a sigh.

"Kiss me, my dear little Engadine," said the talkative one. "You know I'm nothing but a capricious girl." She offered her companion a shrivelled face. "My little husband always said I was such a child!"

Engadine pretended not to hear, and walked faster. Her companion had a certain nauseating smell of the sick about her that repelled her. She walked faster. The sun was hidden by heavy black clouds. A flock of goats and a billy goat passed close, the buck threatening them with a devil's look.

"They frighten me, these goats, they smell so bad. What a brutish smell!" The buck continued to stare at her.

The road became harder. The mountains darkened into rude animal shapes; in the distance they seemed to hear galloping horses.

They rang the bell at the great portal of the convent; it

was opened by a creature that might have come from a lemon, she was so shrivelled and acid. "The Abbot is in the middle of his prayers," she wheezed. "Mother Superior is on her knees. Come, come in the chapel."

They followed her through the corridors, and finally arrived at the chapel. The Abbot had just finished his prayers. The Mother Superior of Jesus's Little Smile of Anguish got up from her knees with difficulty, weighted down by her greyish flesh.

"Poor little girl," whispered the nun. "Come along to the drawing room."

Once there, the enormous woman enveloped the other in a fat, sturdy embrace. Then they talked:

"I've come to die in your convent and win the soul of my dear husband. . . ."

"Board and lodging five hundred francs a month. . . ."

"I'm very ill, very ill. . . ."

"Plenary indulgences are supplementary, a thousand francs."

"My darling little husband will come see me often. . . ."

"Another thousand francs for food, of course."

"I pray morning till night for my little husband."

"A community like ours is very expensive."

They talked like this for several hours.

At half past six an enormous bell rang for the dead and the evening meal, a meal to be taken in rigorous silence. On feast days, Sister Ignatius, headmistress, read aloud. She rang a little bell, and when everybody had something to eat, announced, "This evening is among the greatest of occasions for our community; the Great Saint Alexander himself is coming to speak to us in the chapel at seven-thirty. Afterwards we shall have a meal in the great hall to celebrate the occasion."

The eyes of a hundred nuns shone with joy.

"Now," continued Sister Ignatius, "we continue with chapter one thousand nine hundred thirteen of the twentieth volume of the life of Christ as told to children." The light disappeared in a hundred pairs of eyes.

When the chapel was full of nuns, the organ played a grand, sombre hymn for the saint's imperial entrance. In gold and purple and followed by five little boys, he got down on his knees before the altar.

A voice in the choir began to sing. Perhaps it was a hymn, but it went so fast that most of the nuns were two or three lines behind. The effect was odd; the Mother Superior appeared ill at ease; when the saint mounted the pulpit, followed by six fat cats, she was in a sweat.

"Dear sisters, I have come from far to gladden you with the word of God."

It seemed as if the altar was filling with cats, gold cats and black cats.

"The harshness of life, the temptations of the flesh, the goodness of the good . . ."

A strong wild smell drifted through the church; raising their eyes, the sisters were horrified to see a large badger climbing tranquilly onto Saint Alexander's head. He continued, but every now and again made a movement with his hand as if trying to chase something away.

"Beware of sinful thoughts. . . ."

The voice in the choir was still singing, but it scarcely resembled a hymn; Saint Alexander was obliged to shout to make himself heard.

"The good Lord sees your most secret thoughts. . . ." The ceiling was hidden by a million birds of the night crying: "Death to foul Alexander. . . ."

He descended the pulpit with as much dignity as he could muster, and went out, followed by the nuns, the cats, the badger, and a million birds of the night.

In the refectory a huge table groaned with platters of game, cakes, and great flagons of wine. The saint sat down in the place of honour at the top of the table and asked the good Lord for permission to eat. The good Lord made no reply, and everybody sat down and attacked with good appetite.

The Mother Superior, sitting on the saint's right, whispered, "Holy Father, you weren't disturbed in your magnificent discourse?"

"Disturbed?" he asked in a surprised voice, though his face was covered in scratches. "Disturbed, how?"

"Oh, nothing," the mother replied, blushing. "There are some flies in the church."

"I notice nothing when I talk to the good Lord," said the lady who'd taken up residence at the convent. "Not even flies."

The two ladies exchanged sour looks.

"That, dear madam, is a noble thought," answered the saint. "Are you familiar with a little poem I wrote in my youth:

> *In Paris the Pope*
> *In Aix Lord of the House,*
> *But before the good Lord*
> *I'm but a poor mouse.*

"It's fresh, and yet so strong at the same time," the lady exclaimed ecstatically. How I love real poetry."

"There's more where that came from," said the saint. "I find the lack of true poets forces me to write."

Out of the corner of her eye, the Mother Superior saw seven large cats enter the room silently. They sat down beside the saint, curling their tails around themselves. She grew pale. "Your husband, dear child, must be very busy to leave you alone so often?"

"My husband," the lady replied in a sharp voice, "is very tired. He's having a rest."

"Well then," replied the Mother Superior, "no doubt he's having it on the Riviera? Remember the temptations of the flesh. If my husband were not Our Lord, if I had instead chosen among the poor sinners of this world, I would hardly feel easy with him on the Riviera, especially if I weren't in the first spring of youth anymore, let's be frank."

The lady trembled with rage, and clenched her fingers. "My darling little husband adores me. He does silly things, but we're made for each other."

The moment had come for the roast to be carried in, and everyone looked with anticipation at the door that led to the kitchen. Sister Ignatius stood up and blew a long, melancholic note on a small leather trumpet: "The boar!"

The door crashed open and all the beasts of the forest entered crying, "Kill him, kill him." In the turmoil that followed one could barely make out a human form sitting on a wheel that turned with incredible speed, who shouted with the others: "Kill him!"

—Translated from the French
by Kathrine Talbot

The Skeleton's Holiday

The skeleton was as happy as a madman whose straightjacket had been taken off. He felt liberated at being able to walk without flesh. The mosquitoes didn't bite him anymore. He didn't have to have his hair cut. He was neither hungry nor thirsty, hot nor cold. He was far from the lizard of love. For some time a German, a professor of chemistry, had been eyeing him, thinking he might convert him into delicious *ersatz*: dynamite, strawberry jam, garnished sauerkraut. The skeleton knew how to give him the slip, by letting fall a young zeppelin bone, on which the professor pounced, reciting chemical hymns and covering the bone with hot kisses.

The skeleton's lodgings had an ancient head and modern feet. The ceiling was the sky, the floor the earth. It was painted white and decorated with snowballs in which a heart beat. He looked like a transparent monument dreaming of an electric breast, and gazed without eyes, with a pleasant and invisible smile, into the inexhaustible supply of silence that surrounds our star.

The skeleton didn't like disasters, but to suggest that life did have its hazardous moments, he had placed an enormous thimble in the middle of his fine apartment, on which he sat from time to time like a real philosopher. Sometimes he danced a few steps to the tune of Saint-Saëns's "Danse Macabre." But he did it with such grace, with such guilelessness, in the manner of midnight dances in romantic, old-fashioned graveyards, that nobody seeing him would have thought of anything unpleasant.

Satisfied, he contemplated the Milky Way, the army of bones that encircles our planet. It sparkles, glitters, shines with all its myriad little skeletons that dance, jump, turn somersaults, do their duty. They welcome the dead from the thousand fields of honour, the honour of hyenas, adders, crocodiles, bats, lice, toads, spiders, tapeworms, scorpions. They provide first counsel, guide the first steps of the newly dead, who are wretched in their abandonment, like the newborn. Our repugnant eminent cohorts, cobrothers, cosisters, councles and -aunts who smell of wild boar and have noses encrusted with dry oysters, are transformed upon dying, into skeletons. Have you heard the appalling moan of the dead in slaughter? It's the terrible disillusionment of the newly born dead, who'd hoped for and deserved eternal sleep but find themselves tricked, caught up in an endless machinery of pain and sorrow.

The skeleton got up every morning, clean as a Gillette blade. He decorated his bones with herbs, brushed his teeth with ancestor marrow, and lacquered his nails with Fatma Red. In the evening, at cocktail time, he went to the café on the corner, where he read the *Necromancer's Journal*, the paper favoured by high-toned corpses. Often he amused himself by playing dirty tricks. Once he pretended to be thirsty and asked for writing materials; he emptied the inkpot between his jaws into his carcass: the ink stained and spotted his white bones. Another time he went into a joke shop and bought himself a supply of those Parisian pleasantries, imitation turds. One evening he put some in his chamber pot, and his servant never got over the shock in the morning: to think that a skeleton who neither ate nor drank did his business like the rest of us.

It happened that one day the skeleton drew some hazelnuts that walked about on little legs across mountains, that spit frogs out of mouth, eye, ear, nose, and other openings and holes. The skeleton took fright like a skeleton meeting a skeleton in bright daylight. Quickly he had a pumpkin detector grow on his head, with a day side like patchouli bread and a night side like the egg of Columbus, and set off, half reassured, to see a fortune-teller.

—Translated from the French
by Kathrine Talbot

Pigeon, Fly!

"There's somebody on the road. Somebody's coming to see me, someone strange, though I can only see him from afar."

I leaned over my balcony and saw the figure getting rapidly bigger, for it was approaching at great speed. I thought it was a woman, for its long, straight hair fell down upon its horse's mane. The horse was large, with rounded, powerful bones, and it was a strange kind of pink with purple shadows the colour of ripe plums: the colour called roan in England. Of all animals, the horse is the only one who has this rosy colour.

The person on the horse was dressed in a pretty untidy manner that reminded me of the coat of a mountain sheep. On the other hand the colours were rich, almost regal, and a gold shirt was just visible between the strands of loose wool. True the shirt was full of holes and somewhat dirty when examined closely, but the general effect was impressive.

She stopped below my balcony and looked up at me.

"I have a letter which needs an immediate answer."

The voice was a man's voice, and I found myself at a complete loss in making out the person's sex.

"Who are you?" I asked cautiously.

"I am Ferdinand, emissary of Célestin des Airlines-Drues."

The rider's voice, very soft, was unquestionably a man's voice: a scent of heliotrope and vanilla mixed with sweat rose to my nostrils. I leaned down to him and, taking the letter from his hand, used the opportunity to look at his face, half hidden. It was a very white face, the lips painted reddish purple. The horse shook its fat neck.

"Madam," the letter said, "please have the great kindness to help me in my deep distress. In consequence, you will learn something much to your advantage.

"Entrust your honourable person, as well as your canvases, your brushes, and everything you need in your profession of artist to my emissary.

"I beg you, dear lady, to accept my deepest and most sorrowful respect." Signed, "Célestin des Airlines-Drues."

The writing paper was heavily scented with heliotrope and decorated with several gold crowns transfixed by plumes, swords, and olive branches.

I decided to accompany Ferdinand back to his master, since the promises the letter contained interested me very much, though I'd never heard of Célestin des Airlines-Drues.

I was soon sitting on the broad hindquarters of the emissary's horse behind Ferdinand. My luggage was attached to the saddle.

We took the road to the west, a route that crossed some wild country, rich in great dark forests.

It was spring. The grey, heavy sky dropped a tepid rain; the green of the trees and fields was intense. From time to time I dozed, and on several occasions I could easily have fallen from the horse, but I hung on to Ferdinand's woolly clothes. He didn't appear to worry about me, thinking of other things, and singing "The Sighs of the Dying Rose."

> *Its petals cold against my heart*
> *My hot tears could no warmth impart*
> *To the velvet*
> *Of the soft skin of My Rose*
> *OH MY ROSE.*

These last words woke me completely, for he screamed them with excruciating brutality into my left ear.

"Idiot," I shouted, furious.

Ferdinand laughed softly. The horse had come to a halt. We were in a huge courtyard a few hundred yards from a large house. This house, built in dark stone and of ample proportions, was so sad in appearance that I felt a keen desire to turn round and go back home. All the windows were shuttered, there wasn't a wisp of smoke from any of the chimneys, and crows were sitting here and there on the roof.

The courtyard looked as deserted as the house.

I thought that there must be a garden on the other side of the house, for I saw trees and a pale sky through a big wrought iron gate. The gate was strange, the wrought iron showed a gigantic angel sitting in a circle, its head thrown back in an anguished profile. On the right, towards the top of the circle, a little wave of water, also in wrought iron, flowed towards the angel's face.

"Where are we?" I asked. "Have we arrived?"

"We are at the Airlines-Drues," Ferdinand answered after a moment's silence.

He looked at the house without turning his head. It seemed to me that he was waiting for somebody, something, or some event. He did not move. The horse stood very still, also looking straight ahead.

Suddenly bells began to ring: I've never in my life heard such a ringing of bells. The drawn-out echo hung all about us in the trees like a metallic liquid. Distraught, the crows on the roof flew off.

I was about to question my companion when a coach drawn by four black horses passed by us with the swiftness of a shadow. The carriage stopped in front of the gate, and I saw that it was a hearse, sumptuously fixed with carvings and flowers. The horses were of the same breed as the herald's, round and sleek, but these were black as muscat grapes.

The door of the house opened and four men came out carrying a coffin.

Ferdinand's horse began to whinny and the black horses replied, turning their heads towards us.

The men carrying the coffin were dressed the same way as Ferdinand, the only difference being the colour of their flowing robes: purple, black, and a very deep crimson. Their faces were very white and made up like Ferdinand's. They all had long heavy hair, badly combed, like wigs of long ago that had lain in an attic for years.

I'd hardly had time to observe all this when Ferdinand gave his horse a tap with his whip and we were plunging at full gallop headlong through an avenue, throwing up earth and stones behind us.

This journey went so quickly that I wasn't even able to look around me. But I had the impression that we were travelling through a forest. In the end, Ferdinand stopped his horse in a clearing surrounded by trees. The ground was covered by mosses and wildflowers. An armchair stood some yards from us, draped in green and mauve velvet.

"Get down, won't you," Ferdinand said. "Set your easel up in the shade. Are you thirsty?"

I told him I would like a drink of some sort and slid from the back of the horse. Ferdinand offered me a flask containing a very sugary liquid.

"They'll be along soon." He went on looking into the depth of the forest. "The sun will soon set. Put your easel along here, this is where you'll paint the portrait."

While I was busy setting up, Ferdinand took the saddle and bridle from his horse, then lay on the ground, the horse beside him.

The sky became red, yellow, and mauve, and dusk fell. It began to rain, and large raindrops fell on me and my canvas.

"There they are," Ferdinand suddenly called out.

Soon the clearing was full of people. These people, who were veiled, looked more or less like the men who had carried the coffin. They made quite a large circle around me and the armchair. They talked together in low voices, and every now and again one laughed shrilly. There were about forty of them.

Soon a high, clear voice came from behind the circle: "Like this, Gustave. No, no, no, my poor friend, to the left. . . ."

"Who would have thought she was so heavy," another, lower voice answered. "And yet she wasn't fat."

The laughter sounded like bleating sheep, and looking around me, I had the vivid impression I was surrounded by a flock of bizarre sheep dressed for a gloomy ritual.

Part of the circle moved aside, and the four men I had seen previously entered backwards, carrying the coffin.

A tall, narrow individual followed them, speaking in a high, clear voice: "Put her beside the armchair. Have the draperies been scented?"

"Yes, Monsieur des Airlines-Drues, those were your orders."

I looked with interest at the gentleman. I could not see his face, but I could see one of his white hands gesturing like an elephant's trunk. He wore an immense black wig, which fell in stiff curls down to his feet.

"Is the painter here?" he asked.

"Yes, sir, she's here."

"Ah, so I see. It is very kind of you, dear lady, to honour us thus. Be welcomed."

He came close to me and pushed aside the strands of hair hiding his face. It was indeed the face of a sheep, but covered in soft white skin. His black lips were very thin, and strangely mobile. I took his hand with a certain amount of repugnance, for it was too smooth, much too smooth.

"I've admired your work so much," Monsieur des Airlines-Drues murmured. "Do you think you could get a really perfect likeness?" He gestured towards the coffin, which was now open.

Two men took out the corpse of a young woman. She was beautiful and had a mass of silky black hair, but her skin was already phosphorescent, luminous, and vaguely mauve. A rather unpleasant smell wafted towards me. Monsieur des Airlines-Drues, seeing me wrinkle my nose involuntarily, gave me a charming smile of apology.

"It's so difficult," he said, "to part with the remains of those one has loved . . . adored. I was sure I'd have your sympathy in this matter. My wife died two weeks ago, and with this heavy, humid weather we've been having . . ." He finished the sentence by gesturing with one of his beautiful hands.

"In short, esteemed lady, please be forbearing. Now I shall go and leave you to your Art."

I squeezed the colours from the tubes onto my palette and began to paint the portrait of Madame des Airlines-Drues.

The sheeplike individuals around me began to play pigeon, fly: "Pigeon, fly; Sheep, fly; Angel, fly. . . ."

Dusk seemed to last an interminable time. Night, which had appeared imminent, did not fall, and the dull light in the clearing remained strong enough for me to continue to work. I did not notice until later that the light imprisoned in the circle of trees came from no other source than the body of Madame des Airlines-Drues. The forest was in total darkness. I was completely absorbed in my painting and did not notice that I must have been alone with the dead woman for quite a long time.

I was pleased with the portrait, and I stepped back a few paces to see the whole composition. The face on the canvas was my own.

I couldn't believe my eyes. Yet as I looked from the model to the portrait there was no denying the truth. The more I looked at the corpse, the more striking became the resemblance of these pale features. On canvas, the face was unquestionably mine.

"The likeness is extraordinary, my compliments, dear lady."

Monsieur des Airlines-Drues's voice came from behind my left shoulder.

"It's exactly noon now, but one isn't aware of the sun in this forest. Anyway, Art is a magic which makes the hours melt away and even days dissolve into seconds, isn't that so, dear lady? Do you think you'll be able now to finish the portrait without the model? My poor wife, you understand, has been dead three weeks. She must be pining for her well-deserved rest. . . . It's not often that one has to work three weeks after one's demise."

He laughed a little to underline his joke.

"I can offer you a pleasant and well-lit room at Airlines-Drues. Allow me, dear lady, to take you there in my carriage."

I followed the enormous walking wig like a sleepwalker.

The studio was a big room, with a large cupboard taking up the farthest end. The room had once been luxurious, but the embroidered silk draperies were now torn and dusty, the delicately carved furniture broken, and the gilding had flaked off in places. Several large easels in the shape of swans or mermaids stood about here and there, like the skeletons of other things. Spiders had spun their webs between them, giving the room a fossilized look.

"This is Madame des Airlines-Drues's studio. This is where she died."

I rummaged through the cupboard. A great number of clothes, wigs, and old shoes were jumbled together in great disorder. They all looked like fancy-dress costumes, and some reminded me of the circus.

"She must have played at dress up in her time alone in the studio—it's said she liked acting."

Not the least interesting of my discoveries was a diary bound in green velvet. Her name was on the title page, the handwriting neat but curiously childish.

"Agathe des Airlines-Drues. Please respect this book, its contents is for no other eyes than those of Eleanor. Agathe des Airlines-Drues."

I started to read.

Dear Eleanor,
   How you will cry when you read this little book. I'm

using patchouli to scent its pages, so that you'll remember me better. Our sharpest memories are of perfumes and smells. How you will cry! Anyway, I shall be glad. I should like you to cry a great deal.

Today is my birthday, and of course yours too. What fun to be the same age. I'd like so much to see you, but since that's not possible, I'll tell you everything in this diary—everything. (My God, If Célestin could hear me!) Marriage, of course, is a dreadful thing—but mine! My mother writes, "I'm knitting some tiny things for you, or rather for somebody very close to you, my darling. For a little being who'll surely make his appearance soon."

Oh, Eleanor, I'll sooner have children by one of the chairs in my studio than by Célestin. Listen! The Wedding Night (!), I lay down in the huge bed draped with acid pink curtains. After more than half an hour the door opened and I saw an apparition: an individual dressed in white feathers, with the wings of an angel. I said to myself, "I'm surely going to die, for here is the Angel of Death."

The angel was Célestin.

He threw off his clothes, dropping his gown of feathers to the ground. He was naked. If the feathers were white, his body was blindingly so. I think he must have painted it with some phosphorescent paint, for it shone like the moon. He wore blue stockings with red stripes.

"Am I beautiful?" he asked. "They say I am."

I was too fascinated to reply.

"My dear Agathe," he continued, looking at his reflection in the mirror, "you see you aren't among country folk anymore. . . ." (They call me "madam" here.)

He put on his feathers and wings again. I suddenly felt so cold, my teeth began to chatter. And now listen to me carefully, Eleanor. The more I looked at Célestin, the lighter he seemed to me, light as a feather. He began to walk around the room in a strange way. His feet seemed to touch the ground less and less. Then he began to glide through the door into the corridor. I got up and hastened to the door. Célestin vanished into the darkness . . . his feet weren't touching the ground . . . I'm absolutely sure of what I'm telling you. His wings beat very slowly . . . but . . .

So you see what the start of my marriage was like!

I didn't see Célestin for a week. Furthermore, I saw hardly anybody except an old servant called Gaston. He brought me things to eat, always sweet things. I lived in my studio, and I've lived here ever since. I am so sad, Eleanor, so sad that my body has become transparent, I've shed so many tears. Is it possible to dissolve into water without leaving a trace? I am so often alone that I have struck up a sort of love affair with my mirror image. But Eleanor, here's the worst of it—recently I've found it very difficult to see myself in the mirror. Yes, it's horrible, but it's true. When I look at myself, my face is all hazy. And . . . I believe . . . no, I'm sure, that I can see the objects in the room behind me through my body.

Now I'm crying so much I can't see the paper on which I'm writing anymore.

Every day, Eleanor, I lose myself a little more, yet I've never loved my face more. I try to paint my portrait so as to have it near me still, you understand. But . . . I can't. I elude myself.

And here is another thing: the objects around me are becoming terribly clear and vivid, much more alive than I. You know, Eleanor, I'm afraid. . . . Listen, the chairs in this room are very old, and so is all the rest of the furniture. Last week I saw a little green bud on one of these old chairs, the kind of bud that appears on trees in the spring. And now . . . how horrible . . . it has become a leaf. . . . Eleanor!

A few days later:

The room is full of them. All the furniture has sprouted new green growth, many chairs have already got leaves, small, fragile leaves of a tender green. It's ludicrous to see such young leaves growing on such old, dusty furniture.

Célestin came. He didn't notice anything, but he touched my face with those smooth hands of his . . . much too smooth. . . . He said, "You will always be a child, Agathe. Look at me. I am terribly young, aren't I?" Then he stopped and laughed. He has a very high-pitched laugh.

"Do you put on performances all by yourself?" he asked.

That isn't true, Eleanor. . . . I only put on fancy dress to make myself more solid, more substantial . . . so as not to . . . guess what I was going to say! . . .

"Agathe, when you were a little girl, did you ever play pigeon, fly?"

Célestin asked me this strange question while looking into the mirror. I replied that it was a game that very much amused me when I was little.

Now the room was full of bizarre individuals dressed like sheep. But, Eleanor, they were naked. . . . Their clothes were nothing but fleece. All of them were men made up like whores.

"The lambs of God," Célestin said.

We sat down at a round table, and about twenty pairs of hands suddenly appeared from between the strands of hair. I noticed their nails were varnished but very dirty. The hands were pale, greyish.

This was only a moment's impression, for I really had eyes for nothing but Célestin's hands. I swear to you, Eleanor, that his hands were running with moisture . . . and so smooth, and their colour was strange, like mother-of-pearl. He too was looking at his hands with a secret smile.

"Pigeon, fly!" he cried, and all the hands went up in the air, waving like wings. My hands too were fluttering in the air.

> "Sheep, fly!" Célestin called.
> The hands trembled on the table but didn't lift.
> "Angel, fly!"
> So far nobody had made a mistake.
> Suddenly Célestin's voice rose in a sharp cry, a terrible cry, "CÉLESTIN, FLY!"
> Eleanor, dear Eleanor, his hands . . .

At this point Agathe's journal suddenly stopped.

I turned to her portrait: the canvas was empty, I didn't dare look for my face in the mirror. I knew what I would see: my hands were so cold!

—Translated from the French
by Kathrine Talbot

The Three Hunters

I was having a rest in a deep forest. The trees and wild fruit were ripe. It was autumn. I was beginning to fall asleep when a heavy object fell on my stomach. It was a dead rabbit, blood running from its mouth. It was dead of fatigue. I'd hardly freed myself of the rabbit when, with a leap more agile than a stag's, a man landed beside me. He was of medium height, had a red face, and a long white moustache. From his face, I'd have guessed him to be about ninety.

"You're pretty nimble for your age," I said, but then I looked at his clothes. He was wearing a hunting jacket the colour of Damascus rose, a bright green hat with orange plumes, and very long black boots trimmed with summer flowers. He wore no trousers. He looked at the rabbit with interest.

"I was going slowly, to give the poor beast a chance," he said. "But it just didn't know how to run. In future I'll leave the rabbits to Mcflanagan."

THE THREE HUNTERS

I tried to think of something nice to say to him.

"I like your outfit," I said with a pleasant smile.

"Oh that," he replied. "People with a certain aesthetic appreciation will find that it lacks distinction. But it's only sporting to wear these colours. If the animals see me coming, they have more chance." Then his expression changed. "Is it whisky you've got in that bottle?"

"Yes," I said.

"Oh," he said. "Really?"

"Yes, yes."

"Ah." He sat down beside me and said, staring at the bottle as if hypnotized, "You did say it was whisky?"

"1900."

"A very good year. It's the vintage I prefer."

"Me too."

"Ah."

"Yes." By this time I'd guessed that he'd perhaps wanted a little drink. I offered him a drink. He accepted.

"You know, I've got an extraordinary cellar. Would you like to taste some of my wines?"

"Yes," I said.

"Take this path on the left straight on and cross every path you come to. It's the first manor after the eighteenth crossroads."

"But aren't you coming?"

"I can only travel in leaps and bounds," he replied, disappearing between the trees in leaps five yards long.

I started out. Around midnight I arrived at the manor house. The door was opened by an individual on all fours.

"My brother Mcbologan has been waiting for you since noon. I am Mcflanagan, the Terror of the Forest. Mcbologan is the Curse of the Forest, and Mchooligan the Abomination of the Forest. Mchooligan is the cook."

We went into a room a hundred yards long and fifty wide. Mcbologan was sitting at the table in front of six dozen hares, a hundred wild duck, and nineteen boars.

"Mchooligan," shouted Mcbologan, "we're ready to start eating."

A noise of wind and Mchooligan entered like lightning: he couldn't stop himself before the other end of the room and hit the wall, and sat at the table bleeding. His brothers looked at him with gloom.

"He can never go slower than that," said Mcflanagan, still on all fours. Mchooligan was maybe ten years older than Mcbologan, and exhibited the same profound sadness as his brothers. During the meal they all cried hot tears into their plates.

Towards the end of the meal, Mcbologan said, "Mcflanagan ought to have a shave."

It was the first thing that had been said. An hour later Mcflanagan said "Why?" and two hours after that Mcbologan said, "Because." Mchooligan didn't say anything at all, he was crying too much. Getting on for five in the morning, Mcbologan said, "Let's live it up a bit, shall we? I need some amusement." And since the others still didn't say anything, he turned to me. "I've got some hunting trophies. Would you like to see them?"

Walking through a long gallery, we arrived in a room well lit by some lamps. There was nothing but sausages. Sausages in aquariums, sausages in cages, sausages hanging on the walls, sausages in sumptuous glass boxes. Nothing but sausages. I may have shown a certain surprise. Mcbologan looked at his sausages.

"That," he said to me, "is the hand of destiny." I stood beside him in deep thought. "One's got to realize that nothing is eternal, that nothing"—he contemplated a landscape of sausages—"nothing is finally stronger than goodness. Since my grandfather Angus Mcfruit's first communion, the family has been in dire straits. Jock Mcfish Mcfruit, my poor father, could walk only on his head. Geraldine, my mother (a saint!), could walk only on her . . . ah, but, the details are too personal." He shed a few tears.

"Still, don't let's be sentimental. It all began the day of my grandfather's first communion. He was only a lad, he didn't realize the solemnity of the occasion. The evening before this

Holy Day, the eve before he was to receive his Lord, he ate a plate of beans. And next morning in church . . ." Mcbologan hesitated. "It happened that a certain noise escaped him. . . ." He went on looking at the landscape of sausages. I felt him fighting his emotions. "From that day the judgement of the good Lord has been upon us. Whatever trophy we try to preserve becomes a sausage. And we ourselves . . . well, as you see."

He turned away in great emotion, and I heard his bounding steps disappear into the manor house.

—Translated from the French
by Kathrine Talbot

Monsieur Cyril de Guindre

On a heavy, balmy spring afternoon, Monsieur Cyril de Guindre was resting elegantly on his ice blue couch. Moving like a tired snake, he was playing with his cat. Despite his age, he was very beautiful.

"His face is that of an albino orchid," said his great friend Thibaut Lastre. "His greedy violet mouth is a poisonous bee-orchid like a lunar insect, and where can you find a rare animal with a coat comparable to his hair?"

Monsieur de Guindre sighed in his halo of perfume, thinking of Thibaut, who was already half an hour late for tea.

The garden was so intensely green that he had to shield his eyes. "Your gaze tires me as much as the garden," he said to his cat. "Shut your eyes."

He didn't notice Thibaut, who had come silently into the room carrying a bouquet of moss roses. Thibaut, who was a great deal younger than Cyril de Guindre, had a golden skin like the corpse of a child preserved in an old and excellent liqueur. He wore an elegant dressing gown the colour of trout flesh, and his face, behind the roses, was livid with anger.

"Ah, Thibaut," Cyril said in a weary voice, "whatever have you been doing all afternoon to keep me waiting like this? You know very well that I take tea at five o'clock . . . as does everyone, indeed . . ."

Thibaut threw the roses at the cat, which growled and clawed Cyril's thighs, looking across the flowers with malevolent eyes. "Moreover," continued Cyril, disentangling his cat from the roses, "I have an important project that I've been wanting to discuss with you. . . . But since you seem to prefer nature to my company, I hesitate to tell you what I have in mind."

Thibaut shrugged. "Will you please explain," he retorted, "how it has come about that your garden is infested with nymphs?" His voice hissed with anger.

"Nymphs?" Cyril asked. "Wherever have you been seeing nymphs?" His hand trembled a little as he arranged the lace on his chest.

"I saw a young girl beside the lake," Thibaut said sharply. "Who is she?"

Cyril reflected for a few moments, his eyes closed, but he did not stop fondling his cat. "Ring for a bottle of champagne, dearest Thibaut, and I'll explain it to you."

Thibaut obeyed with bad grace.

"First of all," said Cyril, when he had a crystal goblet full of champagne in his hand, "first of all tell me, was the girl pretty?"

"I hardly saw her," replied Thibaut, looking distraught. "Why should it interest you?"

"It interests me, my dearest Thibaut, because that little girl is probably a very close relation of mine. She could even be my daughter." A painful smile played around Thibaut's lips, which held a cigarette, and his fingers clawed the arms of his chair.

"Really?"

"Yes. Twenty years ago I committed the indiscretion of

taking a woman. Moreover, I married her. She was extremely tiring, an uncivilized creature, painfully lacking in delicacy. Lacking as was her wont, she became pregnant six years after we were married. The grossness of her physique during those nine months made me fall quite ill. I was obliged, my dear Thibaut, to stay in bed for several weeks after her daughter's birth. I suffered greatly, imagining myself pregnant. Thanks only to the massage administered by Wang To, a Chinese, was I finally put back on my feet."

"And then?" asked Thibaut in a blank voice.

"And then," said Cyril, moistening his lips with champagne, "I began to imagine that I had sexual relations with a mermaid who was forever fondling me with her heavy, limp tail, wetting my pink dressing gown. . . ."

Thibaut stopped him with an irritated movement. "I didn't ask for details of your psychological state. I wanted to hear what happened to this domestic idyll."

"I'm coming to that," answered Cyril with a sigh. "My wife never regained her normal state of mind. Actually she's in a sanitorium, a very comfortable one, of course. She suffers from strange hallucinations and an unfortunate simplemindedness. I haven't seen her for ten years."

Thibaut's face was filled with disgust. He swayed like a drunk. "Charming. . . . Charming . . . ," he murmured between dry lips. "And the girl?"

"I placed her in the good hands of the Purple Sisters of the Convent of the Holy Tomb. These excellent nuns have taken care of her moral and worldly education. The little girl's name is Panthilde, a whim of her mother's. Now, darling Thibaut, you know as much about my life as I do myself."

Thibaut got up, very pale, saying he had to go rest.

"Panthilde," murmured Cyril de Guindre, "whatever shall I do if you are ugly? I shall make you disappear gently into the emerald water of my lake, for I can't endure ugliness. She ought to be fourteen, awkward age. . . . If only she doesn't end up looking like her mother. What a disaster! Whatever shall I do with a girl?"

He rang for his servant, who was a bloated young man who looked like a plump hen cooked in aromatic stock. His name was Dominique, and he had the gestures of a Jesuit.

"Monsieur?" he murmured while arranging the cushions behind Cyril's head.

"Dominique, my succulent plant, when you were a lay brother at the Jesuits', did you ever hear of the Purple Sisters of the Convent of the Holy Tomb?"

Dominique looked at the ground with his milky eyes. "There was the Abbot, monsieur, who from time to time went to the good sisters to say mass and hear confessions."

"Ah, and what did he think of them?"

"Brother Coriolan, who assisted the Abbot with his bath, told me that the Abbot was always jaunty after his visits to the Convent of the Holy Tomb. He always scented himself with bitter almonds on the eve of his visits. May I add that the Abbot knew how to savour the agreeable subtleties of life?"

"Dominique, go and prepare my bath of rose water. This evening I shall make up with peacock green powder. Afterwards, go into the garden and find me the little girl who is playing near the lake."

Dominique bowed and went out backwards.

"Lay out my angora gown," added Cyril with closed eyes, "and the Pope's striped socks."

The final detail of Cyril de Guindre's toilet were a few drops of opium essence behind his ears. He looked with satisfaction at his reflection in the mirror. He really had beautiful ears, delicate as geranium leaves. He bent towards the mirror and kissed the reflection of his lips, leaving a crimson mark the shape of a bird in flight.

"Precious mummy," he murmured, laughing. "Who knows? Won't you have fun after all?"

Slowly he went down the marble staircase.

Panthilde was standing in the middle of the drawing room. They looked at each other in silence. Cyril saw a little girl of fourteen, dressed like the pupil of a convent school. Her dress was made of a stiff black material and had a little white collar at the throat. Her skinny legs were covered in thick black wool. A straw hat hid her face. Her long, black hair was braided into correct plaits: an inch or two more and they would have reached the ground.

After a few moments' silence, Cyril advanced towards her and cautiously took off her hat. He was astonished by her perverse beauty: she resembled him very much.

"Panthilde," he said finally, "don't you recognize your father?"

She threw him a vague glance and shook her head.

"No, monsieur, I don't know you."

"How long have you been staying here?" he asked with an immense effort. He was irritated by a slight smile on Panthilde's lips that disappeared immediately.

"I don't know, monsieur. . . . It seems to me I've been here some time. I study every day with the Abbot."

Cyril felt so tired that he went to lie down on the couch. He lit a special myrrh-scented cigarette, and soon fell asleep, though he remained vaguely conscious. He had the feeling Panthilde was sitting near his head singing with a child's high-pitched voice,

> *Daddy don't cry I'll buy*
> *A dolly in a coach one day!*

Across a cloud of sleep he saw Panthilde take a little jar from her pocket, dip her lips into its black and sticky contents, and put her face close to his. Her lips were black and gleaming like the back of a beetle. Then he felt himself compelled, quite against his will, to taste her lips. He opened his mouth and moved towards her, but she moved her head out of reach, laughing: he trembled with horror and desire.

"Papa wants Spring," Panthilde said in a mocking voice. "Papa wants Spring. Papa wants Spring."

She began to chant the monotonous rhythm of the words. "Papa wants Spring."

Cyril went to sleep.

He woke up with Thibaut looking at him, Thibaut in a tight suit that fitted his body as closely as a second skin.

"Good heavens," Cyril said, "is it already time for dinner?"

Dinner was served, as usual, on the terrace of the weeping willows. Cyril sat opposite Thibaut, across a bronze table in the shape of a poppy, dreaming amongst the scents of the garden and the food. His eyes were tired. Dominique prowled around the table with soft steps, serving delicate dishes, a plump fat chicken with stuffing made of brains and the livers of thrushes, truffles, crushed sweet almonds, rose conserve with a few drops of some divine liqueur. This chicken, which had been marinated—plucked but alive—for three days, had in the end been suffocated in vapours of boiling patchouli: its flesh was as creamy and tender as a fresh mushroom.

A chilled asparagus mousse and creamed oysters were followed by a procession of strange and succulent cakes, all white, yet as varied as the animals in a zoological garden. Cyril and Thibaut tasted each, conversing from time to time while listening to music played by a little boy dressed as an angel.

Thibaut spoke of a suit he intended to have made.

"It will hardly be a suit for going out in," he said, "but rather for the privacy of the boudoir . . . tea for two. . . . The trousers are to be made of a rosy beige fur, and very delicately striped in another colour, like the pants of a Persian cat. The shirt will be of a very pale green like the feathers of a dying kingfisher, half hidden by an acid blue jacket, brilliant like the scales of a fish. What do you think of it?"

"Ravishing," Cyril replied, taking a bite out of some fruit. "But I'd have the shirt made in velvet of a green verging on ochre. A moss green." He stopped abruptly, putting his hand to his forehead. On the rose-coloured stone wall, the shadows of two horses were fighting with frightful ferocity.

The terrible battle only lasted a few seconds: the shadows faded, and Cyril, very pale, turned his head and saw, behind him, a priest.

"Monsieur the Abbot of Givres," said Dominique's voice.

The Abbot's soutane was grey with dust, and riddled with the depredations of moths. His chin and shaved skull were blue, his face sombre. De Guindre felt overcome by nausea as the Abbot held out a hand he couldn't refuse to take, a hand long and thin like a woman's and like the cast skin of a snake.

"My dear Monsieur de Guindre," said the Abbot in a gentle voice, "what a pleasure to come to know all this at last." He indicated with a gesture an imaginary circle around him. "My ecclesiastical work has prevented me from meeting you as soon as I would have wished. I have, however, had the great pleasure of being of some little use to Mademoiselle de Guindre in her studies."

With a smile of charming frankness he took a chair and sat down beside Cyril. He ignored Thibaut.

"This heavy weather," continued the Abbot, helping himself to a very large piece of vanilla-flavoured anemone cake, "has a narcotic effect on the spirit, don't you agree, my dear de Guindre? But your delightful garden is a veritable cradle of flowers, and often, when I walk under your flowering almond trees, an animal runs past me on mysterious paths."

"Often? You often walk in my garden?" asked Cyril in astonishment. "Please forgive my curiosity, but how long have you been a regular visitor to my property?"

"Often!" the Abbot repeated in an ardent tone of voice. "I know every flower, every plant . . . every tree. You might say that the Abbot de Givres is the house spirit of the de Guindre garden." He took a branch of honeysuckle from his breast and held it under the nose of Cyril, who smelled it avidly.

His crimson lips became black as they touched the flowers, his face weary and pale with pleasure. Thibaut did not move, but his eyes were dry and fierce. It seemed to him that the new moon descended from the sky and glided between the leaves of the weeping willows, coming to rest at last on the priest's head, its pointed crescent thrusting into his glittering skull.

Panthilde, who at that moment arrived from the garden, remained at a distance. She looked at the three men, however, with a sombre eye.

"Panthilde," asked the Abbot, looking at Cyril and barely concealing a certain anxiety in his voice. "Are you there? Aren't you playing in the moonlight anymore?" She rolled her eyes angrily. "Come," continued the Abbot. "Come and say good evening to your papa."

Thibaut shuddered and clawed at the table. Panthilde did not move; she breathed heavily while looking at the table in an anguished way.

"That smell," Cyril said in a thick voice. "I feel sick."

He tried to get up, but the Abbot held him firmly by the arm and laughed.

—Translated from the French
by Kathrine Talbot

The Sisters

"Drusille," the letter read.

"Drusille, I shall soon be with you. My love is already with you, its wings are faster than my body. When I am away from you, I am only a poor stuffed bird, for you are guardian of my vitals, my heart and my thoughts.

"Drusille, I embrace the south wind because it blows towards you. Drusille, my life! Your voice is more moving than the thunder, your eyes more overwhelming than lightning. Drusille, wonderful Drusille, I love you, I love you, I love you, sitting in the rain, your long and ferocious face close to this letter."

The thunder growled around her, and the wind beat her face with its wet hair. The storm was so terrible that it tore the flowers from their stalks, and bore them in muddy streams towards an unknown fate. The flowers weren't the only victims, for the streams also swept away crushed butterflies, fruit, bees, and small birds.

Drusille, sitting in her garden in the middle of all this havoc, laughed. She laughed a harsh laugh, the letter crushed against her breast. Sitting on her foot, two toads hissed this thought monotonously, "Drusille, my Belzamine; Drusille, my Belzamine."

All at once, the sun tore the clouds apart and poured a fierce yellow heat into the wet garden. Drusille got up and went into the house.

The maid, Engadine, was sitting on the floor, her hands full of the vegetables she was preparing for dinner. She looked at her mistress with her shrewd little eyes.

"Prepare the royal apartment," Drusille said. "The king will be here this evening. Hurry and sprinkle the sheets with perfume."

"I already knew all that," Engadine said. "The letter passed through my hands."

Drusille kicked her in the stomach.

"Get up, garbage." The servant rose, her face rigid with pain.

"Jasmine or patchouli?"

"Patchouli for the pillows, jasmine for the sheets, and musk for the purple blankets. Put the lilac dressing gown on the bed with the scarlet pyjamas. Hurry or I'll smack your face."

In the kitchen, cakes and enormous tarts were put to the flame and taken from the oven. Pomegranates and melons stuffed with larks filled the kitchen: whole oxen were turning slowly on spits, pheasants, peacocks, and turkeys awaited their turn to be cooked. Chests full of fantastic fruit cluttered up the corridors.

Drusille walked about slowly in this forest of food, tasting a lark or a cake here and there.

In the cellars, the old wooden casks gave up their contents of blood, honey, and wine. Most of the servants were lying about the floor, dead drunk. Drusille took the opportunity to hide a demijohn of honey under her skirt. She went up to the attic. The top of the house was engulfed in a deep silence, rats and bats peopled the spiral staircases. Drusille arrived finally before a door which she opened with a large key attached to a chain around her neck.

"Juniper?" she said. "Are you there?"

"As usual," answered a voice out of the gloom. "I don't move."

"I've brought you something to eat. Are you better today?"

"My health is always excellent, sister."

"You're ill," replied Drusille in an irritated voice. "Poor little thing."

"It's Thursday, isn't it?"

"Yes, as a matter of fact, it is Thursday."

"Then I'm allowed a candle. Have you brought me one?"

Drusille hesitated a moment, then she spoke with an effort. "Yes, I've brought you a candle. I am good to you."

Silence.

Drusille lit the candle, illuminating a dirty little attic without windows. Perched on a rod near the ceiling, an extraordinary creature looked at the light with blinded eyes. Her body was white and naked; feathers grew from her shoulders and round her breasts. Her white arms were neither wings nor arms. A mass of white hair fell around her face, whose flesh was like marble.

"What have you brought me to eat?" she asked, jumping on her perch.

The moment she saw the creature moving, Drusille slammed the door behind her. But Juniper had eyes for nothing but the honey.

"You've got to make it last at least six days," Drusille said.

Juniper ate for some time in silence.

"Drink," she said finally. Drusille held out a glass of water, but Juniper shook her head.

"Not that, not today. I need red. . . ."

Drusille laughed. "No you don't. . . . Last time you drank

THE SISTERS
45

red, you bit me. It excites you too much. Water's good for thirst."

"Red," insisted Juniper in a monotonous voice. "Else I'll scream."

With a quick gesture, Drusille brought a knife from between her breasts. She held it to her sister's throat, who jumped on her perch with raucous cries, like a peacock.

A little later Juniper spoke in a tear-choked voice. "I don't mean you harm, I only want a small glass, no more. I'm so thirsty, so thirsty. Dear Drusille, I want only a single drop . . . and afterwards a look at the beautiful new moon for five minutes. . . . Nobody will see me, nobody, I promise you, I swear it. I'll lie on the roof and look at the moon. I won't go away, I'll come back once I've seen the moon."

Drusille laughed silently. "And then what? Perhaps you'd like me to catch the moon to light up your attic? Listen, Juniper. You're ill, very ill. I only want what's best for you, and if you go out on the roof you'll catch cold, you'll die. . . ."

"If I don't see the moon tonight, I'll be dead tomorrow."

Drusille screamed with rage. "Will you please shut up? Isn't what I do for you enough?"

Suddenly the two sisters heard the noise of a car approaching below. The servants began to shout orders and insult one another.

"I have to go now," announced Drusille, trembling. "Go to sleep."

"Who is it?" Juniper hopped on her perch.

"Mind your own business," replied Drusille.

"Rats, bats, and spiders are my business."

"I've given you socks to knit. Go knit."

Juniper lifted her strange arms as if wanting to fly away. "My hands aren't made for knitting."

"Then knit with your feet." And Drusille left so hastily she forgot to lock the door behind her.

Ex-king Jumart stepped from his old Rolls-Royce. His long, iron grey beard flowed over his green satin coat embroidered with butterflies and the royal monogram. On his superb head he wore an enormous gold wig with rose-coloured shadows, like a cascade of honey. A variety of flowers, growing here and there in his wig, moved in the wind. He held out his hands to Drusille.

"Drusille, my Belzamine."

Drusille trembled with emotion.

"Jumart! Jumart!" She fell into his arms, sobbing and laughing.

"Oh how beautiful you are, Drusille! How I have dreamed of your scent and your kisses." They walked in the garden, their arms entwined.

"I am ruined," Jumart said with a sigh. "My coffers are empty."

Drusille allowed herself a triumphant smile. "Then you'll stay with me! I have had nothing but solitude for too long."

The heavy, murky atmosphere of the garden was rent by a long, raucous cry. Drusille turned pale and murmured, "Oh no, it's impossible."

"What is it, my Belzamine?"

Drusille threw back her head with the laugh of a hyena. "It's the sky," she said. "These yellow clouds weigh so much I was afraid they might fall on our heads! Besides, this stormy weather's giving me a migraine."

"Kiss me," murmured the king tenderly. "I shall eat your migraine."

He noticed that Drusille's face was like the face of a ghost. Frightened, he took her hand in his to reassure himself she was alive.

"Your face is green," he said in a low voice. "There are heavy shadows under your eyes."

"They're the shadows of the leaves," Drusille answered, sweat on her brow. "I'm exhausted by my emotions, it's been three months since I saw you." Then she took him violently by the arm. "Jumart, do you love me? Swear that you are in love with me . . . swear it quickly."

"You know it well," Jumart said, surprised. "What is the matter, my Drusille?"

THE SISTERS

"Do you love me more than all other women? More than all other human beings?"

"Yes, Drusille. And you, do you love me as much?"

"Ah," Drusille said in a trembling voice, "so much that you will never know how much. My love is deeper than deepest space."

The king's attention was distracted by something moving amongst the leaves at the end of the garden. His expression became ecstatic, his eyes glittered.

"What do you see?" cried Drusille suddenly. "Why are you looking down there with that strange expression?"

Abruptly, Jumart came back to himself and said a few words in a dreamy voice. He seemed to be waking up. "The garden is so beautiful, Drusille, I feel as if I were in a dream."

Drusille was choking. She gave a painful smile. "Or a nightmare—sometimes one confuses the two. Let's go in, Jumart, the sun has set, and soon dinner will be on the table. We'll eat on the terrace so that you can enjoy the moonrise. Tonight it will be paler and more beautiful than ever. When I look at the moonlight, I think I'm seeing your beard."

Jumart sighed. "The twilight is enchanted, bewitched. Let's stay out awhile. The garden's suffused in magic. One doesn't know what beautiful phantom might appear from these purple shadows."

Drusille's hands went to her throat, and her voice had a metallic ring. "Let's go in, I beg you. Night's going to fall, I'm shivering with cold."

"Your face is a leaf of such a pale green it must have grown under the light of the new moon. Your eyes are stones found in caves at the centre of the earth. Your eyes are grim."

Drusille's voice became acid: "You're moonstruck. You've gone out of your mind. You're seeing things that aren't there. Give me your hand and I'll take you to the house."

"Bang-bang, who's the madder of us two?" replied Jumart, twisting his beard. "Don't preach to me. If my lands and castles are lost, I'm the happiest of men."

Enchanted with his deep reflections, the king rubbed his

hands and did a few dance steps. Drusille looked at the trees and thought the fruit looked like little corpses. She looked at the sky and saw drowned bodies in the clouds. Her eyes were full of horror. "My head is a bier for my thoughts, my body a coffin." She walked behind the king with slow steps, her hands clasped in front of her.

A bell rang for dinner.

Engadine came out of the kitchen. She was carrying a suckling pig stuffed with nightingales. She stopped with a cry. In front of her an exultant white apparition blocked the way.

"Engadine!"

"What the devil, Miss Juniper . . ."

"Engadine, how red you are."

The maid drew back. The apparition approached, bounding.

"I've just come from the kitchen," Engadine said. "It's hot in the kitchen."

"And I—I'm all white, Engadine. Do you know why I'm white like a ghost?"

Engadine shook her head without speaking.

"It's because I never see the light. And now I'm in great need of something, my dear little Engadine."

"What then? What?" the maid whispered, and she trembled so much that the suckling pig fell to the floor, the platter in a thousand pieces.

"You're so red . . . so red." At these words, Engadine let out a long and terrible siren's cry. At that moment Juniper leapt. The two fell to the ground, Juniper on top, mouth pressed to Engadine's throat.

She sucked, sucked for long minutes, and her body became enormous, luminous, magnificent. Her feathers shone like snow in the sun, her tail sparkled with all the colours of the rainbow. She threw back her head and crowed like a cock. Afterwards she hid the corpse in the drawer of a chest.

"Now for the moon," she sang, leaping and flying towards the terrace. "Now for the moon!"

Drusille, naked to her breasts, had her arms around Jumart's neck. The heat of the wine warmed her skin like a flame, she gleamed with sweat. Her hair moved like black vipers, the juice of a pomegranate dripped from her half-open mouth.

Meat, wine, cakes, all half eaten, were heaped around them in extravagant abundance. Huge pots of jam spilled on the floor made a sticky lake around their feet. The carcass of a peacock decorated Jumart's head. His beard was full of sauces, fish heads, crushed fruit. His gown was torn and stained with all sorts of food.

—Translated from the French
by Kathrine Talbot

Cast Down by Sadness

Cast down by sadness, I walked far into the mountains where the cypresses grew so pointed one would have taken them for arms, where the brambles had thorns as big as claws. I came to a garden overrun by climbing plants and weeds with strange blooms. Through a large gate I saw a little old woman tending her untidy plants. She was dressed in mauve lace and a large hat from another age. The hat, decorated with peacock feathers, sat askew, and her hair escaped on all sides. I stopped my melancholy walk and asked the little old woman to give me a glass of water, as I was thirsty.

"You may drink," she said coquettishly, putting a flower behind her large ear. "Come into my garden."

With extraordinary agility she leapt towards me and took me by the hand. The garden was full of old sculptures of animals, all more or less dilapidated. Plants of every kind mingled in profusion, growing with tropical splendour. The little old woman jumped right and left picking flowers, which in the end she put around my neck.

"There you are, now you're dressed," she said to me, looking at me with her head to the side. "We don't like people coming in here without being dressed. Personally I take a great deal of care with my toilet, one could even say I was something of a coquette." She hid her face behind a little dirty hand, looking at me through her fingers. "Not bad, what," she murmured. "My coquettishness is quite innocent, and no one can say different." At these words she lifted her long skirt an inch or two, and I saw her tiny feet, in little deerskin boots. "I've been told that I have very beautiful feet, but I beg you not to tell anybody that I let you see. . . ."

"Madam," I said, "innumerable troubles have befallen me, and I am very grateful to you, as you have shown me the most beautiful feet I have ever seen. You have little feet like knife blades."

She flew into my arms and kissed me several times. Then she said with great dignity, "I can see that you are a person of exceptional intelligence. I would like to invite you to stay with me. You will not regret it."

That's how I came to know Arabelle Pegase. I shall never forget her black eyes or her feet. She led me to a small lake in the garden and invited me to drink. This lake was surrounded by weeping willows that trailed into the clear water. Arabelle looked at her reflection in the water.

"I have wept so much here," she said. "I find that my beauty is very touching. For entire nights I have trailed my luxuriant hair in the water, and washed my body, telling it, 'You rival the moon, your flesh is more brilliant than its light.' I said all this to give it pleasure, for my body's so jealous of the moon. One evening I'll invite you to meet it."

Trembling, I looked deeply into the water.

I saw a group of peacocks passing on the other side of the lake. I heard their raucous cries.

"I always wear peacock blue underwear," continued Arabelle. "Silk, of course, with eyes embroidered all over. The eyes are there for looking—guess at what."

I shook my head. "I can't guess," I said.

She covered her face with her hand once more, blushing like a young girl.

"But . . . my body!" she said. "They see it morning to night, aren't they the lucky ones?" I was so disturbed by this question that I couldn't reply. Arabelle didn't notice and went on. "I wear a lot of petticoats of all shades of blue and green. And if you saw my knickers, every pair more beautiful than the last. I speak to you as an artist, you understand, simply as an artist. I have a dress made entirely of the heads of cats. It's very beautiful. If you were to see it . . . At one time that was just the height of fashion."

The evening shadows, long and blue, became thicker around us. Arabelle's face was in a haze like some landscapes on a summer day. Somewhere from the other side of the lake a bell rang.

"Dinner," said Arabelle, taking me suddenly by the arm. "And I'm not dressed. Let's hurry, Dominique is going to scold me again." She dragged me along, talking all the time.

"He's so sweet, Dominique, but so nervous. . . . One has to be careful with such sensitive creatures. He's been praying all afternoon, and now he's hungry, and here we are, late. The good Lord help us."

We went along paths overgrown with grass and moss. We found ourselves in front of the house, a large mansion covered in sculptures and terraces descending from it one beyond the other in a stupefying state of confusion.

When Arabelle opened the front door, we found ourselves in a great marble hall, furnished with fruit trees, which grew everywhere. A long table in the middle of the room was set for dinner.

"I'll leave you here for a moment while I change my dress," Arabelle said. "Help yourself to wine and cake while you're waiting." She left me with an enormous carafe of red wine and a quantity of rich cakes. I helped myself to some wine and was looking around tranquilly when I realized I was not alone: a young man was standing beside me, looking at me with hostile eyes. This young man was so pale that I could hardly believe he was alive. He was dressed like a priest, a Jesuit I think, and his cassock was spotted with food and all sorts of filth. His presence made me recoil involuntarily.

"Explain yourself," he said, making the sign of the cross. "I don't like strangers here. Moreover I'm very nervous and it's bad for my health." He poured himself a litre of wine and drank it at a single gulp.

"I don't know what I'm doing here," I replied. "My head feels so heavy I can't think properly, and all I want is to leave immediately."

"You can't go . . . now," he said. "This isn't the right time."

I was disconcerted to see that big tears were rolling down his cheeks. "I understand you so well," Dominique continued. "Don't think I don't know what you are after in this terrible house; I've even prayed for you all afternoon." He hesitated, his voice choked with pain. "I've wept so much for your poor soul."

At this moment Arabelle Pegase made her appearance, dressed in the most extravagant fashion, with ostrich feathers, lace, and jewels, all slightly dirty and very crumpled. She went up to Dominique, took his ear between her lips, and said, "Don't scold me, Dominique darling, I was making myself beautiful for you," and then it seemed to me that she suddenly noticed my presence, for she quickly withdrew.

"Dominique is my little son," she said. "A mother's heart is so tender."

"The garden is so beautiful now," she said. "Dominique, darling, I dream of nothing but walking along the lake with you." Dominique threw her a terrified look. I thought he would faint.

"We are very close in spirit, my son and I," said Arabelle, turning to me. "And we share a great feeling for poetry, isn't that so, Dominique, darling son?"

"Yes, mother of my heart," replied Dominique in a trembling voice.

"Do you remember how when you were a child we played together, and I was as much of a child as you? You remember, Dominiquino?"

"Yes, darling little mother."

"They were lovely, those days we had together. You hugged me all day long and called me Little Sister."

I was embarrassed. I wanted to go, but it was impossible.

"When one has an only son," continued Arabelle, "one thinks and dreams of nothing else."

By the light of the candles I suddenly saw a young girl standing beside Arabelle. She had come in silently and mysteriously. She was beautiful. Her black dress blended with the shadows around her, and I had the impression that her face was floating in space. When Dominique saw this girl, he was taken with such a fit of trembling one might have thought his bones would fall apart. Suddenly Arabelle seemed very old. The girl looked at mother and son with a fixed expression. They got up, and I followed without knowing why. Finally the girl walked towards the door. We went out into the garden and arrived at the lake, still in silence. I saw the reflection of the moon in the water, but was horrified to see there was no moon in the sky: the moon had been drowned in the water.

"Let us see your beautiful body," the girl said, addressing Arabelle.

Dominique gave a cry and fell to the ground. Arabelle began to undress. Quickly there was a heap of dirty clothes beside her, but she kept on taking off more with a sort of rage. At last she was completely undressed, and her body was nothing but a skeleton. The girl, arms crossed on her chest, waited.

"Dominique," she said, "are you alive?"

"He's alive," cried the mother. I had the feeling I was at a spectacle that had already been played out a hundred times.

"I am dead," Dominique said. "Leave me in peace."

"Is he dead or is he alive?" asked the girl in a sonorous voice.

"Alive," cried the mother.

"And yet he's been buried a long time," replied the girl.

"Come let me kill you," the old woman shrieked. "Come let me kill you for the hundred and twentieth time."

The two women threw themselves upon each other and fought savagely. They went into the water administering ferocious blows to each other.

"The moon is immortal," the girl shouted, with her hands around the old woman's throat. "You've killed the moon, but she doesn't rot like your son."

I saw the old woman growing weaker, and she soon disappeared into the water, followed by the girl. With a sigh, Dominique crumbled into a heap of dust. I was alone in a night without light.

—Translated from the French
by Kathrine Talbot

White Rabbits

The time has come that I must tell the events which began in 40 Pest Street. The houses, which were reddish black, looked as if they had issued mysteriously from the fire of London. The house in front of my window, covered with an occasional wisp of creeper, was as black and empty looking as any plague-ridden residence subsequently licked by flames and smoke. This is not the way that I had imagined New York.

It was so hot that I got palpitations when I ventured out into the streets, so I sat and considered the house opposite and occasionally bathed my sweating face.

The light was never very strong in Pest Street. There was always a reminiscence of smoke, which made visibility troubled and hazy—still it was possible to study the house opposite carefully, even precisely. Besides, my eyes have always been excellent.

I spent several days watching for some sort of movement

opposite but there was none, and I finally took to undressing quite freely before my open window and doing my breathing exercises optimistically in the thick Pest Street air. This must have made my lungs as black as the houses.

One afternoon I washed my hair and sat out on the diminutive stone crescent which served as a balcony to dry it. I hung my head between my knees and watched a bluebottle suck the dry corpse of a spider between my feet. I looked up through my long hair and saw something black in the sky, ominously quiet for an aeroplane. Parting my hair, I was in time to see a large raven alight on the balcony of the house opposite. It sat on the balustrade and seemed to peer into the empty window. Then it poked its head under its wing, apparently searching for lice. A few minutes later I was not unduly surprised to see the double windows open and admit a woman onto the balcony. She carried a large dish full of bones, which she emptied onto the floor. With a short appreciative squeak, the raven hopped down and poked about amongst its unpleasant repast.

The woman, who had very long black hair, used her hair to wipe out the dish. Then she looked straight at me and smiled in a friendly fashion. I smiled back and waved a towel. This served to encourage her, for she tossed her head coquettishly and gave me a very elegant salute after the fashion of a queen.

"Do you happen to have any bad meat over there that you don't need?" she called.

"Any what?" I called back, wondering if my ears had deceived me.

"Any stinking meat? Decomposed flesh meat?"

"Not at the moment," I replied, wondering if she was trying to be funny.

"Won't you have any towards the end of the week? If so, I would be very grateful if you would bring it over."

Then she stepped back into the empty window and disappeared. The raven flew away.

My curiosity about the house and its occupant prompted me to buy a large lump of meat the following day. I set it on the balcony on a bit of newspaper and awaited developments. In a comparatively short time the smell was so strong that I was obliged to pursue my daily activities with a strong paper clip on the end of my nose. Occasionally I descended into the street to breathe.

Towards Thursday evening I noticed that the meat was turning colour, so waving aside a flight of rancourous bluebottles, I scooped it into my sponge bag and set out for the house opposite. I noticed, descending the stairs, that the landlady seemed to avoid me.

It took me some time to find the front door of the house opposite. It turned out to be hidden under a cascade of something, giving the impression that nobody had been either in or out of this house for years. The bell was of the old-fashioned kind that you pull, and when I pulled it rather harder than I intended, it came right off in my hand. I gave the door an angry push and it caved inwards, admitting a ghastly smell of putrid meat. The hall, which was almost dark, seemed to be of carved woodwork.

The woman herself came rustling down the stairs, carrying a torch.

"How do you do? How do you do?" she murmured ceremoniously, and I was surprised to notice that she wore an ancient beautiful dress of green silk. But as she approached me I saw that her skin was dead white and glittered as if speckled with thousands of minute stars.

"Isn't that kind of you?" she went on, taking my arm with her sparkling hand. "Won't my poor little rabbits be pleased?"

We mounted the stairs and my companion walked so carefully that I thought she was frightened.

The top flight of stairs opened into a boudoir decorated with dark baroque furniture and red plush. The floor was littered with gnawed bones and animal skulls.

"It is so seldom that we get a visit." The woman smiled. "So they all scatter off into their little corners."

She uttered a low sweet whistle, and transfixed, I saw about a hundred snow white rabbits emerge cautiously from every nook, their large pink eyes fixed unblinkingly upon the woman.

"Come, pretty ones! Come, pretty ones!" she cooed, diving her hand into my sponge bag and pulling out a handful of rotting meat.

With a sensation of deep disgust, I backed into a corner and saw her throw the carrion amongst the rabbits, who fought like wolves for the meat.

"One becomes very fond of them," the woman went on. "They each have their little ways! You would be surprised how very individual rabbits are."

The rabbits in question were tearing at the meat with their sharp buck teeth.

"We eat them of course occasionally. My husband makes a very tasty stew every Saturday night."

Then a movement in the corner caught my attention and I realized that there was a third person in the room. As the woman's torchlight touched his face I saw he had identical glittering skin, like tinsel on a Christmas tree. He was dressed in a red gown and sat very rigidly with his profile turned towards us. He seemed to be unconscious of our presence or of that of a large white buck rabbit which sat and masticated on a chunk of meat on his knee.

The woman followed my gaze and chuckled. "That is my husband. The boys used to call him Lazarus—"

At the sound of this familiar name, he turned his face towards us and I saw that he wore a bandage over his eyes.

"Ethel?" he enquired in a rather thin voice. "I won't have any visitors here. You know quite well that I have strictly forbidden it."

"Now, Laz, don't start carrying on." Her voice was plaintive. "You can't grudge me a little bit of company. It's twenty-odd years since I've seen a new face. Besides, she's brought meat for the rabbits."

She turned and beckoned me to her side. "You want to

stay with us, do you not, my dear?" I was suddenly clutched by fear and I wanted to get out and away from these terrible silver people and the white carnivorous rabbits.

"I think I must be going, it's suppertime—"

The man on the chair gave a shrill peal of laughter, terrifying the rabbit on his knee, which sprang to the floor and disappeared.

The woman thrust her face so near to mine that her sickly breath seemed to anaesthetize me. "Do you not want to stay and become like us? In seven years your skin will be like stars, in seven little years you will have the holy disease of the Bible, leprosy!"

I stumbled and ran, choking with horror; some unholy curiosity made me look over my shoulder as I reached the front door and I saw her waving her hand over the banister, and as she waved it, her fingers fell off and dropped to the ground like shooting stars.

Waiting

Two old women were fighting in the street, pinching each other like a pair of angry black lobsters. One or two nighthawkers watched them appreciatively.

Nobody knew how the quarrel had begun.

A young woman on the other side of the street also observed the fight but she was more absorbed in the windows above, which went dark one by one. It was the hour of sleep, and with the extinction of each light the night became longer.

People had given up staring at her, she had been standing there for so long. She was like a familiar ghost, but she was strange looking; her clothes were too long and her hair much too untidy, like those of a person barely saved from drowning. Somebody, a little earlier, had quickened his step and looked away because a winged creature was clinging to her mouth and she had not stirred.

Now the creature had flown away on its own mysterious business, leaving the red on her mouth slightly smudged.

She wondered how it was that the people in the street were not dancing, dancing to the monotonous rhythm in her head. It was loud and dangerous and it made wonderful music.

A tall woman came striding around the corner and stopped near her. On a leash she had two big blonde dogs the same colour as her hair, itself like a separate animal sitting on her head.

The dogs were excited and pulled her over to the young woman.

"What are you doing?" she said. "At this hour . . ."

She bent down and seemed to address the dogs.

"They have been dancing for hours you know, the hounds . . . they led me here."

"I am waiting for Fernando."

"And you have no tears left?"

"No, I haven't any more," admitted the young woman. "Although I tried pinching my breasts and thinking of death, it was no good. So I came out here."

The blonde woman took a sheepskin off her arm and wrapped it around the other. "Come," she said, "you must get free, free to kill and scream, free to tear out his hair and free to run away only to come back laughing."

"His hair is so long and straight and almost blue, blue grey, I love it so much."

She relapsed into infatuated silence.

"Be careful. I shall slap you . . . ," said the blonde woman irritably.

"You can't love anyone until you have drawn blood and dipped in your fingers and enjoyed it."

They were being pulled along by the big blonde dogs and occasionally dragged zigzagging across the street to another fascinating stink.

"My name," said the blonde woman, "is Elizabeth . . . a beautiful name which suits me admirably."

"Margaret," said the young woman sadly, "is my name. Margaret."

"Musical Margaret," said Elizabeth, giving a loud triumphant laugh, which sent the dogs bounding forward.

"Not yet!" screamed Elizabeth. "Not yet. . . . But they always obey me in small things, although I am directed in others. . . . They lead me, my trust is implicit."

They were pulled into a small square, charming with trees and elegantly windowed houses; the dogs went straight to Number 7. In they went and up a rather bleak marble staircase. Up and up to the highest landing and finally in through a small blue door to a diminutive hall littered with beautifully coloured and rather soiled clothes. Their entrance provoked a flight of large moths, which had been grazing peacefully amongst the more mature fur coats.

Somewhere a musical box played a very old song.

"The past," said Elizabeth, unleashing the dogs. "The adorable living past. One must wallow, just wallow in it. How can anybody be a person of quality if they wash away their ghosts with common sense?"

She turned on Margaret ferociously and laughed in her face.

"Do you believe," she went on, "that the past dies?"

"Yes," said Margaret. "Yes, if the present cuts its throat."

"Those little white hands could cut nobody's throat."

Elizabeth laughed so much that she reeled around the room.

"How old is Fernando?" she asked suddenly. "Older than you?"

"Yes," said Margaret, who looked ill. "Fernando is forty-three."

"Forty-three, that makes seven . . . a beautiful number."

The dogs rolled about voluptuously amongst the silks and furs.

Elizabeth pulled Margaret into the kitchen, where the long-dead stove was littered with cooking utensils or half full of what looked like green food; but Margaret saw that the green-ness was a fluffy growth of fungi. Most of the crockery on the floor was covered with the same feathery vegetation.

"We just had dinner," said Elizabeth. "I always cook too much. . . . You see, I don't like meals, I only eat banquets."

She dipped a spoon into the nearest dish, after having examined it closely. . . .

"It dropped into the lavatory the other day," she explained, "while I was washing up. Hungry?" she asked.

Margaret said that she was not hungry.

"Then come . . . ," said Elizabeth. "We will talk."

The musical box started to play again and Margaret remembered the tune because Fernando had always hated it. He had once said that he preferred to pour boiling oil into his eardrums than listen to that tune; it was called "I Will Always Come Back."

The third room was a bedroom whose dark strawberry walls were stained with age. The disorder was possibly greater than that in the kitchen and hall and the bed was rumpled and looked as if it was still warm from lovemaking.

Elizabeth stood at the door smiling and looking at the bed, then she bent down and picked up a satin shoe and threw it across the room. Margaret screamed as two mice jumped out of the wrinkled sheets and scuttled down the counterpane with the smooth legless rapidity that terrifies women.

"There has been so much love in here that even the mice come back," said Elizabeth. "It is like the ticking of a clock; you have to listen to hear and then when you listen you can't stop hearing."

"Yes," said Margaret. "Yes, that's right."

She kept wiping her hands on her skirt, they were damp. The two dogs were sitting near the end of the bed, they were listening.

"I always wear cotton wool in my ears," Elizabeth went on. "Otherwise the sounds outside distract me. I am only human, not like them. . . ." She looked at the dogs.

"I cut his toenails myself. And I know every inch of his

body and the difference between the smell of his hair and the smell of his skin."

"Who?" whispered Margaret. "Not Fernando?"

"Yes, Fernando," answered Elizabeth. "Who else but Fernando."

The Seventh Horse

A strange-looking creature was hopping about in the midst of a bramble bush. She was caught by her long hair, which was so closely entwined in the brambles that she could move neither backwards nor forwards. She was cursing and hopping till the blood flowed down her body.

"I do not like the look of it," said one of the two ladies who intended to visit the rose garden.

"It might be a young woman . . . and yet . . ."

"This is my garden," replied the other, who was as thin and dry as a stick. "And I strongly object to trespassers. I expect it is my poor silly little husband who has let her in. He is such a child you know."

"I've been here for years," shrieked the creature angrily. "But you are too stupid to have seen me."

"Impertinent as well," remarked the first lady, who was called Miss Myrtle. "I think you had better call the gardener,

Mildred. I don't think it is quite safe to go so near. The creature seems to have no modesty."

Hevalino tugged angrily at her hair as if she would like to get at Mildred and her companion. The two ladies turned to go, not before they had exchanged a long look of hate with Hevalino.

The spring evening was lengthening before the gardener came to set Hevalino free.

"John," said Hevalino, lying down on the grass, "can you count up to seven? Do you know that I can hate for seventy-seven million years without stopping for rest. Tell those miserable people that they are doomed." She trailed off towards the stable where she lived, muttering as she went: "Seventy-seven, seventy-seven."

There were certain parts of the garden where all the flowers, trees, and plants grew tangled together. Even on the hottest days these places were in blue shadow. There were deserted figures overgrown with moss, still fountains, and old toys, decapitated and destitute. Nobody went there except Hevalino; she would kneel and eat the short grass and watch a fascinating fat bird who never moved away from his shadow. He let his shadow glide around him as the day went by and over him when there was a moon. He always sat with his hairy mouth wide open, and moths and little insects would fly in and out.

Hevalino went to see the bird dining the night after she was caught in the brambles. A retinue of six horses accompanied her. They walked seven times around the fat bird in silence.

"Who's there?" said the bird eventually, in a whistling voice.

"It is I, Hevalino, with my six horses."

"You are keeping me awake with your stumping and snorting," came the plaintive reply. "If I cannot sleep I can see neither the past nor the future. I shall waste away if you won't go away and let me sleep."

"They are going to come and kill you," said Hevalino. "You had better keep awake. I heard somebody say you would be roasted in hot fat, stuffed with parsley and onions, and then eaten."

The corpulent bird cast an apprehensive eye on Hevalino, who was watching him closely.

"How do you know?" breathed the bird. "Just tell me that."

"You are much too fat to fly," continued Hevalino relentlessly. "If you tried to fly you'd be like a fat toad doing his death dance."

"How do you know this?" screamed the bird. "They can't know where I am. I've been here for seventy-seven years."

"They don't know yet . . . not yet." Hevalino had her face close to his open beak; her lips were drawn back and the bird could see her long wolves' teeth.

His fat little body quivered like a jelly.

"What do you want of me?"

Hevalino gave a sort of crooked smile. "Ah, that's better." She and the six horses made a circle around the bird and watched him with their prominent and relentless eyes.

"I want to know exactly what is going on in the house," said she. "And be quick about it." The bird cast a frightened look around him, but the horses had sat down. There was no escape. He became wet with sweat and the feathers clung, draggled, to his fat stomach.

"I cannot say," he said at last in a strangled voice. "Something terrible will befall us if I say what I can see."

"Roasted in hot fat and eaten," said Hevalino.

"You are mad to want to know things that do not concern you . . . !"

"I am waiting," said Hevalino. The bird gave a long convulsive shudder and turned his eyes, which had become bulging and sightless, to the east.

"They are at dinner," he said eventually, and a great black moth flew out of his mouth.

"The table is laid for three people. Mildred and her husband have begun to eat their soup. She is watching him suspiciously. 'I found something unpleasant in the garden today,' she says, laying down her spoon; I doubt if she will eat any more now.

" 'What was that?' asks he. 'Why do you look so angry?'

"Miss Myrtle has now come into the room. She looks from one to the other. She seems to guess what they are discussing, for she says: 'Yes, really, Philip, I think you ought to be more careful whom you let into the garden.'

" 'What are you talking about?' he says angrily. 'How do you expect me to stop anything if I don't know what I am stopping?'

" 'It was an unpleasant-looking creature half naked and caught in a bramble bush. I had to turn my eyes away.'

" 'You let this creature free, of course?'

" 'Indeed I did not. I consider it just as well that she was trapped as she was. By the cruel look on her face I should judge she would have done us serious harm.'

" 'What! You left this poor creature trapped in the brambles? Mildred, there are times when you revolt me. I am sick of you pottering around the village and annoying the poor with your religious preamble, and now when you see a poor thing in your own garden you do nothing but shudder with false modesty.'

"Mildred gives a shocked cry and covers her face with a slightly soiled handkerchief. 'Philip, why do you say such cruel things to me, your wife?'

"Philip, with an expression of resigned annoyance asks, 'Try and describe this creature. Is it an animal or a woman?'

" 'I can say no more,' sobs the wife. 'After what you have said to me I feel faint.'

" 'You should be more careful,' whispers Miss Myrtle. 'In her delicate condition!'

" 'What do you mean "delicate condition"?' asks Philip irritably. 'I do wish people would say what they mean.'

" 'Why surely you must know,' Miss Myrtle simpers. 'You are going to become a daddy in a short time. . . .' Philip goes white with rage. 'I won't stand these fatuous lies. It is quite impossible that Mildred is pregnant. She has not graced my bed for five whole years, and unless the Holy Ghost is in the house I don't see how it came about. For Mildred is unpleasantly virtuous, and I cannot imagine her abandoning herself to anybody.'

" 'Mildred, is this true?' says Miss Myrtle, trembling with delicious expectation. Mildred shrieks and sobs: 'He is a liar. I am going to have a darling little baby in three months.'

"Philip flings down his spoon and serviette and gets to his feet. 'For the seventh time in seven days I shall finish my dinner upstairs,' says he, and stops for an instant as if his words have awakened some memory. He puts it away from him and shakes his head. 'All I ask is that you don't come whining after me,' he says to his wife and quits the room. She shrieks: 'Philip, my darling little husband, come back and eat your soup, I promise I won't be naughty anymore.'

" 'Too late,' comes the voice of Philip from the staircase, 'too late now.'

"He goes slowly up to the top of the house with his eyes looking a long way ahead of him. His face is strained as if in the effort of listening to faraway voices chattering between nightmares and dead reality. He reaches the attic at the top of the house, where he seats himself on an old trunk. I believe that the trunk is filled with ancient laces, frilly knickers, and dresses. But they are old and torn; there is a black moth making his dinner on them as Philip sits staring at the window. He considers a stuffed hedgepig on the mantel piece, who looks worn out with suffering. Philip seems to be smothered with the atmosphere of this attic; he flings open the window and gives a long . . ."

Here the bird paused, and a long sickening neigh rent the night. The six horses leapt to their feet and replied in their piercing voices. Hevalino stood stock-still, with her lips drawn back and her nostrils quivering. "Philip, the friend of the horses . . ." The six horses thundered off towards the stable, as if obeying an age-old summons. Hevalino, with a shuddering sigh, followed, her hair streaming behind her.

Philip was at the stable door as they arrived. His face was luminous and as white as snow. He counted seven horses as they galloped by. He caught the seventh by the mane, and leapt onto her back. The mare galloped as if her heart would burst. And all the time Philip was in a great ecstasy of love; he felt he had grown onto the back of this beautiful black mare, and that they were one creature.

At the crack of dawn all the horses were back in their places. And the little wrinkled groom was rubbing off the caked sweat and mud of the night. His creased face smiled wisely as he rubbed his charges with infinite care. He appeared not to notice the master, who stood alone in an empty stall. But he knew he was there.

"How many horses have I?" said Philip at last.

"Six, sir," said the little groom, without ceasing to smile.

That night the corpse of Mildred was found near the stable. One would believe that she had been trampled to death . . . and yet "They are all as gentle as lambs," said the little groom. If Mildred had been pregnant there was no sign of it as she was stuffed into a respectable black coffin. However nobody could explain the presence of a small misshapen foal that had found its way into the seventh empty stall.

II
THE
STONE
DOOR

The Stone Door

I

September 15.

Cancer. Illness, New York. Cancer. Tropic of (Mexico). Cancer, fourth place in the circle. Water Father. Spider-Crab. Mizte-cacihautl's box, (6) Scorpion-crab for funeral paraphernalia. Tiger-spider-crab in dream.

The star follows her strange course in the mountains, in the round temples, through green, lukewarm woods and penetrating hedges and walls. She lies hard, bright, and cold under the beds of lovers or under bodies of sleeping cattle.

I never cease spying on the star's course.

Pedro came in drunk again, I made him a screeching sordid scene and yet I am stuck like a rat in a trap. Will I ever be free? What secret craving keeps me near him?

Day.

The cuckoo clock is driving me wild. I am always alone, that is what makes me suffer. Damn that bird.

Words are treacherous because they are incomplete. The written word hangs in time like a lump of lead. Everything should move with the ages and the planets.

The time has come for the star to appear once more. Perhaps I will dress in wolfskin, sitting in a tree watching the circle, waiting for the next step to be traced in the mud.

All these shadows from the unknown. I am ignorant, but soon I shall begin to know.

It is still October.

A clue, October, the scales. The man and woman in the egg. The house of the Sleeping Winds. They hang together like witchstones made into a broken necklace. Clues because they smell of the same sensation, how or why I cannot say.

The ivory box lined with sandalwood which I used to sniff when nobody was in the drawing room. The ivory box awakened unnamed memories.

The last days of October.

Divination is difficult with isolated incidents. Weaving them together into prophecy is an arduous labor. Hazard a word dropped out of the unknown. Several hazards sometimes make a whole sentence. My memory twitches into a sharp image of something never seen, yet remembered and so acutely alive that I am possessed.

A pine forest white with snow in a country where the people are dressed in bright colours. A noise of smashed glass. Little ragged horses as swift and powerful as tigers. Snow, dust, and cinnamon.

Wearing a mask I am on all fours with my nose almost touching the nose of a wolf. Our eyes united in a look, yet I remain hidden behind myself and the wolf hidden behind himself; we are divided by our separate bodies. However deeply we look into each other's eyes a transparent wall divides us from explosion where the looks cross outside our bodies. If by some sage power I could capture that explosion, that mysterious area outside where the wolf and I are one, perhaps then the first door would open and reveal the chamber beyond.

Last night in a dream It returned. A creature wearing a shaggy skin and smelling of dust and cinnamon. Screaming I entered the fur, wool, or hair, crying tears that were dark and sticky like blood. Tears thick with centuries of agony remembered all at once, they matted the furry coat and stank of birth and death. Shamelessly abandoning all that anguish to this man, animal, vegetable, or demon. Then I was in entire possession of the five sensorial powers and their long roots were as visible as the sun. The light of a vision or a dream is united to any given luminous body outside. No longer alone in my own body.

Thoughts and dreams but not a particle of dust to prove their reality. Meanwhile I am wasting each living day in captivity.

All Saints' Day.

Sorcerers and alchemists knew about animal, vegetable, and mineral bodies. To hack away the crust of what we have forgotten and rediscover things we knew before we were born.

November 16.

I rode a white horse through the woods of Chapultepec. A grey early morning and few people were about. I galloped around the Palace thinking all the while of my loneliness and of the creature dressed in wool and smelling of cinnamon and dust. Try as I would I could not evoke his real presence and he remained a thought. The formula for this evocation is somewhere hidden inside of me, I feel small and ignorant and this pleases me not at all. I cannot accept this, I want to feel enormous and powerful. (I secretly believe that I am a goddess with very short moments of incarnation.) At the moment Pedro and I loathe each other. We scream ourselves to sleep like fishwives. This is a terrible waste of good energy. Yet I dare not go. Return, ghost, animal, or man. I cannot bear this loneliness, I am sick of being alone with myself.

November 20.

Several nights ago I was alone, Pedro being absent as usual. Making a cup of coffee I resolved to be firmly indifferent to his neglect. It is difficult not to feel like an abandoned kitchen maid. Drinking my coffee in my dreary little hole of a kitchen, I pondered about myself.

"I am sitting here alone. I am a fool, a person letting herself starve to death because the odor of food is usually more exquisite than its taste. No philosopher ever told me if one could capture in taste the aroma of roasting coffee."

While I was busy telling myself this, in a futile attempt to shut out my loneliness, a small white packet on the table caught my eye. Undoing it curiously I found several sticks of cinnamon. I did not remember having bought cinnamon that day.

Cheered, yet afraid, I took myself to bed and placed the cinnamon under my pillow, to give any passing succubus a sporting chance.

When I closed my eyes the following dream, memory, or vision unrolled: I was crossing Mesopotamia on foot and carried a load on my back. It is difficult to say if the load was heavy or light because I already seemed to be accustomed to carrying loads and this had become a function of my body.

My destination was Hungary, which apparently shared a frontier with Mesopotamia. The country in which I travelled was barren, with hardly a tree to be seen. The dusty waste was interrupted here and there by tombs of all shapes and sizes, beautifully decorated and painted like tropical fish. Looking around me I noticed that the people were not entirely

THE STONE DOOR

human but on the contrary were partially of clay. They glided slowly through the dust, now and then colliding and one or both shattering to smithereens.

The Mesopotamians, thought I, are a savage and lazy race. Approaching what looked like a town or very large cemetery I noticed a person detach himself from the group of human pottery and run to me. Actually it was more of a shuffle than a run, as the tight wrapping which swathed him from head to foot encumbered his movements. As he shuffled one of his feet fell off like a dry leaf from a tree.

As he drew near he started shouting: "What news, Stranger? What news?"

His appearance was ancient but he was young: the cracked brown face was that of a boy not much older than twelve.

"You are from Baghdad, no doubt?" he asked, panting clouds of dust into my face. I waited to see what I would reply.

"From Baghdad, Master. I have been walking for twenty days."

"Are you dead?"

"No, I think not. The Lord Mayor of Baghdad paid me three farthings to take this present to the Jewish King who lives on the frontier of Hungary. I pass through here as a shortcut."

"You are a slave?"

"Why, no," I replied stiffly. "I am a beggar."

"What will you do if you can never get out of the country of the Dead? The stone door of Kecske is jealously guarded."

"I will shriek till *doomsday*, till my voice is written all over the centre of the Earth like the drawings on the wall of a lavatory."

"Still, Kecske may never open."

"Kecske will open."

He put out his tongue, a mere black thread, and uttered a laugh like the last crow of a decrepit rooster.

"What does the Lord Mayor of Baghdad send to the King of the Jews?"

"A toy, Master."

"Besides the toy, what is there in your bag?"

I gave him a cunning smile and shook my matted hair.

"That is a secret; there are twelve thousand treasures in my sack."

Giving another laugh as dry as the wrinkled skin on his young face, he put his head close to my ear and said: "Tell me a story and I will give you a slice of funeral cake."

"Must the story be true?" I asked, setting down my burden.

"All stories are true," he said. "Begin."

"One night while passing through the desert by the light of a fat moon I saw a hump on the horizon. Before I was near I could make out more humps, which grew in size and complexity till I could see that it was really the encampment of a large caravan. The tents, embroidered with foreign letters, were grouped about a central pavilion like chicks around a hen.

"A hundred slaves armed with musical instruments squatted all around this centre tent, blocking my approach.

"A slave passed near the boulder, and with a quick snatch I imprisoned her ankle in my hand.

"'I am the devil,' I said, 'and you must do my will.'

"'Command,' replied the terrified slave.

"'I wish to see your master.'

"'That is difficult,' replied the slave. 'No living being may look at my master, for he is the wise King of all the Jews.'

"'If you cannot arrange what I ask I shall release the fire in my fingers and roast you here and now.'

"'Then you must climb onto the royal tent and peep through the hole gnawed by the Chancellor's pet rat.'

"'How shall I pass through the servants and climb such a height without being noticed?'

"'You must disguise yourself as a bird. The King always travels with a drove of Mexican wild turkeys.'

"'Then bring me some feathers.'

"When she had gone I lay in the warm earth, which still smelt of the sun. The chill dawn had not yet arrived. Soon the slave returned with a sack of feathers and a jar of honey and I set about disguising myself as a turkey.

"Once I rolled in the honey and the feathers were stuck on, the slave tied a string around my neck and led me through the groups of servants, while I hopped and clucked like an outraged fowl.

" 'What have you there?' they asked. 'That is a very ugly bird.'

" 'It's a turkey,' replied the Egyptian slave, 'a turkey for the King's supper.'

"Behind the tent hung a silk ladder. The slave indicated this, saying: 'I can help you no more, you must escape as you can when you have seen the King. This was your wish, although you may be cursed to the end of your days for this adventure.'

" 'I shall perch on the King's tent and crow my triumph,' I replied. 'The wise King may not pass through the desert till I have seen him.'

" 'That is a great impertinence,' said the slave sadly. 'Moses was blasted to bits for less.'

" 'Leave me in peace,' I told her.

"I climbed the silk ladder with some tremor. What if I should be discovered? I startled some vultures which had been sitting immobile on top of the tent, like gourds staring vacantly into the night.

"The Chancellor's pet rat gnawed a passably large hole in the roof, and without losing a second I peeped through.

"There stood the King, admiring himself in a sheet of brass. I could well understand the rapt admiration of the King for his own image. Such a beautiful being never stepped out of a female belly. His great curling beard swept the earth at his feet, black as night herself. The Monarch of All Ravens never had such a majestically curved nose, nor any stag a darker or more liquid eye.

"The nightshirt which hung in long folds from his tall body was embroidered with all the secrets of the cabala in scarlet letters.

"Looking deeply into the face reflected in the sheet of brass the King murmured: 'I am as bored as I am exquisite. Is it a source of pleasure to possess a beauty which cracks any ordinary mirror? Perhaps I eat too much during dinner, perhaps I am depressed because the talking bronze head from Persia will not talk. . . . I have no new toys and no desire to learn more of the Universe. Play and study are devoid of interest. I am bored and sad . . . even fear would be a release.'

"Listening to the King I leaned too far through the hole and fell, landing a few paces from his feet.

"The Monarch leapt into the air with the grace of a goat. The ends of his moustache twitched with fright.

" 'An angel of God or Satan?' said the King after he recovered his poise.

" 'I am an errant angel banished from Heaven with Lucifer. Out of Hell I crept to find the King of Kings they call Solomon.'

" 'No ordinary being may look at me,' replied the King. 'So I must believe you have passed through Heaven and Hell.'

" 'I have been feeling a certain soreness in my shoulder blades, which makes me think I'm growing a pair of wings.'

" 'With what you have learned in Heaven, in Hell, upon and under the Earth, you should possess twelve wings.'

"His words shook me. Dreams and nightmares were contained in the King's hermetic smile.

"I was greatly troubled and I asked: 'You and I can swim back and forth in time, but are we condemned to remain alone?'

" 'It is a great thing to be errant in time and space,' said the King. 'The frontiers into the unknown are constructed in layers. One layer opens into a fan of other layers, which open new worlds in their turn. It is true that there is an infinite empty space somewhere beyond the Universe. It is equally true that that space is as richly peopled and inhabited as this very Earth. The space is dark, with no beginning and no end. The space is light, it begins, ends, and continues like life.'

"The King sat down and I noticed that a brood of small transparent roots grew from the soles of his feet. 'Yes, I am also errant. My roots can find no soil and this is why they are visible.'

" 'You are a prophet,' I said. 'Tell me, where is the promised land of the Jews?'

" 'Far beyond Mesopotamia and Hungary. Those who find the promised land will be few and they must arrive hundreds of years before and after it has been used as a word. The world only recognizes truth after it is dead and gone. . . . I should say a million truths, or a particle of reality.'

"He curled strands of beard in his fingers as he spoke. I was astounded at the shining texture of his whiskers. He continued: 'Words are more useless than the dust of the desert because language has also died, and dead things have movements that are difficult for an eye to perceive.'

"He then gave me a small wooden wheel in the centre of which was a spider. 'The eight legs of the spider are love and death. The eight spokes of the wheel are triumph, movement, and life.'

"I was shaken by my encounter, and I moved out of the camp without taking any note of my direction. I was sure that I had a mission but I could not remember what it was. As I racked my brain my feet covered great distances; then I realized with a shock that the bearded King was my mission and that I had left him. It was he I had been seeking in Heaven, on Earth, and in Hell.

"Shouting insults at myself for my stupidity I turned tail and ran till I felt sick back to where the King had pitched his camp.

"All that remained of the sumptuous camp was a little hole in the dust containing a stick of cinnamon, a skein of black wool, and five iron nails."

When I had ended my story, the creature in tight wrappings laughed till he shook and his body rattled like a dry gourd.

"My heart," he explained mirthfully, "is dry as a nut, and rolls about inside me when I laugh."

He gave me a slice of funeral cake as he had promised,

and when his mirth had abated I asked: "Is there such a black-bearded King in the great cemetery yonder?"

But the only reply was the frantic rattling of his heart.

The dream left a sensation of such bitter loss that I felt life could only be lived in sleep. Occupations like washing, dressing, eating, and talking became so laborious that the sun revolved more slowly on its orbit. Every human creature I saw filled me with repugnance, till I did not dare approach the window to look into the street. When anyone chanced to knock on the door I hid, shuddering with horror in the bathroom. I have never loved my fellow beings but that day the very sight of them became tedious. As long as the light lasted my nerves chattered like parakeets; little by little darkness came and the suffering was less acute. When I saw the lamps light in the street I went to bed and shortly found myself back in Mesopotamia.

Standing on a hill and looking back along the road I saw the city of tombs still visible in the distance. Before me the road continued like a dusty ribbon whose borders were marked by heaps of broken sculpture and miscellaneous rubbish such as partially unwrapped mummies in different stages of mutilation, painted tablets in every known and unknown language, books and parchments dried into convulsive gestures, old shoes, sandals, and boots, and any number of pots and casks, urns and dishes in whole or small pieces.

As I walked slowly along the road I examined these rich heaps of rubbish, stopping now and again to root about, putting anything that happened to please me in my sack.

The only tracks in the road leading away from the city were my own. A constant stream of beings passed by, all bent on the same destination. Their appearance was confused and some were transparent. There were animals, vegetables, men and women. Some of them had an individual outline but others were joined like Siamese twins in twos or threes or in greater numbers, forming geometrical shapes and objects such as five-, six-, eight-, nine-, or twelve-sided polygons, triangles, squares, circles, or kitchen utensils and articles of furniture. I saw a five-legged table composed of two fox terriers, a field of daffodils, and three middle-aged women in an embrace. Flapping over them was the carcass of a sea lion.

The motley throng streamed by without noticing me. I supposed they must be ghosts.

After walking some distance putting this and that in my sack I became hungry, and sat down on a Druid's head to eat the funeral cake I had been given in payment for my story. It was hard and dry and difficult to eat. I would have thanked my destiny for a cup of cold water instead, but no liquid was in sight, so I ate what I could and put the rest in my sack for hard times.

Looking back along the road I saw that a vague shape was forming in the distance and advancing in my direction. This gave me some hope for a companion along the lonely road. The thing or person was difficult to define; as it approached it became larger, but it remained a vague form. Only when this fluid and embryonic shape was within a few yards of me could I distinguish a perfect oval containing a moving object within. A light from the centre of the object threw out five rays, forming a star. The oval hopped along like somebody walking on one foot, though it did not lack grace.

"That," I said aloud, "is the Egg. The Egg within the Star, the Star within the Egg."

These words seemed appropriate, for it hesitated a few yards away and hopped nimbly onto a painted tombstone, where it perched.

"Our meeting must explain why I lost the black-bearded King. That I know."

This produced no effect on the Egg so I realized that I must dive deeper to find the right words. When I could utter these words the reply would follow as day follows night.

Taking a small trowel out of my sack I began to dig in the roadside for the word that would open the secret of the Egg. As I worked I repeated all the long words I knew, such as *federation*, *conspicuous*, *anthropology*, and *metamorpho-*

sis. The Egg did not budge an inch. I tried one-syllable words like *am*, *art*, *it*, and *off*. The Egg trembled very slightly, without communicating any meaning to me. I then understood that the word to address such a primitive and embryonic body would have to come from a language buried at the back of time. The very moment that I understood this my trowel grated on a hard thing in the earth, and with a cry of joy I pulled a small pipe out of the ground. I put it to my lips and blew some notes, which started low but mounted the scale rapidly till they reached such a high pitch that my ear could scarcely catch the thin sound. An umbilical cord unrolled slowly out of the center of the Egg and wriggled along the ground towards me. When it reached my left foot I picked up the end and knotted it firmly around my neck. Thus united, the Egg and I started along the road in Indian file. As we advanced I played the pipe. Our movements coincided in a kind of elementary dance, facilitating the journey so much that we travelled far before I felt any fatigue.

A lonely pair we made, the Egg and I, in the great dusty plain of Mesopotamia.

So long as I made my thin tune on the pipe the Egg hopped along behind me willingly, but if I hesitated for a moment it would halt and the umbilical cord would tighten around my neck.

We continued for a long time, until I noticed that the music became slower and the notes lengthened, sounding finally more like shrieks than music. The Egg was drastically affected: the Star stretched and broke the oval contour; each one of the five prongs became a sense and each sense shot out five bright rays, which bit into the earth and up into the air like long sharp teeth. The umbilical cord withered and dried till it hung about my neck like a piece of straw.

The Star and the Egg had become a small white child, who stood frail and luminous in the road. All that remained of the Star was a five-pronged crown of root and bone on the child's head.

The music had not been still for long when the child spoke: "Be fed by my death; I am half born but my death will be complete. All the colors on Earth have made me white; all the animals under the sky have made my body, but my soul is the rope which hangs from the half circle of light into the half circle of darkness above and below the horizon." When it had spoken the White Child wrapped its hair around its face and walked on ahead of me. I followed in silence, knowing that our steps would go towards the person that I must find.

The country changed gradually into hills and ravines. Occasionally a wan tree became visible here and there. The painted tombstones thinned out to single dots and were replaced by rocks carved into animals or people or sometimes left in their jagged shapes.

The Child and I were alone. The ghosts had disappeared. As we advanced I began to notice high mountains on the horizon, their peaks white with snow. Then far along the road the dust rose and I could distinguish six horsemen riding hell-for-leather in our direction.

The six men were dressed in coloured rags and metal jewels, their shaggy horses covered with embroidered blankets haphazardly affixed with chains or rope. As they came they hurled armfuls of Bohemian glass on the road, making a great clatter. The noise of broken glass and the thud of the horses' feet delighted them, and as they ground to a halt in front of the White Child each man shrieked with mirth in six different keys. The foremost of the six men held aloft a wheel. I counted the spokes. They were eight, like a spider's eight legs.

"I am Calabas Kö," said the man who held the wheel. "We have come out of Hungary to take the White Child."

"Then we must move in time," it piped. "I am afraid."

Whereupon one of the men grabbed the Child and tied it to his horse's girth by its hair and they whirled around to gallop back towards the snow-topped mountains.

The morning has been tedious. I have not been able to move away from the window, watching the street, waiting for some sign outside my dreams.

The street is empty and foreign except at night. Outside everything is tainted.

How shall I ever get to the market to buy lunch?

The sign can only appear when I have ceased to need my will. I lurk around the mystery murmuring maledictions on the feebleness of my words.

Hardly daring to touch what I want to say, yet knowing that if I had enough space around me it would be a piercing shriek. White, long, sharp as the crack of a whip.

This is a love letter to a nightmare.

For centuries they dressed up love for easy digestion in the body of a fat little boy with wings, pale blue bows, and anaemic-looking flowers. Behind this bland decoration Love snarled its rictus through the ages. With shrieks of adoration it flung itself on human breasts, "to crush you, to suck your life away. I cannot drag my own weight over the crust of the Earth so you must carry me on your back so that in time you will be crippled with my weight." These words are in every heart in the mating season.

Is this the result of loving a fellow creature? Somewhere I am frightened of my loneliness and feel incomplete with myself.

Love, goat, tiger . . .

Blind Jug, tell the future?

A time, a date, when?

"Midnight," replies the Blind Jug.

Under what sign, Blind Jug?

"Under the sign of Fire and of Air, Ivory and Milk."

How many will see the Sign?

"Four, the Moon."

And how shall we know?

"Urin, the microscopic ocean."

In some mysterious way these words will enter life.

The air was rare and chill so I thought that I was already amongst the highest mountains. Heavy snow burdened the branches of the fir trees. Streaming grey clouds crept along the Earth and about the rocks, leaving icy teeth where they passed.

Built into the mountainside a few yards from me was a

great stone door, on which was crucified an immense black parrot. As I approached I could see that the bird was still alive, though a long iron nail pierced its heart and the blood oozed out in a scarlet rope. The heavy head hung motionless between its shoulders and the hard yellow eye gave an occasional blink.

"This is the frontier of Hungary," said my thought. "I must walk, swim, creep, or sail through the Mountain Kecske to the source of the Danube, which flows into Hungary from a subterranean ocean."

The parrot screamed. It began to speak in a rapid nasal voice, but I could see in its eye that it did not understand what was said.

"Anybody who knows may enter but time begins so harness your memory."

It repeated this phrase six times and died.

Try as I would I could find no way to open the door. I kicked and knocked and shouted: "Let me in, Let me in."

The pipe which had enchanted the Egg into motion had disappeared. I was bitterly alone in the land of the Dead, on the wrong side of the great stone door.

Several days have passed. I have only slept a few hours, an empty black sleep.

Since the death of the black parrot I have remained alone outside the stone door in the mountain, kicking and knocking and shouting: "Let me in, Let me in."

All through the night I try to get back; to no avail, I can find no means of opening the stone door.

In the daytime I wander about the marketplace thinking, but the Indians keep their world tight and closed over a secret they have probably forgotten for centuries.

The long tentacles of vision and understanding have withdrawn and all that is left to me is the ragged black hole of my loss. Loss and the world around. A noisy puzzle whose solution is another puzzle noisier and more stupid. The circle widens towards nothing.

An answer is hiding somewhere, if I could only read.

A green shawl has fallen on the arm of a chair. It draws the contours of a horse, a green silk horse, a horse hiding under my shawl.

Lovers get drunk on bitter milk; I am a hermaphrodite in love with one of my own dreams. Beast fed with the shade of a dry funeral cake.

Oh Satan, let me love myself again, loving the nightmare of a dead King has made me hate life.

Good night, good night, I am lost forever in the country of the Dead.

II

"Always be dignified, remember to be polite. You are going to study and learn many things which will help you in the world. Now you must blow your nose, so. . . ."

Rebecca demonstrated the adult method of blowing a nose in a huge white handkerchief, rubbing her streaming eyes impatiently as she did so. They were already red and sore.

"Remember that you are a Jew and always remember this with pride and dignity, no matter what the world outside may do or say."

She was kneeling before her little boy, putting on his socks. He was passive and soft with sleep and watched her face with wide black eyes.

"My fingers fumble so with the cold. Stretch your foot, Zacharias."

Grandmother came in and placed a brown paper parcel in the child's hands. He clutched it to his bosom like a doll.

"It's seven o'clock, Daughter, you must hurry. They will be waiting. Is he ready?"

Rebecca nodded and scrambled heavily to her feet. "I will get my shawl. Aaron, Aaron, are you dressed?"

"Yes, Mother." The other boy appeared in the doorway and stared in awe at his brother. Rebecca hurried out.

"Will he ever come back, Grandmother?"

"Yes, of course, child. He will return a great learned man."

"Is he going far away from Budapest?"

"Hold your tongue, Aaron."

There was silence for a while as she bustled about the room making small packages.

"Grandmother?"

"Are you a child or a parrot? Always talk, talk, talk."

Aaron was startled and relapsed into silence. They hurried along on the slippery pavement. A horse drawing a sledge trotted past, tinkling agitated little bells. Aaron wished that they could be riding behind the horse and its gay bells, but he did not dare speak for he was frightened of the terrible stranger his mother had become. She strode along, dragging the children at her side with her cold hands, her face almost invisible inside the black shawl.

The sun was up as they arrived at a square building whose large doors stood open to a crowd of Jewish women and their children. Some were in rags and some, like Rebecca, were dressed in threadbare but respectable clothes, held together precariously by much diligent mending.

Two long benches in the bare entrance hall accommodated the women, while an attendant hustled the children through a stained-glass door.

When he came to Rebecca she clutched her son roughly and kissed him once between the eyes. Then looking up at the attendant she asked: "Shall I wait?" He was a young man with a forlorn moustache and empty blue eyes.

"As you please." He seemed impatient and stood with a hand on the boy's shoulder as if wishing to be gone.

"Name?" He scribbled in a shiny little red book. "Address?" And after a short hesitation he asked: "Are you a widow?"

Rebecca had hardly time to nod before her son was hustled through the stained-glass door and disappeared after the other little boys.

They went down a passage which smelt acridly of poverty

and some strong disinfectant. The walls, distempered green, were occasionally decorated with brown and white prints of the largest monuments in Budapest.

About a hundred and fifty boys were seated on wooden chairs in a long chilly room. Five men with shears and white aprons passed with surprising rapidity from child to child, shaving each small head to a grey stubble. The floor was covered with dark curly hair, as if a flock of black sheep had been shorn to their skins. When the haircutting had finished they hurried the children to the baths. Each child made a small packet of his home clothes, which were afterwards given back to their parent or relations.

Because he was only four, the youngest of all the children, Zacharias was dressed after the bath by the forlorn attendant. He was put into long striped trousers of a harsh material and a jacket buttoned up to the chin with the number 105 sewn on the left sleeve in the same place where people wear the black band of mourning. Each foot was folded in a square of navy blue calico and pushed into a pair of brand-new boots made of rigid black leather. When he stood on his feet he looked like some oddly dressed puppet made by a mad doll maker.

Once the shearing, bathing, and dressing were over the children streamed back through the stained-glass doors. Some clattered to their parents' sides while others stood about self-consciously in their new stiff clothes, stamping their shiny boots.

Rebecca took her child in her arms and kissed his face and hands.

"Be a good boy, be a good boy." She could think of nothing else to say. "I'll come and visit you soon. Be a good boy."

Then taking Aaron by the shoulders she pushed him into the street and they hurried away as they had come.

He tried to run after her, but his new boots slipped on the stone flags and he fell on his face. He was picked up, crying bitterly. At that time he did not mind that others saw him cry and the tears came easily.

An hour later when they were on the train bound for the Northern mountains, he vomited all the breakfast Grandmother had given him over his new trousers and shiny black boots.

105 sat up in bed and screamed. A hundred and forty-nine children stirred, murmured, or sat up, then sank back to sleep as they understood that it was only another of 105's frequent nightmares.

105, however, did not follow their example. He could not go back to sleep. He lay sweating in his narrow bed, pinching his thighs through the coarse nightshirt. He knew it was against regulations to put one's arm under the cover: the offence was severely punished.

The long dormitory did not offer a rich field of contemplation. Beds in two rows against either wall were divided by a strip of linoleum which was worn thin down to the middle. The oblong windows, placed much too high to look out, let in a pale light when there was a moon. Then the linoleum glistened and 105 pretended that it was the Danube and his bed was a boat that would sail him back to Budapest. Tonight however, there was no boat. The horror was too near, it was inside him, all around and over the bed.

Once at a local fair he had crawled unobserved into the chamber of horrors; he had been attracted by a serious-looking black-and-white printed card which said: ADULTS ONLY. The boys had been strictly forbidden to enter. For once in his life 105 regretted having broken one of the rules of the Institution.

Inside was an orgy of horror. A beautiful lady lay in her nightdress on a silk bed. She was made of wax and looked so much alive that 105 turned back several times to see if she had moved. In her long golden hair sat a demon, a dwarf, a monkey, and a serpent. He whispered temptations into her pale pink ear. After this came colored photographs of people eaten away by syphilis, unborn foetuses in different stages, and finally a scene from the Spanish Inquisition which had haunted him ever since: at night he was constantly apprehensive that it should return.

As his memory of this scene became older it gathered in detail and richness, finally far surpassing the original in fantasy and horror. It usually began with a vaulted cellar furnished with a somewhat confused assembly of giant meat mincers, iron armchairs with adjustable spikes in the seat and back, long man-shaped boxes, and a thing which looked like a monster sewing machine with a needle as long as a man's body and stained with clots of blood. This object awoke the painful memory of his mother's sewing machine; she earned their living as a dressmaker. From early morning to late night during the short holidays she pedalled away on expensive yards of soft material belonging to somebody else. 105 went stiff with hate when he thought of the monotonous chuffing of the sewing machine. His mother seemed to pedal away on a long painful journey, leaving him when he wanted to tell her so many important things and the time was so short. She pedalled away to Poland, where his father lay dead under the snow.

Somewhere in the thick mobile shadows a door clicked so audibly that he jumped. Eight pale-faced priests scampered lightly about the terrible vaulted chamber, pressing buttons and twirling handles; they were trying out the machines. They were going to sew him into a bloody pair of combinations for a little cream-faced Spanish Prince.

105 screamed and the vision disappeared abruptly, leaving him weak with terror and determined not to fall asleep till dawn. Then for hours he fought not to see the picture lurking in the back of his mind. He tried to evoke the Danube at midday, or another more powerful spell against the moon-faced priests.

Walking up a long avenue of trees towards a castle whose windows were glittering orange squares. Walking: but if all went well he would be wafted off his feet at the fifth tree. Counting them as he passed: one, two, three, four, five; then deliciously wafted off his feet a short distance from the ground. It was not really flying because he used no effort at all. It was being lifted by some power not his own.

The doors of the castle opened as he approached and in the vague interior stood a bright pink damsel. Her high colouring resembled that of a rose-coloured sweet called krumplicukor made out of sugar and potatoes, which 105 had eaten on several memorable occasions. The bright pink sweetmeat quality of the lady was mixed with something else no less fascinating and which he dimly recognized as being female. Trembling with a strange warmth which began in his cheeks and which crept heavily downwards, 105 drifted into her arms. The caress was unlike anything that he had ever known; this, he imagined, was woman, the faraway skirted creature who held the unique power over loneliness, nightmares, and warmth.

As he lay with tightly closed eyes trying to evoke the pink lady something touched his arm and said: "Shhhh." He kept his eyes closed and waited. Something sat on the bed, it bent and kissed his cheek.

"You had another," whispered the voice. "I know you are not asleep, so don't pretend."

99 sat shivering beside him.

"You'll catch cold," said 105, relieved and disappointed. "And if the Lurcher takes a midnight stroll, you'll get a beating."

"Let me get in your bed," said 99. "I'm cold."

"No," said 105. "There isn't room. I can't even turn over myself without nearly falling on the floor."

"All right then I'll stand, even if I do catch pneumonia. Let's talk."

"The Lurcher will catch us. It isn't worthwhile."

"I feel cold inside too and I can't feel my feet anymore."

"Then go back to bed."

"Look, I've got a present for you," said 99, pressing five iron nails into 105's hand. "They're the heavy kind and hardly rusted at all. I traded them with 62 for my green toothbrush. He wanted it to clean machinery."

Iron nails were used for a game called boki, which consisted of throwing nails into the air and catching them with various methods. Horseshoe nails were the most prized—and these were the kind 99 gave to 105. He tied them cautiously into the corner of his nightshirt and thanked 99.

"Now please go to bed, tomorrow I'll let you see my compass."

The little boy crept silently back to his own bed and soon afterwards 105 fell asleep.

He dreamt that he was walking up a drive bordered with tufted green trees. The place was quite different from the residence of the Pink Lady and the flowering shrubs along each side of the avenue were a kind he had never seen. Hearing the sound of hoofs beating on the gravel, he hid behind a bush and waited. A little girl rode into view on a fat Shetland pony. She joggled up and down on the saddle chanting: "Gee up, Bessie! Gee up!" The pony suddenly broke into a gallop and rushed past 105 at an astonishing pace for such a beast.

"She never galloped before," he heard the little girl say. "She's too fat even to trot properly."

When they had disappeared around a bend in the drive, 105 stepped out of his hiding place and followed the direction taken by the girl and pony.

He met them returning rather slowly. The girl looked surprised, and her mouth hung open.

"Who are you?" she said. "I hadn't counted you in and there you are, uninvited like Tomey."

105 felt embarrassed and his head seemed full of numbers. "She is younger than I," he said to himself.

"Who are you?" asked the girl again. "I knew I was going to dream of Black Bess but I hadn't counted in anyone else. It's rude. I don't know you, do I?"

"Yes, you do!" shouted 105. "You know you do, how could you have forgotten? Remember the five horseshoe nails you gave me?"

She frowned and looked puzzled, then after a while she said: "No, you left them for me and I never could give them back." She began to cry for no reason, and wiped away her tears with her hair.

"Who are you? Who are you? I can't remember you, you must tell me."

"Who are you then?" replied 105. "And why do we go on asking all the time when we know?"

"We know but we can't remember," said the little girl. "What else did you give me? There were two things, I know."

105 shook his head. "It's too far away to remember precisely. . . ."

Then she jumped off the pony and hopped around chanting: "If you can't guess you'll have to go away, it's a game."

"The nails were enough for today," said 105. "Is this your garden?"

"It's my father's garden. We use it all the time but he hardly ever does, he works."

"Where are we?" asked 105. "I mean what country?"

The little girl rolled about cackling with mirth: "Ha ha ha, he doesn't even know where he is, ha ha ha, what an ignoramus!"

"Stop that or I'll twist your arm till you plead for mercy."

She stopped obediently and put her lips to his ear—"We're in England, of course, SILLY!"—suddenly jumping away after shouting the last word into his eardrum.

"England?" said 105, turning the word over in his mind. "Of course, you are in England now, and I am in Hungary."

"Of course," said the girl and stopped suddenly, staring at him. "In Hungary, in Hungary, now I seem to remember something. How old are you?"

105 was going to say that he was twelve but different words came out of his mouth: "Very old."

"I'm six," she said. "But I'm in my seventh year."

The pony had disappeared and they had turned off the drive into a wood.

"We are going to the Big Pond." She ran in front of him, leading the way. "They don't allow us to go when we're awake, but in dreams you do what you want unless they're nightmares. Jim Gardner says the Big Pond has no bottom." They were pushing through rhododendrons to a small lake covered with floating green weed: "Nanny says they're called rodidandrums, Jackie had some in the garden in Ireland and my sister-in-law had blue ones. There aren't any blue rodidandrums in England."

They sat together near the water on the moss.

"This is a dangerous place," said the girl. "It's haunted. That's why Gerard and I love to come here. Gerard is my younger brother."

"So you are not alone." 105 felt cheated.

"Yes I am!" she said violently. "They all hate me because I'm a girl. Little girls can't do the same things as little boys, they say. It isn't true. I can kick harder than Gerard and I don't allow him to draw horses. Mummy told me I have such a bad temper that I'll be an old witch before I'm twenty. I don't care if I do wrinkle up before I'm twenty. I'll still climb trees and come to the Big Pond whenever I like."

The stagnant coat of weed seemed to shift, but the girl took no notice: "I have three brothers, one mother, and one father. They all do whatever they like because they are boys. It isn't fair. When I grow up I'll shave and put hair oil on my face to grow a beard. Pat has a moustache and at school he says they call him Bobby whiskers. He says he kicks them whenever they call him that. Once I called him Bobby whiskers and he kicked me. I'm the only one that has to practise the piano for hours, wash all day, and say thank you for everything. You should see the clothes they make me wear."

105 started to laugh. He couldn't stop, and the tears rolled down his cheeks till he didn't know if he was laughing or crying. The little girl stared at him horrified, then scrambled to her feet and ran away. 105 was panic-stricken. He leapt to his feet and followed her as fast as he could. When he caught her she was crying and struggling in his arms: "Let me go you Damn Pig!"

"Shut up," said 105. "You're nothing more than a silly baby. Why waste all our time complaining? Don't you realize we have to wake up?"

She became suddenly quiet and afraid. "We won't go back, we'll refuse. Can't we escape now that we're together?"

"Come on back to the Big Pond," said 105. "Something was going to happen when you started babbling all that nonsense." They walked back together hand in hand to the Big Pond and sat down once more near the water. "Jim Gardner calls it mucky. Mummy says its vulgar to say 'Mucky,' but we use it in secret."

They watched the stirring weed expectantly. "Soon we shall know," said the little girl. "Now do you remember what you gave me?"

"Five Iron Nails, a Stick of Cinnamon, and a Skein of Black Wool."

The water was parting. Two curved horns, then the head and neck of a black ram emerged. In its mouth hung a pair of golden scales.

The little girl drew a circle on the ground and filled it with different polygons, then pointing first to the left and then to the right, she exclaimed: "Fire and Air, you and I, Little Brother; our mother is Earth and our father is Water. In twelve houses we lived, through twelve houses we will pass. When we hold hands across the circle, yours is Air, mine is Fire."

The black ram picked its way daintily out of the Big Pond and stood in the center of the circle.

The girl handed the boy a sharp triangular stone, which he took in his left hand. Kneeling before the ram he caught its spiral horn in his right hand, twisting back its head and exposing the beating pulses of its neck. He cut its throat with the triangular stone. The girl caught the blood in her cupped hands, saying: "Drink the scarlet milk of Paradise, Little Brother, it is ours."

He bent his head and drank the blood out of her cupped hands. When he had also drunk he said: "The Old Gods are our food, the New Gods will be revealed to us in time and out of time. The Old Gods are dead; Earth, the Goat will renew the lifeblood of the Myth and will violate the Garden of Paradise. The Goat will deliver us the New Myth and she will be clothed with animal, vegetable, and mineral; nothing dead, alive, or unborn will she lack and nothing on this Earth or in the Nine Planets around will remain untouched by her or she by them."

The girl took the triangular stone and cut two meshes of wool from the head of the dead ram; one she entwined around the boy's neck, and the other she hid inside her nightdress. "This is a jewel and also a weapon: black wool rope into the center of the Earth, where our roots were entwined at the beginning of life.

"Black wool, Black hair, Air roots for the night. Our roots into the Air, our roots into the Earth. We shall knit a ladder of Black hair and climb into the center of the Earth to our roots and when these long strands join again we will Hear, Taste, See, Smell, and Touch."

They joined hands over the carcass of the ram and sang a song to the music of an old tune: *"Buj buj zöldag, zöld levelecske. . . .* Open, open, little green leaf, Open, open, great stone door, You are the black ram, I am the black ram, It is dead so I am no longer I but you are I and I am you. Secret Enemy, we have quit the first house and have entered the fifth in the dark water."

"Water the place, we have met in Time."

When 105 awoke he was horrified to find that he had wet his bed. The dawn had already made the windows pallid and in an hour's time the waking bell would ring. He rolled around trying to dry the wet patch with the warmth of his body. Afterwards he would try and smooth out the telltale wrinkles in the sheet. They would find out, he thought, feeling his heart shrink to the size of a hazelnut. He would be humiliated and punished; they would make him sleep in the youngest children's dormitory, there would be no water for three days, everybody would know. Even humble 99 would despise him. They would whisper behind his back in class and in the Synagogue, he would be branded forever as the twelve-year-old boy who still wet his bed. He lay there miserably, imagining the consequences till the sharp peels of the morning bell brought him rudely out of bed and into the day's work.

The clubfooted monitor preceded 105 up the strip of linoleum to his bed. He stopped suddenly with a clump of his shoe and indicated the damp wrinkled patch on the sheet. The bed was the only one now uncovered in the dormitory; 105 thought it looked white and guilty.

"What's that, Boy?" he asked, still pointing at the patch of the sheet with a thick and rather dirty finger. 105 was dripping chilly sweat inside his striped coat, but he looked the monitor in the eye and did not reply. "Well then, I'm speaking aren't I? Are you deaf? You've got a tongue in your head, speak up!"

105 remained silent and the monitor's voice started to sharpen dangerously. "Come on, Boy, I am asking you a question. I want you to explain just exactly what that is. Come along!"

Something in the persistent question suddenly stabbed 105 into a great rage. He felt the blood beating like a hammer behind his eyes. From without they looked like two hard black stones.

"I will give you five seconds to speak," said the monitor. He began to count out loud, still pointing at the patch on the sheet: "One, two, three, four . . . now one more chance . . . *five!*" He grabbed 105's thin arm on the last word and slapped him hard on the face.

105 did not move. He stared straight in front of him with one side of his face red and the other white. The monitor released his arm and limped away: something in the boy's face frightened him.

Once he was alone again, 105's teeth began to chatter and his body shook convulsively with dry sobs. When the tears began to fall he took refuge in the latrine. He let himself cry and rubbed his face on the grimy walls.

Far away in the building he heard the bell ring for morning lessons. Hurriedly dabbing cold water on his face to remove the tearstains, he ran to class, arriving a few seconds after the history master, who gave him an unpleasant stare.

"Well, Number 105, so we've become a gentleman and arrive for class at the hour we please? I suppose one would say we are one of nature's gentlemen? Ha ha."

105 tried to shift into his seat beside the fat boy, 20, but the history master had not finished his little joke. "Take the chalk, Boy, and write." He had already detected the signs of tears on 105's pale face. "And what do we see here?" His voice sounded damp and unctuous. "The gentleman of the class has been crying? At your age, 105, I am surprised! At age twelve tears are for females, or are we becoming girlish in our old age?"

One or two boys sniggered, but most of the class kept stolid cold faces. They hated the teacher, and 105 was generally popular because he was brave and modest.

"Very well, Boy, take the chalk and write in even clear letters the exact date and description of the coronation of Szent István."

When 105 turned towards the blackboard he had a clear picture of the date and circumstances of István's coronation, but when the chalk touched the smooth black surface he drew a large perfect circle with a sweep of his left arm. The boys drew in their breath with a hiss, but 105 went on drawing as if oblivious to everything apart from his strange occupation. He filled the circle with polygons placed in different positions. Their points touched the circumference of the circle in twelve places. The diagram was mathematically correct. He could not have said how long he had been drawing when the click of the opening door made him turn his head; he found himself face to face with the Director of the Institution. The wrinkled countenance behind the old man's long grey beard was impassive. They stared at each other for a long time.

"Zacharias," said the Director, "seems to have mistaken Szent István's coronation for higher mathematical calculations. Zacharias, you have never shown an aptitude for mathematics up till now and the least I can say is that the time and place are ill chosen. Follow me."

105 wondered how he knew his name. Following the old man with some misgiving down the corridor, he turned over in his mind different plausible explanations for his exploit on the blackboard.

They entered the Director's study, which seemed luxurious and awesome to the twelve-year-old boy. True, the carpet was somewhat thin in places. Still it was a carpet and nearly covered the entire floor. Well-filled bookcases reached to the ceiling, giving the whole room a sober atmosphere which was not disagreeable. The ceiling was painted dark cream and had decorative molds in each of the four corners.

The Director made a sign indicating that 105 should take a chair while he sat himself behind a very large desk.

"Zacharias," he began, joining his fingers just under his large nose, "reports lately on your behavior have been far from good; your teachers complain of a continuously rebellious attitude and a refusal to apply yourself to study. This cannot continue, Zacharias. Boys in your situation may not allow themselves the luxury of wasting their time. You are dependent on the State for your education and this is an eminently important factor for your future life. Moreover, remember that we are Jews and our lot is hazardous and difficult, not only in Hungary but unhappily in many parts of the world. Your life, like the lives of thousands of other Jews and gentiles, will not be easy. Lives are seldom easy, but a good foundation of knowledge is a strong weapon against the stones in the path of life; an aid in earning your bread—and let it be an honest bread!—and in preserving your dignity amongst your fellow men."

He paused and scrutinized the boy, who was impressed by the measured tones of his voice. They looked into each other's eyes with a certain understanding and mutual respect.

"Now, Zacharias," continued the old man, "you are not a stupid boy, I might even say the contrary. But you are proud and wilful, and these faults will be the source of great suffering when you take your place in the world. Pride is a form of blindness and therefore a kind of stupidity. The sage sees himself with such lucidity that the word *pride* ceases to have any meaning. He sees himself as a phenomenon amongst thousands of other mysteries great and small. A humble and dignified attitude is therefore the logical inheritance of his vision. A strong will is sometimes an asset in his life, Zacharias, but beware, for that element we call strength is often a mere assertion of a personality which blinds itself to reality and only seeks to obtain power and domination over its fellow men. Domination, Zacharias, is not only a great sin but also a great waste of time because one becomes a slave of power, and life degenerates into a continuous struggle to maintain something which is no more than a conventional abstraction or word which men have made in a futile attempt to glorify their own ignorance and weakness. In learning the true nature of your faults you will have made the first step towards knowledge, and knowledge, my child, is the doorstep of Paradise. Someday you will understand my words if you grow in the direction I suspect; you shall see what an immense and varied thing is real wisdom, how many and how strange are her faces. Never tire of seeking her, and do not despise her humble costumes."

He stopped speaking, apparently occupied with his own thoughts. The boy was embarrassed and pretended to find something on the toe of his boot. The old man took a piece of paper and made some diagrams, then he called 105 to his side.

"Can you tell me what this is, Zacharias?"

"Yes, sir, it is similar to the drawing I made on the blackboard in the history class."

"Quite so. Do you know what it signifies?"

Zacharias went red and hesitated before he replied. "No, sir, not exactly, sir."

"But where did you learn such a thing?"

There was a long pause, during which 105 shifted his weight from one foot to the other.

"I cannot say, sir. I don't exactly know."

"Zacharias," said the Director sternly, "you must not lie to me."

"I cannot say, sir."

The old man examined his face and finally told him to be seated.

"I believe you, Zacharias, though it is most remarkable. Most remarkable."

He pulled his watch as the bell rang, ending the first lesson.

"You may retire now, my child, do not keep your teacher waiting. You may say that I detained you in my study. Go now, Zacharias; we will continue this conversation at another opportunity."

105 saluted the Director and left the world of learning.

At eleven the boys were allowed ten minutes' recreation before returning to their lessons. Black bread was served on a long wooden table in the school yard.

105 was no sooner outside than he was joined by 99, who wore a worried frown. "What happened, Zed?" he asked, taking his friend by the arm. "Did the Old Geezer jaw?"

"Not exactly," said 105, who was reluctant to disclose the details of the interview with the Director. "The usual stuff about work, behaviour, and manners. He was quite nice really."

"Quatch! You had guts to pull Dung Heap's leg like that! When you left he was shaking like a leaf."

105 gave a forced laugh. "Do him good, the old stinker. He's had his knife into me the whole term."

"What was it?" asked 99. "It looked like some sort of geometry."

105 walked along whistling and throwing the five iron nails into the air and catching them again deftly. "Oh, something like that," he replied indifferently. "It just came into my head, any old thing."

"Well, it certainly made him waxy; better look out next time, he'll have you out if he can."

The bell summoned them back to class.

When night came, 105 waited in vain for the little girl and pony; perhaps his fear of repeating the previous night's accident kept her away. Many months passed, during which he was obliged to evoke the Pink Lady to keep away dreams of the Inquisition and the scampering, moon-faced priests. The Pink Lady was still able to exorcize nightmares, but she herself grew evasive and unreal. Her castle thinned to a flimsy structure like a painted theatrical backcloth. It had lost two of its dimensions.

105 passed the winter yearning; a yearning which became acute and anguished towards spring. He strove to ease his nostalgia by taking violent physical exercise and concentrating his affection upon 99.

The evenings grew longer and became warm. Sometimes the boys were permitted to take short excursions to the banks of the Danube, where some of them bathed and others sat around inventing stories of drowned strangers and beautiful female suicides, stories of the Danube. . . .

During one of these excursions 105 and 99 discovered a huge orchard near the river. The exuberant display of half-ripe fruit tempted them. The orchard was guarded by vigilant keepers and wide dykes, but this only served to make the fruit more desirable to the two boys.

"Who could own such a big orchard?" asked 99. "And what a large family he must have to eat all that fruit."

105 was pensively eating the tender stalks of young grass. When he had them chewed to shreds he spat them as far as he could.

"It belongs to a Patriarch," he explained, "who has six wives and ten children to each wife. The only meat he gives them is cow's ears, and they eat the fruit so as not to starve to death."

"You're talking through your hat," said 99. "It belongs to a General who only eats meat and all that fruit is for the pigs. He has millions and trillions of jet black pigs."

105 spat a piece of chewed grass at least a yard. "Well I don't see why all that good fruit should go to the General's pigs or to the Patriarch's wives. After all we're as good as pigs, or nearly as good because we're probably not edible after the food we've been absorbing for the past ten years. . . . Why

not pay them a visit? A friendly visit of course, merely to leave our cards."

"At night," said 99 excitedly. "We could muster a gang under oath. . . ."

"Entire secrecy," replied 105, "is demanded, under pain of Chinese torture."

The expedition was arranged for the following night and was to include 19, 60, and 38 among others. The boys were to meet at the stroke of midnight in the school latrine and make their exit by the narrow window obscured by shrubbery and conveniently situated on the ground floor. Once outside the Institution they would take off their clothes and rub themselves with the grease 60 would obtain from the kitchen. Capture would be almost impossible, as anybody knows who has taken part in the greased-pig competition in a fair.

Each member of the expedition was to carry a small book sack. Once in the orchard the boys would divide and obtain as much fruit as possible before the alarm was given, then each would save his skin as best he could. They were to meet again at the end of the drive, where their clothes would be hidden.

The latrine was to be the center for dividing the spoils. Here 105 would supervise an even distribution of the stolen fruit.

Each detail of the plan was carefully examined and accepted, and on the following night the five boys went to bed in a state of high excitement.

A thin new moon was making her way across the dormitory window. Zacharias knew that when she reached the third pane midnight would strike and he would slip out to the school latrine. Thinking about it he realized that he did not really care for the fruit, but an hour's freedom in the night was as precious as a whole holiday.

The moon, slight and sharp as a knife, gave enough light for them to pick their way into the centre of the orchard. They spread fanwise, each choosing a tree at a different point of the compass. Their pale forms moved as quietly as shadows.

105 pushed his way through the long damp grass with his

head bent and alert. Alone, he moved as surely as any nocturnal animal intent on his business. He stiffened to hear a foreign sound winding here and there, approaching him deviously. 105 crouched low and waited. In a short while he saw a small white object moving busily in the grass. On close inspection it proved to be a little dog, which sprang towards him, wagging its tail and giving other signs of welcome and recognition. The animal pranced about like a diminutive white horse cutting capers, but when he bent to stroke it it danced away, waiting till he came near to prance off again. They played a circular game, drawing each time nearer to the oldest apple tree.

"Are you there at last?"

105 crept forward on his hands and knees; he saw somebody or something perched high in the branches of the oldest apple tree.

"Come quickly," it said. "I have been waiting so long amongst the tricks of time."

Afraid and excited, 105 started to climb the tree. Over his head crouched a young woman with long dark hair. She appeared not to see or hear him so he stayed still and listened to her voice, a bodiless sound that seemed to come from far away. Yet he heard it intimately in his ears.

"I need you now. Quetzalcoatl the serpent is sucking me dry. Wise King open the stone door, now I understand the black parrot's dying words. Man must open the door, for alone I am impotent. Alone I am a pitiful and incomplete creature."

Looking down the young woman saw him. She spoke to herself: "Who is this? Is it the White Child of Mesopotamia?"

He answered without knowing the source of his words: "I am the White Child, the wise King, the Jew, the Black Ram, and the scales."

She stretched her hands out, willing. "I cannot touch you. We are separated by time. Let me in! Let me in!"

He cried out in anguish and tried to climb to her side, but the twisted branches held him like a fish in a net. The young woman turned her face towards the moon and he saw that she was blindfolded.

"The Bohemian is surrounded by shadows. If my eyes weren't covered I could read his past. The Bohemian was there when you were King on the frontier of Mesopotamia, the land where people are crockery. Mesopotamia faces Hungary across a mountain and a deep ravine, each spying on the other.

"Mesopotamia, huge arid cemetery, whose cities are tombs, whose trees are shaped lions and astrological artifacts. Holy, Holy Land, so holy that it is infested with prayers in the form of black butterflies swelling to the size of turkeys' eggs and forged with the life of the Mesopotamians; for seven decades their vitality has been sucked down the gullets of black butterflies. Even the wind is dead, leaving the prayer wheels motionless; the prayer wheels which once spun like tops. Facing this embalmed country across the mountain and ravine you lived, My Love, in a country of trees and snow.

"The stone door is closed against me, let me in, Oh my Love, let me in."

She shook the tree so violently that the fruit fell thumping to the earth in abundance.

105 lost his footing and fell amongst the apples. When he looked up the young woman had entirely disappeared. As he bent to pick up the fruit and fill his sack he heard somebody whistling in the distance, but the sound was so far and faint that he thought that it only existed in his mind's ear.

III

He made a dejected figure against the snow-crusted street; haggard and dirty, his clothes ragged and torn, a mixture between a young scarecrow and the crows it was supposed to scare. The sole of his boot hung loose and the piece of newspaper inside soaked up the water and made a filthy pulp under his foot.

"My feet are so cold now I can't feel them anymore. So much the better, perhaps they'll drop off with frostbite."

"Zed! Zed!" He stopped at the sound of his name but did not turn.

"Zed!" Elias, Number 99, caught him by the shoulder and looked deeply into his face. "Did you hear me call you?"

"Hello, El."

"Where have you been, Zed? I've looked for you all over Budapest for months."

Zacharias smiled bitterly and started to walk as the cold slunk back under his clothes. "I came out of prison last week," he said. "There are so many jobs in Budapest I haven't been able to make up my mind."

El directed him into a café and they took a small table near the wall.

"Drink?"

"Offer me a bun and some coffee," said Zacharias. "Rubber dropped a pengö this morning on the stock exchange."

"Zed, you must tell me what happened. I might be able to help."

They ordered coffee and szamorodni. El left a packet of cigarettes on the table: whole cigarettes, not damp butts picked out of the gutter and dried surreptitiously on the chestnut man's fire.

"Tell me all about it, you know I'm your friend, Zed."

"There's nothing to tell." Zacharias sipped his coffee, warming his fingers on the hot cup. "There's nothing to tell. I would much rather you tell me your own adventures; stories only make good telling once they've ended. My story hasn't begun yet. I'm still mere offal among the extinct ungulate mammals, waiting to learn slow movement. When the stone age begins—it seems to be a long way off—when it begins come ask about my past. Till then I'll confine myself to asking for bread and insulting policemen."

El gave him a cigarette and sighed. "You haven't changed a great deal, Zed. Still the same old petrified Zed so stuffed with humility and pride that he prefers to starve rather than ask for the help he needs.

"Never mind, if you prefer I'll tell you my own adventures.

"Old Aunt Sari died five months ago. With her went the

pension. Having sold the little we had, paid for the funeral and the debts she left, I found myself on the street with five pengö in my pocket. A few hard and dirty jobs here and there, you know the type, then as luck would have it I was drunk one night in a café over by Hokay Ter and I got talking with a balmy Chinese. He wound up offering me a job and to my great astonishment the next day he remembered me and kept his word. I've been working for him ever since. He pays pretty well, he's not over exigent, and even if he is a bit cracked I'm thankful for his pay."

"What does he make? Sell? Steal? Cook? Grow or knit?" asked Zacharias, who felt revived by the hot coffee. "And where does he live?"

"Precisely near Hokay Ter, on a side street called O Ucca. The Chinese always seem to live on side streets, however wealthy they are. Perhaps because they're a secretive people, or we imagine them to be.

"In any case, this particular Chinaman is a queer case. He makes dolls, toys, music boxes, cheap paper fans, and what not. He can make almost anything go with a sort of clockwork that he invented himself. There's nothing in the way of toy trains, soldiers, dolls that he can't make go in any way he pleases. He's a nice fellow though in his own way. I haven't quarrelled with him yet, and on thinking it over I don't think I should like to."

"You are lucky," said Zacharias. "Employers are always swine; either that or insidious stinking dogs. There's no happy medium. I'd be content with just a slightly dirty swine, but they don't seem to exist."

"Well you don't have to starve. I have a small room in Lovag Ucca and earn enough to keep body and soul together. We will share and share alike. Remember the sour apples in the school latrine? What bellyaches we all had! It's funny to think we're the product of an orphan asylum."

"Yes, I suppose we are," said Zacharias, "though I always thought of an asylum as a place where people with unkempt hair, wild eyes, and long nails gibber through iron bars. I suppose our institution wasn't so far off. . . . Twelve years locked up in a place like that is enough to give anyone a start in life. Quatch! What a start!"

"You remember the night don't you? Remember the General's orchard?"

Zacharias suddenly became sad and silent. How empty his nights had been since he'd crouched in the oldest apple tree. He had tried to sift that painful hope out of his blood, but it had clung to him through the years.

"Yes," he replied at last, "I remember very well. Are we supposed to forget just because we're what they call grown up?"

"You will never grow up."

"I've had plenty of opportunity. Tell me, El, have you got a girl?"

"No," said El. "No, I haven't got a girl, and you?"

"Girls, yes, I have girls when I have money. No money, no girl. There's not many who want to go bed with a scarecrow. Not that I'm fastidious, but between hunger and a brothel I usually choose my stomach. It's not a question of principle but necessity. When the fat days come along again, I shall pick a nice blonde and put her in a bed-sitting-room which I shall visit at my will. I always had a fancy for plump blondes. There's lots to catch hold of and they wear well."

"Women are a poor use for our hard-earned money," said El. "Give me a nice bottle of szamorodni any day."

He paid the bill and they walked out into the street laughing. It was snowing again.

"Come to my place and I'll cook some supper. The bun you ate wasn't enough to fill a canary. I've become a good cook since my café days, you'll see."

Zacharias followed him with his bitter smile. The day was darkening and it was deadly cold; the snow capped his head and shoulders. Under the cold crown his raven's face was still and indifferent.

Chung Ming Lo used a basement in O Ucca as his workshop. During the winter days when the snow piled high outside, a long twilight reigned in the shop, but at night the petrol lamps gave off a warm yellow light. At eight o'clock every evening Ming Lo pulled down the red blind to the disappointment of the children outside, who loved to gather and spy on his workshop. Between six and eight however they could feast their eyes on piles of cheap toys, musical boxes, wooden soldiers, and a long carpenter's table furnished with saws, chisels, hammers, paint pots, and sharp wheels spitting chips of wood.

Zacharias went to fetch his friend El at the workshop the evening after their encounter. He paused outside and peered in along with the children. He felt slightly guilty peeping into the workshop unseen. El was sitting at a side table painting half a dozen wooden trains bright red. A cigarette on the edge of the table sent up a thin line of smoke.

If I lived alone on top of the highest tree in the world, thought Zacharias, I could not be more outside the lives of human beings. Though if anyone ever asked me where I am, I doubt I could reply. He felt rather heroic, then depressed. It was cold.

"Let me in, let me in."

The nostalgia always returned monotonously when the sun went down.

"Won't you come in?"

Zacharias stiffened at the sudden words. Looking around, he saw the Chinaman at his elbow, a brick red scarf wrapped around the lower part of his face.

"Come in," said the Chinaman. "I was expecting you. The cold is intense out there. It's not difficult to come in. . . ."

"I'm a beggar," said Zacharias.

"Begging is a profession like any other, it takes a certain skill. Even living is a form of commerce: we absorb the fruit of the Earth and pay energy back into the Earth. Work or art merely apes the natural order. You are a Jew, are you not?"

"Yes, I am a Jew."

"Then you understand me. That which is called forgetfulness in others is to a Jew a long shriek traversing his race from the beginning of Time. Among the Jews are those who can read the spoor of the road, hieroglyphs along the wayside containing the footprints and the knowledge of errant Jews. The Stars too can be read by man."

The Chinaman took a key out of his pocket and opened the door. Zacharias followed him after a short hesitation.

They were in a small poorly lit hall furnished with ornate furniture on fragile legs. Bric-a-brac clung to every possible space, leaving the walls invisible.

The Chinaman continued talking as he hung up his coat on a brass hook protruding from the jaws of a tiger.

"When a tiger kills his prey," he said, pointing to the hook, "he first tears out the liver and devours it. That liver is the best nourishment for the tiger. But how many other elements are contained in the body of an antelope?"

"Most enlightening," said Zacharias, who did not remove his coat, "but I should appreciate it if you offered me dinner rather than philosophy. Philosophy is an after-dinner game. Perhaps I am rude, but then I have nothing to lose if I never see you again."

"Frankly, if not altogether tactfully spoken," said the Chinaman. "Though you may gain more from me than you think. You will eat dinner here; we might interest each other. I am neither proud nor stupid, as you will see."

"Then you have my respect," replied Zacharias. "Real dignity cannot be affronted."

"You shall join your friend in my workshop," said the Chinaman, making for a curtain at the far end of the hall. "I am my own cook, slave and master. Please excuse me."

As the small man disappeared, Zacharias walked thoughtfully down the stairs to the workshop.

"Any luck?" asked El as Zacharias sat down on a wooden stool beside him.

"I haven't eaten since breakfast. There's no work, no hope of work. I'm cold and tired."

El looked up from his painting with a sly smile. "The Chinaman needs another assistant to catalogue the knick-knacks upstairs."

THE STONE DOOR ──────────────────────────── 115

"He seems to like me," said Zacharias thoughtfully.

"I'm not surprised. He's a garrulous sort, and you did pretty well at school on the type of thing that amuses him."

"What type of thing amuses him?"

"Just talking."

"Well, I would sooner be paid for talking than for shovelling coal, washing dishes, or doing arithmetic. We must fill our stomachs somehow. With our high-class education I suppose it's best not be too delicate."

"You're difficult to please," said El. "I took anything I could get."

"And what have I got?" asked Zacharias. "A cold in the head and an old suit of clothes."

"Look at my department upstairs." It was the Chinaman speaking. They did not know how long he had been standing in the doorway watching them.

"Upstairs I have toys for adults. Please follow me."

They mounted three flights of stairs and finally arrived in a dusty attic packed with junk or precious objects.

"Some I made myself," said the Chinaman, holding a candle aloft, "some are presents, and some are objects found or bought. Should you enter my employment it would be to catalogue and sort out the saleable items from the rubbish and to clean the former."

"You need only look at me to know that I need work," replied Zacharias. "But how do you know I'm honest?"

The Chinaman smiled. "Yes, I think you are honest, though my judgement could be in error." He lit an oil lamp. "Have a look around while I finish dinner. I shall be with you shortly."

When he was gone Zacharias crossed the room to a dusty convex mirror which hung on the opposite wall. Zacharias could not decide whether the mirror was black or so dirty that it appeared black. As he looked at his distorted reflection a sudden star-shaped crack burst in the center of the mirror where he had seen his face.

Frightened, Zacharias looked about for a place to hide the

cracked mirror. On second thought, he realized that a gap on the wall would be even more conspicuous.

He turned away and hunted among the nearest knick-knacks for something to divert his thoughts. He found an old musical box which was made in the form of a coach-and-four; he wound it up to see if it still worked.

"*Buj buj zöldag,*" sang the box in its creaky little voice. "*Zöld levelecske nyitva van az aranykapy. Kapuljatok rajta nyistd ki rózsam Kaputat kaputat hadd öleljem valadat, szita, szita peutek, szerelmes csütörtok bab szerda. . . .* Open, little green leaf, Come in through the golden doors, For I miss the shoulders of my love. Wooden sieve, Friday, Thursday, green leaves, Wednesday, my love. . . ."

The song has more words, thought Zacharias, yet try as he could he could not remember the second verse. Winding and rewinding the music box, he played "*Buj buj zöldag*" a half dozen times. The thin tune evoked a nostalgic pain. He went back to stare at himself in the black mirror.

"You look like a scarecrow, I hate you. One cannot be astonished that such a jackdaw's face cracks mirrors. Ah, my soul and heart have withered up so small that both would fit inside the skin of a fried bean. You are a particle in a senseless malady called life: a puzzle made by a lunatic, the winding circles lead to another puzzle sillier and more puzzling yet."

He turned around and felt foolish: Ming Lo had entered the room.

He thinks I was admiring myself, thought Zacharias. I wish I could feel happier.

"Strange what a puzzle one's own face is," said the Chinaman, who did not appear to notice the crack in the mirror. "How detached we are from our own faces."

"When I looked it cracked." After a rapid calculation Zacharias had decided that the truth would be prudent. "I am sorry, you will take it out of my wages."

"It is not a wilful fault," said Ming Lo. "Perhaps you have been accustomed to see your reflection on another surface?"

"I don't think my face merits a great deal of attention."

"I wonder if you always thought so. Opinion is infectious when we are young, either high or low depending on the outside world's opinion."

"Perhaps one must be loved to love oneself."

"To be loved is a necessity while we drink our mother's milk. During adolescence when our virility is unformed we need to be admired, when that virility is formed but not satisfied, to hate. Later all these things fall into their right place, little tools hacking out one's form before our fellow men."

"As a matter of fact," said Zacharias, "I do not agree with you. Dreams, thought, love, virility, and hate are too intimately entwined. To say one can exist without the other is like saying the perfume of roast coffee exists independently of the coffee."

"In which case," said Ming Lo, "you are destined to a great misery."

He took Zacharias by the arm and led him below; they were greeted with the pleasing odour of a roasting animal. At that moment Zacharias felt the kitchen was the most delightful place in the world.

On a sunless Wednesday morning Zacharias began to work in O Ucca. Furnished with a small black book and a pencil he set about sorting the varied, dust-ridden possessions of Ming Lo. While scrabbling around in an ornate tin trunk, he came upon a triangular box covered with black feathers fixed one upon the other as cunningly as if they grew on a bird. With some difficulty he opened the box and saw that it contained a stone key of Mexican workmanship.

Zacharias listened to the box, which chanted: "Let me in, let me in. Open the stone door." He hid the box in his breast pocket.

Towards midday Ming Lo visited the attic, accompanied by a small man with a foreign accent.

"Monsieur Mangues," he explained, "is the secretary of Docteur le Fauvenoir, a French gentleman who is a collector. He wishes you to show him some objects of value which might interest the Docteur. You have not had a great deal of time yet to catalogue our possessions, but if you have happened upon any boxes, mirrors, or keys please show them to Monsieur Mangues; Docteur le Fauvenoir is especially interested in keys."

Zacharias showed them a few small boxes he had found; they were in bronze, ebony, or ivory, and of various origins. While Monsieur Mangues examined them, Zacharias could feel in his pocket the weight of the box and the stone key.

"You're sure that is all you have found?" asked Ming Lo. Zacharias nodded, without speaking. "There are nothing but empty boxes."

"I do have other objects which you could show to the Docteur," said Ming Lo. "Is he in Budapest?"

"Monsieur le Docteur is not in town at present," replied Mangues. "He is taking a rest cure in his country house. I am here on a small business transaction and intend to return to the country this evening. Whenever I visit town I have the habit of bringing a small present to the Docteur."

Ming Lo unlocked a mahogany cabinet and showed the Frenchman several objects in jade.

"You could take these pieces of jade to the Docteur. If they do not please him I will change them for something else."

When they had gone Zacharias went to the black mirror and smiled at his reflection.

"Locked doors," he said to his face in the black mirror, "are opened by keys. Stone door, stone key."

Towards seven o'clock the same evening Ming Lo joined Zacharias, who was still sorting dusty treasures; he was holding a small package. "Stupidly I overlooked this this morning when Monsieur Mangues was here. It is a small ivory of ancient workmanship and I think it would please Docteur le Fauvenoir very much; I know he has no such piece in his collection. Would you be so good as to run out to Duna Palota Salloda and see if Monsieur Mangues has not already left? If he is still there give him this note and packet: I recommend this as entirely after the Docteur's taste."

THE STONE DOOR

When Zacharias was outside in the street he stopped under a lamp to read the note: *The other is not presently in our possession; the enclosed is hermetically sealed, there is no cause to worry. Further particulars later. Do not be impatient, I shall join you within three weeks at Kentaur.*

Zacharias broke open the seal on the packet and found a small ivory doll. It was obviously ancient. He wrapped the doll in its cloth and put it in his trouser pocket, then he walked about for a half hour whistling. He returned slowly to O Ucca and was surprised to find the Chinaman waiting in the street. "Well?" he asked with unusual impatience. "Was Monsieur Mangues at the Hotel?"

"He had left," said Zacharias. "The clerk said he had checked out at five o'clock."

Ming Lo considered this news in silence and finally shook his head. "That is very strange. I particularly wished Docteur le Fauvenoir to see that piece. I must ask you to do me a favour."

"What do you want?"

"I want you to take a small journey. I would like Docteur le Fauvenoir to receive the packet this evening. There is a train which goes as far as Pilisvörösvár and from there you will find a sledge to the residence of the Docteur. The journey will take several hours and if you agree to leave this evening you could return tomorrow. The train leaves Budapest at nine-fifteen."

Zacharias was pleased to oblige; a journey outside Budapest was always an adventure. So at 8:45 that evening he pulled his fur cap down over his ears and set out for the station with the packet carefully buttoned into his pocket. At 9:20 the train clanked painfully out of the station.

Zacharias shared a carriage with a man who wore a black suit and dark glasses. He held a small leather book defensively before his face. His hands were pallid and unsteady. He must be a foreigner, thought Zacharias, because his clothes are cut in a narrow and unfamiliar manner. And how can he read through those spectacles? wondered Zacharias. A plain, elegant leather suitcase sat on the rack over the foreigner's head.

Something seemed to go wrong with the lighting in the compartment, and it became so dim that the white world moving outside was visible through the windows. The stranger lowered his book and looked outside. In the half-light, the lower part of the man's face seemed to be featureless. Zacharias could not distinguish his mouth, even when he spoke in a mumbling, broken Hungarian.

"Do you mind if I open the window?" he asked. "The carriage is rather stuffy."

He is English, thought Zacharias, rising and opening the window. Where is his mouth? . . .

"Are you travelling in Hungary?" he asked, politely offering him a cigarette. If he takes it then I shall see, thought Zacharias.

The Englishman refused. "I never smoke, thank you. I suffer from chronic bronchitis. I find this climate very trying for the bronchial tubes."

"I believe you are an Englishman?" continued Zacharias. "You are visiting Hungary on a pleasure trip?"

"Yes, I am English. I am here not entirely for pleasure, but I am a great believer in mixing business with enjoyment."

"Are you going to Pilisvörösvár?"

"Thereabouts. They say it is a mining district."

"Are you interested in mining?" asked Zacharias, to make conversation. He still could not see an opening in the stranger's face.

"No, I can't say that I am. Old mines are of course interesting to me, as I am an archaeologist."

He handed Zacharias a neatly engraved card: PETER STONE. STONEHENGE.

"I am employed by the British Museum."

"I have never been out of Hungary," said Zacharias, "but I always wanted to travel. London, Paris, Madrid . . . they are like magic words to me. Someday I shall go to Paris."

"Well, do not miss the train. They say anybody who misses a love tryst or a journey to Paris dies without knowing they ever lived."

"I am sure that is true," said Zacharias. The train dived into a tunnel and above the clattering darkness he thought he heard the Englishman shout something.

"I beg your pardon?" said Zacharias, as the train clanked into the open night. "Did you say something?"

"I used to be frightened of tunnels," replied the Englishman. "When I was a child. They still have a disagreeable effect on my nerves."

"I was horribly frightened of the dark." Zacharias thought about his school days. "Frightened and fascinated. I saw things in the dark which were more terrible and more beautiful than anything I have ever known."

"Most children are frightened of the dark because they have a more acute vision than grown-up people. Sometimes I think that a person who kept a child's sensibility as he aged would die of fright when the sun went down."

The wheels of the train squealed and drew to a noisy halt.

The Englishman let down the window and leaned out to see what had happened. Somebody was shouting.

"We're in a snowdrift," he told Zacharias. "They are going to shovel it away. We may be stuck for some time. What a nuisance. I was anxious to reach Pilisvörösvár this evening."

Five horsemen rode past the compartment window, looking into the train.

"Travelling in Hungary during winter is always rather hazardous," said Zacharias. "In England I suppose you don't get so much snow?"

"Fortunately we do not. A French poet once said: 'Pour ne pas que ça se perd, je vais vous dire mon opinion sur la neige: c'est de la merde qui fait sa première communion.' I must admit I share his point of view. The only merit of snow is it is white."

The five horsemen returned and stopped at the window of their carriage. "Hey you!" called one of them. "Give us a cigarette." Zacharias tossed him what he had left in his packet. The man caught it deftly.

"Got a light too?"

"I wouldn't talk to them if I were you," mumbled the Englishman. "They might be bandits."

"What happened?" Zacharias asked the first horseman. "Are we snowed in?"

"Like a pig in a poke."

The Englishman was pulling at his arm, trying to drag him away from the window. "Be careful, don't talk to them. You never know, they might be gypsies."

Zacharias shook him off impatiently and continued talking to the horsemen: "Will it be long?"

"It'll take them three hours or more. Maybe you'll see Pilisvörösvár by morning!" He let out a great hooting laugh and the horse tossed its shaggy head.

"If you let me get up and ride behind you I'd get there quicker."

"Jump up!" bellowed the horseman. "I'll give you a run for your money." One of the others had pulled a zither off his back and was plucking tunelessly on the strings.

"What did I say?" hissed the Englishman. "Gypsies."

"Give us a tune," called Zacharias. "You with the zither." Five wild voices broke into song together: "*Buj buj zöldag, zöld . . . levelecske. . . .* Let her in through the stone door. White Child. Wouldn't you kiss the shoulders of your love?"

"Come back! You can't do that!" yelled the Englishman, plucking at the disappearing tail of Zacharias's coat. But he had landed unhurt on the snow. The horseman stretched out a dark hand and helped him mount. Whirling about, they took to the forest at a gallop.

"Fool!" screamed the Englishman in the distance. "The penalty for opening the door is . . ."

"Freedom!" yelled the horseman over his shoulder.

They lost the stopped train behind the trees and galloped along a winding track. Later they stopped to rest the horses and light a fire.

"My name is Calabas Kö," said the first horseman. "My four companions are Ivor, Tej, Fa, and Vas. They can only speak to music, otherwise they are dumb."

At these words the four men put out their tongues, which were cloven and coloured like blackberries. The wagging black tongues made them look like cobras.

"Ivor, play the zither," commanded Calabas Kö. "Tej, Fa, and Vas, sing what you see."

"We see the sky, a spangled skin stretched domelike over the world and her companions. The world is a fur ball. The moon is a nest of feathers."

"Enough astronomy!" shrieked Calabas Kö, flinging snow into Ivor's impassive face. "They're always talking about astronomy. It makes me sick."

The four men dangled their dark tongues stupidly. Ivor continued plucking at his zither.

"Calabas Kö," he sang, "you are an imbecile. Someday you will give up your soul like a belch of boiled cabbage. Your destiny is not even written in the sky."

"You'll pay for that!" screamed Calabas Kö, spitting in the singer's face. "I'd kill and roast him if the fire was big enough."

The four men in turn spat into the fire and started to sing once more.

"Hungary shares a frontier with Mesopotamia."

"There they go again," said Calabas Kö with disgust. "Geography."

But Zacharias leaned forward to catch each word they sang. "Leave them alone." To his surprise Calabas Kö held his peace.

"Hungary and Mesopotamia are divided by a deep ravine. Facing the desert you lived, my Love, in the mountains. Your palace on the highest peak in Hungary was surrounded by trees. Three kilometres from the Mesopotamian frontier. In your land the snow is your only cloak now, dear Love, but mine is my own wrinkled skin. *Buj buj zöldag, zöld levelecske.* Open, open, little green leaf, Open, open, stone door."

Tej and Fa stood up and danced around the fire, clapping

their hands to the rhythm of Ivor's zither. When they had danced around three times, they sat down abruptly and Vas rose to his great height and sang alone in a penetrating treble voice: "Sweet Love, Dear Love, Eternal Love, listen to my rhyme. *Buj buj zöldag, zöld levelecske.* Hungary's hairy men on their shaggy tiger-horses. Calabas Kö! Igen! Ivor! Igen! Tej, Fa, and Vas. Igen! Igen! Igen! Stone, ivory, milk, wood, and iron, but where, My Love, are Fire and Air?"

He sat down abruptly. Ivor twanged his zither for a while before they started singing again: "White horse, red horse, black horse, Motion is the horse, there is no motion without the horse. The Moon is my love and my love is a horse. Five horsemen, Calabas Kö, Ivor, Tej, Fa, Vas, to whom do you come to do homage?" Each man touched his lips, eyes, ears, nose, and fingertips while his voice rose to a shrill treble: "We come for the Böles Kilary. To salute him we throw armfuls of glass on his path. The road is written with characters from the feet of errant Jews."

They threw pieces of glass into the fire and leapt to and fro over the flames without stopping their song: "His city is the forest. They burn whole fir trees for the Böles Kilary. But who lives in a bier covered with wolfskin? The Old Böles Kilary! Old Böles Kilary."

The five men circled around Zacharias and the fire, spinning together like a wheel. They called out like night birds: "Who are you? Who are you?"

"Zacharias, a Jew."

"No more?"

"I am Zacharias, a Jew."

"Then marry Fire, for she is yours. Take her, take the Fire."

Zacharias bent over the blazing logs and stretched out his hands; the flames leapt up to meet his fingers and disappeared into his hands, leaving nothing but cinders and black charred wood on the ground.

Calabas Kö took a decagonal stone from his bosom and handed it to Zacharias singing: "Jew, this is your heritage from

Solomon." Zacharias placed the stone in the pocket over his left breast. They mounted the horses again and took the road East.

They climbed a steep slope and the air grew rare and thin. The snow-ridden trees in the waning moonlight resembled script. Wolves' cries echoed over the steady beat of the horses' gallop.

Sweating, the five horses at last halted of their own accord before a solitary lighted tavern at a crossroads. As they dismounted Zacharias could hear a voice inside the tavern chanting, and the slow clapping of hands to the long wail of a mourner.

"Hey there, János!" yelled Calabas Kö. "Come out, you limping spotted tyke!"

A man with a wooden leg hopped out of the tavern, his head and shoulders obscured by a black-and-scarlet hood. He addressed himself to Calabas Kö. "We have been waiting for three days, and the embalmers have not yet arrived."

"You stink like a corpse, Jancsi."

"I tell you the embalmers are three days late and Sari insists on keeping him warm with big fires. . . ."

"Take the horses, feed and stable them, and get out of my sight."

János gathered the horses' reins without a word and led them around the corner of the tavern.

"You are the Young Böles Kilary," said Calabas Kö, placing his hand on the head of Zacharias. "Beyond a doubt."

When they opened the door a large black ram charged past them.

They entered a large kitchen lit by six candles. On a sexagonal bier lay the enormous corpse of a bearded king. The great recumbent body was clad in a long black shirt exquisitely embroidered with scarlet letters, circles, and polygons. His curling black beard reached as far as his feet.

The five men stood back as Zacharias walked slowly to the bier. He slapped his hands over his face: the dead King's features were identical to his own.

A red-headed woman who piled wood ceaselessly on the fire started to chant, keeping rhythm by striking the poker against the stone flags: "Böles Kilary, Böles Kilary, *Buj buj zöldag, zöld levelecske.* Die Old Böles Kilary, for the stone door cannot open till Young Böles Kilary lets you into the country of the Dead. Open, open, little green leaf, for when you open the Earth must open too."

She peeped through her hair at Zacharias with pale inquisitive eyes.

Calabas Kö and his four companions stepped forward and squatted around the corpse with closed eyes. The woman rose, took five red handkerchiefs out of the pocket of her skirt, and blindfolded them. Then, sticking their fingers in their ears and spitting, they prophesied war.

"And when the massacre is done, the juice will germinate in the center of the Earth and split her crust and leap up on Land, in Water, in Fire, and in Air. The old powers will seek to suppress it."

When they fell silent, the red-haired woman gave them warm water from a large jar, then wine from a stone jar, and finally milk from an ivory goblet. Taking her place once more by the fire, she lit a pipe. As she puffed a thin music issued with the smoke.

Zacharias was so moved by this music that tears ran out of his eyes and with them went twenty years of bitterness. The red-haired woman watched him weep with a sly smile. When she had stopped smoking the music she put the pipe in his hands. "It is yours," she said. "Use it well."

Zacharias put the singing pipe to his lips and blew, but the only sound that came out was his own breath. The woman let out a peal of laughter. "Ah, no! You cannot use it to charm yourself! Young Böles Kilary, you must grow up! For you it has other uses."

She went back to the fire laughing and Zacharias, annoyed, hid the pipe in his pocket.

Having fed the flames with more pine logs, the woman walked over to the dead King and covered his closed eyes with her hands. "Böles Kilary, your old body must return amongst the dead. Your castle, which was vomited out of the mountain, will sink back from whence it came. The house of shadows: in the light between twilight and dawn, imprisoned in your castle, walk the bodiless shadows you loved and tamed. Remember your castle, Böles Kilary. Listen . . . constructed of black-and-red stones spat from the crater of live volcanos through the Earth's shell. The stones were as huge as seven camels, three elephants, and two horses squashed into a great cube.

"The stones that built your house contained old mineral knowledge from the nine planets. The walls of your house were wise, covered with presents, stolen objects, and lost property. From the ceilings hung embalmed yaks from Tibet stuffed with preserved fruit, as well as piñatas and country sausages. So many things hung from those ceilings, Böles Kilary! You could see all the animal, mineral, and vegetable kingdoms in the Universe looking up at your ceiling, Böles Kilary.

"Your furniture of precious woods, prehistoric bones, mammoths' ivory, and fur covered with lunatic drawings; the tables of turquoise glass with all the tints and reflections of the lake. Bouquets of Egyptian mummies stood like dry flowers in Syrian and Greek vases. Metals and jewels, heaps of jewels as high as the garbage dump outside the walls of Baghdad. This was your house, Böles Kilary, Wise King.

"At night you combed your beard before nine trees burning in the grate, and you jumped a little when a wandering shadow tickled the nape of your neck. The shadows threaded softly through your hair, lost shadows. . . .

"Coming and going from the hall were slaves laden with wine, rich cakes, milk, honey, and succulent little birds. You gorged yourself, sometimes you threw whole cakes to your creatures. Animals sat in every corner and followed the slaves distractedly. Wolves and hyenas and exotic dogs from China, naked and no larger than a grown lizard; giant white poodles from France, with ears like huge rose-coloured butterflies; dogs of every race and kind. Abundant cats and small black pigs, a mandrill and his female, three does and a stag, an Assyrian bull with a human head, owls as big as lions; ducks, turkeys, and geese as fat as priests. All these creatures wandered near you because of your wisdom and tenderness.

"Sometimes you watched your beautiful face in a polished sheet of steel. You looked into your eyes for hours on end, Böles Kilary, but they said nothing. Still you talked to yourself: 'Gorgeous creature, Fascinating Wise King, Exquisite Jew, Savoury Body, what does she say, my lover, the Moon?' You laughed and your creatures gathered around you.

"One of those silent nights, when the snow fell outside, you looked deeply into your steel mirror and your image said: 'I hear.'

"Let me in, let me in, Stone Door."

The red-haired woman lifted her hands from the king's closed eyes and covered her own face.

"Böles Kilary, may these ten fingers suck up the perfume of your great wisdom."

A six-toned bell rang out; János limped through the kitchen to the door. They heard him call: "The embalmers have arrived!"

Everybody stood away from the corpse and the eight embalmers trooped into the room. Each bore a jar on his head containing sweet elixirs for preserving the dead; each man carried a Theodolite and a twig sprouting nine little green leaves. They wore masks and long yellow shirts girdled with swines' tails sewn into a rope.

The woman pointed over her head to the granary and the eight embalmers picked up the bier and followed her upstairs.

Calabas Kö and his companions let out a long sigh and lit their pipes. Zacharias sat down near the fire and fell into a reverie which eventually deepened into sleep.

Dawn had scarcely arrived when Zacharias was awakened by a black cat who rubbed itself against his ear.

Hearing sounds overhead, he guessed that the embalmers were still at work, though he had slept for several hours. The five horsemen snored soundly in their mantles. On the fire a pot of milk started to rise and froth. He leaned forward to pull it off the fire. No sooner had he moved than Sari ran down the stairs.

"He's hanging by the feet from the rafter," she told Zacharias. "He looks like a dead stag, his beard reaches the floor!"

She took the milk off the fire and scooped up a gobletful, which she handed to the Jew. "Drink, Little Brother. The goat yielded a full bucket at three o'clock this morning."

"When will they be done?" asked Zacharias, drinking the milk gratefully. "Will it be long now?"

"They will have done at sunrise, when men are hanged. Listen, Young Böles Kilary. Millions of dead have passed through here and I have seen them lose their past and future. I would not have you do likewise. Now hear me, when the sun rises I shall call the eight embalmers down to the kitchen and feed them milk and bread. While they are still eating you must say to me: 'Sari, I hear a rat in the attic, let us hope he is not gnawing at the Wise King.' I will then reply: 'Why yes, I also hear something in the attic, take this broom and frighten it away.' Upon these words you will gather your cloak and run upstairs, where you must cut down the Wise King and escape with him as fast as you can: the quickest way out is through the window."

"Very well," said Zacharias, "but where should I go?"

"If all is well a black ram will be waiting under the window; as soon as you jump he will take to his heels and you may follow him, for he was bred where you are going."

She wrapped up a piece of cake and gave it to Zacharias saying: "A piece of cake the mourners overlooked. How I cannot say, they nearly ate me out of house and home. Six geese and two sheep; seventy-five kegs of wine; most of them crawled home drunk as swatted cockroaches."

Suddenly she ran to the window and pulled aside the curtain. "Hey! The Sun is about to rise! Gather your wits, Young Böles Kilary, soon you will have to set them loose again."

With her hands she formed a horn in front of her mouth

and bellowed: "Come, Master Embalmers, the Sun will be risen in an instant and I have prepared you milk and bread."

A few minutes later there was a shuffling overhead and the eight embalmers came down the stairs. They brought with them a peculiar, sickly-sweet odor. Their long yellow shirts were stained. Without uttering a word they squatted on the floor in a rough circle and Sari served them mugs of milk and chunks of bread.

Calabas Kö stirred in his sleep and muttered: "Hyenas and tuberoses! Stinking beasts!"

"Sari," said Zacharias nervously, "I hear a rat in the attic, let us hope he is not gnawing at the Wise King."

She shook her head and replied: "Then take this broom and frighten it away."

Zacharias snatched the broom and his cloak and ran upstairs, stumbling. He found himself in a large granary. It had been tidied but still reeked of embalming fluids. The floor was stained and had been roughly swept. A great stone jar in the corner contained the King's entrails. Zacharias looked about for the King, but all he could see was a small object, about the size of an otter, hanging from the ceiling. Looking closer he saw that it was indeed Böles Kilary, shrunken to the dimensions of a newborn babe. He took a stool and cut him down, then, cradling him in his arms, he climbed through the little window and leapt into the air. He almost landed on the woolly back of a black ram, who trumpeting with rage, galloped off down the road East.

Zacharias followed as swiftly as he could, holding the tiny bearded King in his arms like a baby. Zacharias soon found it less cumbersome to clutch the King by his beard and swing him in one hand, which, if not altogether respectful, was a good deal more practical and allowed him to run faster. He still held Sari's broom in his left hand, thinking it might be useful.

The twinkling black buttocks of the ram cut forked tracks in the crusted snow ahead of him. The early morning was beautiful with a gaudy sky and the glittering white hide of the Earth.

Without looking at the country, Zacharias became conscious of the road rising; the forest had already thinned to an occasional tree. He seemed to be gaining the summit of a mountain. A hundred yards ahead the black ram disappeared around a bend in the road; when Zacharias got to that point the ram had disappeared, but his tracks led up to a small plot of ground which seemed to dominate the whole world. The mountains rolled away to the sky; below, in a ravine between the two highest mountains, lay the Danube, frozen and still.

Zacharias looked around, recovering his breath. He let his eyes follow the course of the Danube, which seemed to eat a huge portal between the two mountains.

"The Danube emerges from a subterranean ocean," he said to himself.

He searched awhile in the snow and finally found the ram's tracks, which led downwards towards the ravine. He started off at a trot along the same course. The narrow, twisting path led down between trees and boulders. By dangling the Wise King from his fingers and using Sari's broom as a staff, Zacharias managed to descend swiftly without breaking his neck.

The mountains leaned over him as he descended to the Danube. The path threaded its way along the banks of the river to the gorge ahead, but the tracks of the black ram ceased suddenly. Here the snow was beaten hard by the different footprints of man and beast; the tracks of claws, hoofs, and boots were entangled along the way. After gazing awhile at his feet, Zacharias continued towards the opening in the rocks.

Far along the path he saw a huge man walking towards him. The creature was naked except for a black skin slung over his shoulders, which dripped blood down his torso and legs to his feet. As he drew near Zacharias recognized the skin of a newly slain ram. The man's face was disfigured by a harelip. He had the pointed features of a dog.

"What-ho, young man, where are you going?" The words

whistled through his harelip. He had blocked the path with his huge body. Zacharias rapidly hid the Wise King under his cloak and held up Sari's broom like a weapon.

"Where are you going?"

"What's it to you, brother?"

"My business. Where are you going?"

"I am free to go where I wish."

"Free until something stops you," whistled the harelip giant. "I can stop you if I wish."

"How?" asked Zacharias, trying to edge past.

"Not so fast." The giant blocked the way. "If I skinned you I could have the pair of pants I lack."

Zacharias realized the giant meant what he said. "They would be too small," he suggested nervously. "Besides, I haven't any fur."

"True," said Harelip, "but leather suits me just as well."

"You need two cart horses to make you a pair of pants. My skin wouldn't make you much more than a truss."

"There's no reason you should go on living. You're more useful as a truss, a handbag, or even stuffed on my chimney place. So why should I let you live?"

"Several reasons," said Zacharias, thinking rapidly. "First, because in my own quaint way I like living; second, because I must find somebody before I die; and third, because even to you I am more use alive than dead."

"What use are you to me?" asked Harelip. "Because that seems your only valid reason for living."

"With my hands I could make you trousers, sing you songs, and cook you dinners more delicious than you ever tasted in your life. Also, I would bring you luck."

Harelip considered Zacharias for some time and eventually nodded his head several times. "Very well then, let us see if what you say is true."

"Hurry," said Zacharias, "if you want the pants by nightfall."

Harelip turned and led the way towards the portal in the

mountains. Every now and then he looked back over his shoulder to make sure Zacharias was following.

As they drew near Zacharias could see through the gorge. Beyond the rocks he saw a frozen loch hemmed in on all sides by mountains; the light fell indirectly from the sky, which now seemed infinitely far away. In the distance on the opposite mountain he saw a castle.

Harelip stopped and pointed at the castle. "He's dead and they took him away." His voice whistled sadly. "But he will return."

On the near side of the gorge they came upon a construction resembling a cromlech. The low opening was covered with a sack, which was frozen stiff. Harelip pulled this aside and, crawling in on his hands and knees, beckoned Zacharias to follow. The gloomy dwelling cut into the rock contained nothing but bones and rotted skins strewn about the floor. A heap of dirty straw in the corner evidently served the giant as a bed. The air in the cavern was heavy and fetid. Harelip collected some wood and, striking a flint with some dexterity, lit a fire in the middle of the floor.

"Now," he said, "I want my trousers."

"As you please," replied Zacharias, wondering desperately how he would make a pair of trousers amongst so much garbage. "But remember that trousers are the first rung down the ladder of degeneration."

"I want a pair of pants," said Harelip firmly, "and if you cannot or will not produce them I shall have to make them myself, and you know how."

"All right," Zacharias fumbled, "but if I had such beautifully shaped legs as you I would not hide them under an ugly pair of trousers." He looked around the dwelling at the rotted skins and realized they were unfit to make clothes. Then the beard of Böles Kilary tickled his hand and a terrible idea came into his head. He remembered the dimensions of the King's body before it had been embalmed; if it had once been so large perhaps it could grow again. The least he could do was try. In its present condition however, he thought in despair, it would hardly cover the haunches of a decent-sized tomcat. He looked again at the expectant giant and decided he would try the experiment.

"Listen to me," said Zacharias. "I will make you a pair of trousers, but I must be alone for this and I shall need a cauldron full of snow. You must give me your word not to enter till I give you permission."

"How long will it take?" asked Harelip suspiciously. "You already promised they will be done by nightfall."

"Get me the cauldron full of snow and you will soon see," insisted Zacharias. "And bring another armful of wood."

The giant pulled a large iron pot out of a recess in the wall and carried it outside. He soon returned with a pot full of snow. Zacharias told him to set it on the fire.

"Now," said Zacharias, "get out and do not return till I call."

When the snow had turned to water and the steam began to rise, Zacharias cut a thong of leather from his jacket and hung the Wise King over the pot.

Humidity, he thought, will make him swell.

The pot boiled, and in the humidity and warmth of the steam the Wise King began to swell. Zacharias could hear Harelip stamping about outside. Like a plant growing before his eyes, the body of Böles Kilary filled the space above the pot. His nails and hair grew as rapidly as his body. Then with a sudden loud pop the Wise King burst: a cascade of spiced juices poured into the boiling pot. The whole cavern stank of musk, cinnamon, and other spices. The Wise King's empty skin flapped huge and feeble over the fire.

Now, thought Zacharias, I can begin to make the trousers.

He took down the skin and with his pocketknife fashioned it into the rough form of a pair of trousers: cutting it in two at the waist and joining an arm and a leg as the trouser leg, the head and buttocks serving as the joining piece in the fork. He wove the King's beard into thread and, piercing holes with his knife in the skin, he sewed the pieces together into a creditable pair of pants.

Now and then Harelip called out: "Have you done yet? The sun is already low in the sky. Remember what you promised." And Zacharias replied: "They will be ready at nightfall. Be patient till the first star appears."

As the sun finally set Zacharias put the last stitch in Harelip's trousers and called out to the impatient giant: "Come in, Harelip, you have a pair of Royal breeches!"

Within a few seconds Harelip had entered the cavern and, grunting and swearing, wrapped his limbs in the Monarch's skin. He walked slowly around the cavern before making any remark, then he went up to Zacharias and embraced him, spraying him with fetid breath, and said: "You are my brother and my friend." Then, almost dipping his face into the boiling pot he exclaimed: "Ah, soup! And spiced like the King's own dinner!" He walloped Zacharias on the back. "You're a wizard, let us celebrate!"

Dipping a colossal mug into the mixture, he swallowed the boiling liquid at one gulp. "Delicious! Fit for a King! Help yourself, my friend." Zacharias explained that he was not hungry and that he had already eaten. Harelip rapidly tossed off five mugs full of the embalming broth. Then, belching loudly, he sat himself down on the straw. Zacharias waited with interest to see the result of the giant's repast. He continued, however, in apparent health and even seemed disposed to talk. "Brother, you have shown yourself a superior creature. I surmise therefore that your mission must be of great importance, you are . . ." He stopped suddenly and stared at Zacharias in sudden recognition. He covered his face with his hands and muttered: "It had to be. Salamander's double has returned among us."

"The Danube is born across the loch, isn't it?" asked Zacharias.

Harelip raised his head as if it bore a great weight. "That

is correct; the subterranean ocean lies under the mountain Kecske. Beyond Kecske is Mesopotamia, the country of the Dead."

"Between Kecske and Mesopotamia, is there a stone door?"

"Yes," he replied heavily. "But the stone door only admits the dead into Mesopotamia."

"Just suppose," said Zacharias, "that a wanderer should wish to come out of the land of the Dead to the land of the living through the stone door. . . ."

Harelip's great body trembled. "It would be disastrous, the Masters would never permit such a thing."

"I recognize no master," said Zacharias.

"That is what they wish. They govern without being recognized, nobody knows who they are. That is the secret of their great power."

"Do you know who they are, Brother Harelip?"

The giant fingered his mouth, still viscous with the broth. "I know and I do not know."

"And where did you get such knowledge?"

"Across the loch, in the castle you can see from the doorway of my cavern, lived a Böles Kilary. This king was a prisoner because he escaped through the door, Kecske, from the dead. Those who return forget nothing, and so he was full of dangerous wisdom. The Masters set me to guard him; that was my work till he died."

"Once dead," said Zacharias cunningly, "they feared him no more?"

"Some say that when he passed through the door he was a twice born. They still fear the Böles Kilary."

"And do the twice born possess the wisdom of memory?"

"They possess a half wisdom buried in dreams and omens."

"A whole could have two bodies," said Zacharias.

"The Masters would never permit that," answered Harelip. "They would arrange such a terrible fight between the two bodies that knowledge would always be obscured by hate. One would destroy the other, so only one half would be truly alive."

"These masters are powerful," said Zacharias. "Their power lies in the unit. The belief is one."

"You will be destroyed for knowing that."

"Why?"

"Because as long as man thinks that he is whole in his one body he can never achieve the wisdom which would endanger the Plan. Believing that he is one keeps him in perpetual combat with another half of himself. Once he could see and accept that other half without combat, the Plan would totter like a ninepin."

"That," remarked Zacharias, "would not meet with the Masters' approval?"

"It would not be permitted."

"Why do you tell me all this?"

"Because you already know and because I know who you are."

"Then why don't you kill me?"

Harelip stretched out his arms. As the ram's skin fell away, Zacharias saw that he had many luminous moles on each arm, which twinkled like a constellation.

"You are Air seeking Fire. To find her you must ride your Mother Earth over your Father, Water. The sacrifice of the ram is over; Ram must become woman and Air must become man. Then crossing hands in the center of the Egg and alternately touching Fire and Air, their feet will be joined under Water."

So saying, he rose and went outside. Zacharias heard him playing a shepherd's pipe. This was followed by the bleating of a goat. At that moment a gust of cold night air blew the sacking away from the doorway; the fire reddened and sprang into flame, and Harelip stepped into the cave leading a white-bearded goat.

"She is the Earth, your Mother, and she is also a goat."

Harelip released the goat, which stood bleating and emitting white drops of milk from her full teats.

Zacharias knelt down and was suckled by the goat. When he had drunk his fill she started to walk around the fire in ever-smaller circles, till her feet were in the flames. Then she threw back her head and screamed from the centre of the fire.

"Time is." said Harelip. "You must cut her throat and drink her blood."

Zacharias took the decagonal stone, the gift of Calabas Kö, from his pocket and cut the exposed throat of the goat, who offered no resistance. Then cupping his hands he caught the blood and drank it. Harelip pulled the dead goat out of the fire and flayed her with a knife shaped like a gnomon. He put the carcass whole in the cauldron and set it to boil.

"She will be your boat, Brother," he told Zacharias. "In her you will cross the subterranean ocean to Kecske, the stone door."

After some boiling the goat's flesh dropped off the bones. Harelip lifted the skeleton out of the broth and stretched the hide over it, forming a light boat.

"You must take to the water at moonrise," he told Zacharias. "Her skeleton is Saturn and will ride farther across the water at that hour."

Harelip then slowly stripped off his breeches and handed them to Zacharias, saying: "Brother, your boat must have a sail to catch the subterranean wind. Take my most prized possession and use them well."

They fixed Sari's broom as a mast and the skin of Ancient Böles Kilary as a sail. The little brig stood ready for her journey.

The moon rose. Harelip and Zacharias dragged the goat-ship through the gorge and onto the ice of the loch. They trudged toward Mount Kecske, which loomed before them like a pale featureless head.

Harelip drew the small vessel behind him, the ram's skin flapping around his shoulders and his great arms twinkling with luminous moles.

When they had almost reached the foot of Kecske, Zacharias saw the mouth of the cavern which led inside the mountain. The ice around the opening was hacked into chunks, creating a passage on the water.

"I shall wait till you return, Brother," said Harelip.

He pushed the boat off the brink of the ice and handed Zacharias a board. The boat floated like a leaf. Taking a huge breath, Harelip blew powerfully into the skin of Böles Kilary. It billowed and the ship skimmed over the water and into the cavern.

Here darkness was different from night: it seemed full of the movement of water. Then as the boat penetrated farther inside the mountain, subterranean bodies became luminous. Lights appeared around the goat-ship and slowly began to move before Zacharias. He saw the bodies shudder and shift; a sound moved through the mountain. It was the echo of a voice.

Somewhere in the recesses of the Earth a light wind struggled free and tugged at the sail. The boat skidded easily over the water with a soft lapping.

The echo freed other sounds; muffled shrieks and screeches, hoots and crashes followed upon one another. Light and sound bounced off the cavern walls.

The wind dropped as suddenly as it had started and the boat, after trailing a few yards slowly, lay still on the water.

Zacharias sat and waited. As time lengthened he began to worry, then worry turned into fear. The boat heaved slightly on the water. It was the only movement as the luminous bodies petrified around him.

The space around seemed square. To his panic, Zacharias repeated over and over: "North, South, East, West. The four corners of the Earth."

The slight heaving of the boat became almost imperceptible, then it ceased altogether; the panic inside Zacharias became a hard solid knot. He thought he was hanging in eternity with no beginning or end, where life and movement no longer existed. He sat powerless and immobile with his panic, waiting for nothing.

A rigid and mortal battle was taking place amongst the subterranean forces: they were so finely matched that they did not move a hair's breath.

The scales quivered. Like a finger passing through a tree

of hair, a gentle sound began in the head of Sari's broom; the gentle sound turned into a rustle and the rustle into a thread of smoke. Tiny sparks as small as insects' eyes appeared in the tuft of the broom and dropped into the water. Then little tongues of flame like agitated leaves on a tree: Sari's broom was on fire.

With a shriek Zacharias plucked the mast off the boat and dipped it into the water. It sizzled. He paddled forward, softly crying warm salt tears of release.

With the first movement of the boat light, darkness, and sound vibrated with a quality Zacharias had known but never seen.

The Earth itself seemed to yield up its own life.

He heard the roots of trees over his head suck their life from the minerals and putrid vegetation. He felt the struggle of death becoming life. He tasted acrid fear in the darkness. He smelt the stench of all beasts' desire. He saw all gradations of light, even those that vibrate in pitch darkness. And among all these things the voice continued calling: "Let me in!" It echoed a thousand times in the far recesses of the Earth until it traced itself as a fossil in the stone.

Zacharias did not need to row anymore; the voice's magnetic power pulled the boat towards its source. He sat still, holding the broom on his knees.

They came in sight of a great stone door feebly lit by a large luminous egg hung lamplike on a pole.

The goat-ship reached the edge of the subterranean ocean. It ground against a rough wharf hewn in the rock. It was made of jasperite and as red as blood. Zacharias leapt ashore and tied up the boat to an iron ring.

By the light of the luminous egg he searched for the keyhole. But he could find no keyhole, no opening of any kind in the smooth red face of the rock. The stone key hung impotent in his hand.

"I am here," he shouted. "We are only divided by the stone door." A long silence followed his words. Then with a sigh the voice replied: "Who are you? Have you come for me?"

"I have come out of snow, through the Earth, and over

the Water to find you. Our roots were linked before Time began. I am Air, the Scales. Who are you?"

"I am Woman, Fire, and Ram. Where are you, Dear Love?"

"I am in the mountain, Kecske, in the subterranean ocean which fills the Danube."

"I must be with you."

Zacharias searched the surface of the rock again, but there was no keyhole.

"How can I open the door," he shouted, "when there is no keyhole?"

"Break through it with words, blows, prayers, or music. I've been waiting too long and it is breaking my heart."

These words were followed by a cry which ended in a bleat. Still holding the broom he thought of Sari and remembered the musical pipe and Ivor's zither; the tune echoed through his head: *"Buj buj zöldag, zöld levelecske.* Open, open, little green leaf, Open, open, great stone door."

He took the pipe from his breast pocket and put it to his lips. With the first breath the pipe uttered a long high shriek and burst along the stem into nine little green leaves. A great creaking, the sound of stone rending, sent shivers into the marrow of the Earth. The goat-ship heaved and curled up like burning paper. Before his eyes a string of light opened; the stone door wheezed inwards as if pressed by a great weight. Then the air shuddered and vibrated with the bleating of five hundred white sheep, which poured into the Earth like a deluge of curdled milk. Zacharias was swept aside by the stampede. He clutched a piece of rock which jutted out over his head.

The white flock took straight to the water and swam west. Zacharias recovered the goat-ship and hastened after the sheep, paddling swiftly with the broom.

A hot wind charged with dust, cinnamon, and musk blew behind him from the country of the Dead. The great stone door, Kecske, swung rumbling on the wind and closed with a crash.

Zacharias, rowing with all his might, followed the sheep west.

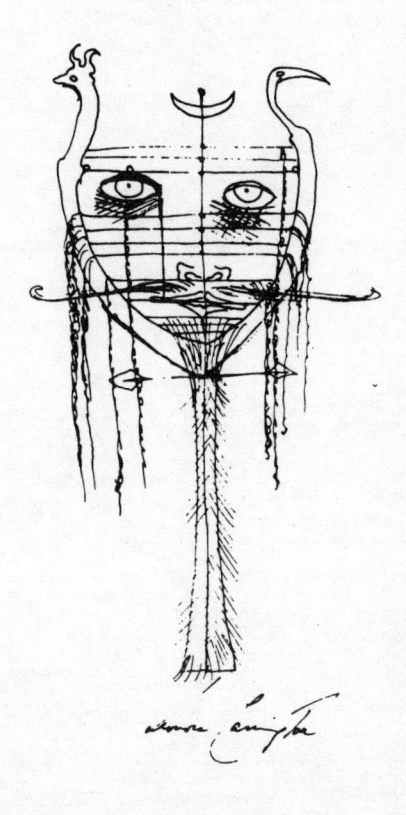

III
THE NEUTRAL MAN

The Neutral Man

Although I've always promised myself to keep the secret regarding this episode, I've finished up, inevitably, by writing it down. However, since the reputations of certain well-known foreigners are involved, I'm obliged to use false names, though these constitute no real disguise: every reader who is familiar with the customs of the British in tropical countries will have no trouble recognizing every one involved.

I received an invitation asking me to come to a masked ball. Taken aback, I plastered my face thickly with electric green, phosphorescent ointment. On this foundation I scattered tiny imitation diamonds, so that I was dusted with stars like the night sky, nothing more.

Then, rather nervously, I got myself into a public vehicle which took me to the outskirts of the town, to General Epigastro Square. A splendid equestrian bust of this illustrious soldier dominated the square. The artist who had been able to resolve the peculiar problem posed by this monument had embraced a courageously archaic simplicity, limiting himself to a wonderful portrait in the form of the head of the General's horse: the Generalissimo Don Epigastro himself remains sufficiently engraved in the imagination of his devoted public.

Mr. MacFrolick's mansion occupied the entire west side of General Epigastro Square. An Indian servant took me to a large reception room in the baroque style. I found myself among a hundred or so guests. The rather charged atmosphere made me realize, in the end, that I was the only person who'd taken the invitation seriously: I was the only guest in disguise.

"It was no doubt your cunning intention," said the master of the house, Mr. MacFrolick, to me, "to impersonate a certain princess of Tibet, mistress of the king, who was dominated by the sombre rituals of the Bön, rituals fortunately now lost in the furthest recesses of time. I would hesitate to relate, in the presence of ladies, the appalling exploits of the Green Princess. Enough to say that she died in mysterious circumstances, circumstances around which various legends still circulate in the Far East. Some claim that the corpse was carried off by bees, and that they have preserved it to this day in the transparent honey of the Flowers of Venus. Others say that the painted coffin did not contain the princess at all, but the corpse of a crane with the face of a woman; yet others maintain that the princess comes back in the shape of a sow."

Mr. MacFrolick stopped abruptly and looked at me hard and with a severe expression. "I shan't say more, madam," he said, "since we are Catholics."

Confused, I abandoned all explanation and hung my head: my feet were bathed in the rain of cold sweat that fell from my forehead. Mr. MacFrolick looked at me with a lifeless expression. He had little bluish eyes and a thick, heavy, snub nose. It was difficult not to notice that this very distinguished man, devout and of impeccable morality, was the human picture of a big white pig. An enormous moustache hung over his fleshy, rather receding chin. Yes, MacFrolick resembled a pig, but a beautiful pig, a devout and distinguished pig. As these dangerous thoughts passed beneath my green face, a young man of Celtic appearance took me by the hand and said, "Come, dear lady, don't torment yourself. We all inevitably show a resemblance to other species of animals. I'm sure you are aware of your own equine appearance. So . . . don't torment yourself, everything on our planet is pretty mixed up. Do you know Mr. D?"

"No," I said, very confused. "I don't know him."

"D is here this evening," the young man continued. "He is a Magus, and I am his pupil. Look, there he is, near that big blonde dressed in purple satin. Do you see him?"

I saw a man of such neutral appearance that he struck me like a salmon with the head of a sphinx in the middle of a railway station. The extraordinary neutrality of this individual gave me such a disagreeable impression that I staggered to a chair.

"Would you like to meet D?" the young man asked. "He is a very remarkable man."

I was just going to reply when a woman dressed in pale blue taffeta, who wore a very hard expression, took me by the shoulder and pushed me straight into the gaming room.

"We need a fourth for bridge," she told me. "You play bridge, of course." I didn't at all know how, but kept quiet out of panic. I would have liked to leave, but was too timid, so much so that I began to explain that I could only play with felt cards, because of an allergy in the little finger of my left hand. Outside, the orchestra was playing a waltz which I loathed so much I didn't have the courage to say that I was hungry. A high ecclesiastical dignitary, who sat on my right, drew a pork chop from inside his rich, crimson cummerbund.

"Take it, my daughter," he said to me. "Charity pours forth mercy equally on cats, the poor, and women with green faces."

The chop, which had undoubtedly spent a very long time near the ecclesiastic's stomach, didn't appeal to me, but I took it, intending to bury it in the garden.

When I took the chop outside, I found myself in the darkness, weakly lit by the planet Venus. I was walking near the stagnant basin of a fountain full of stupefied bees, when I found myself face to face with the magician, the neutral man.

"So you're going for a walk," he said in a very contemptuous tone. "It's always the same with the expatriate English, bored to death."

Full of shame, I admitted that I too was English, and the man gave a little sarcastic laugh.

"It's hardly your fault that you're English," he said. "The congenital stupidity of the inhabitants of the British Isles is so embedded in their blood that they themselves aren't conscious of it anymore. The spiritual maladies of the English have become flesh, or rather pork brawn."

Vaguely irritated, I replied that it rained a great deal in England, but that the country had bred the greatest poets in the world. Then, to change the subject: "I've just made the acquaintance of one of your pupils. He told me that you are a magician."

"Actually," said the neutral man, "I'm an instructor in spiritual matters, an initiate if you like. But that poor boy will never get anywhere. You must know, my dear lady, that the esoteric path is hard, bristling with catastrophes. Many are called, few are chosen. I would advise you to confine yourself to your charming female nonsense and forget everything of a superior order."

While he was speaking to me, I was trying to hide the pork chop, for it was oozing horrible blobs of grease between my fingers. I finally managed to put it into my pocket. Relieved, I realized this man would never take me seriously if he knew that I was walking about with a pork chop. And though I feared the neutral man like the plague, I still wished to make a good impression.

"I'd like to learn some of your magic, perhaps study with you. Until now . . ."

"There is nothing," he told me. "Try to understand what I'm telling you. *There is nothing, absolutely nothing.*"

It was at this point that I felt myself dissolving into an

opaque and colourless mass. When I got my breath back, the man had disappeared. I wanted to go home, but I was lost in the garden, which was heavy with the scent of a certain shrub which people here call "it smells at night."

I had been walking along the paths for some time when I arrived at a tower. Through the half-open door I noticed a spiral staircase. Somebody called me from inside the tower, and I went up the stairs, thinking that after all I didn't have a great deal to lose anymore. I was much too stupid to run away like the hare with its triangular teeth.

I thought bitterly, At this moment I'm poorer than a beggar, though the bees have done all they could to warn me. Here I am, having lost a whole year's honey, and Venus in the sky.

At the top of the stairs I found myself in Mr. MacFrolick's private boudoir. He received me amiably, and I couldn't explain to myself this change in attitude. With a gesture full of old-fashioned courtesy, Mr. MacFrolick offered me a china dish (quite fine) on which rested his own moustache. I hesitated to accept the moustache, thinking that perhaps he wanted me to eat it. He's an eccentric, I thought. I quickly made my excuses: "Thank you very much, dear sir," I said, "but I'm not hungry anymore after having eaten the delicious chop the bishop so kindly offered me."

MacFrolick seemed slightly offended.

"Madam," he said, "this moustache is not in any way edible. It is meant as a souvenir of this summer evening, and I thought you might perhaps keep it in a cabinet suitable for such keepsakes. I must add that this moustache has no magical power, but that its considerable size sets it apart from common objects."

Understanding that I'd made a faux pas, I took the moustache and put it carefully in my pocket, where it immediately stuck to the disgusting pork chop. MacFrolick then pushed me onto the divan, and leaning heavily on my stomach, said in a confidential tone of voice, "Green woman, know that there are different kinds of magic: black magic, white magic, and, worst of all, grey magic. It is absolutely essential that you know that amongst us this evening is a dangerous grey magician. His name is D. This man, the vampire of velvet words, is responsible for the murder of many souls, both human and otherwise. After several attempts, D has succeeded in infiltrating this mansion to steal our vital essence."

I found it difficult to suppress a little smile, since for a long time I had been living with a Transylvanian vampire, and my mother-in-law had taught me all the necessary culinary secrets to satisfy the most voracious of such creatures.

MacFrolick leaned more heavily on me and hissed, "It is absolutely crucial that I get rid of D. Unfortunately the Church forbids private assassination. I'm therefore obliged to ask you to come to my assistance. You're a Protestant, aren't you?"

"Not at all," I replied. "I'm not a Christian, Mr. MacFrolick. Besides, I've no wish to kill D, even if I had the chance of doing so before he pulverized me ten times over."

MacFrolick's face filled with rage.

"Leave this house immediately," he screamed. "I don't receive unbelievers in my house, madam. Go away!"

I left as quickly as I could on those stairs, while MacFrolick leaned against his door, insulting me in language that was pretty rich for so pious a man.

There is no proper ending to this story, which I recount here as an ordinary summer incident. There's no ending because the episode is true, because all the people are still alive, and everyone is following his destiny. Everyone, that is, except the ecclesiastic, who drowned tragically in the mansion's swimming pool: it's said he was enticed there by sirens disguised as choirboys.

Mr. MacFrolick never again invited me to his mansion, but I am told that he is in good health.

—Translated from the French
by Kathrine Talbot

A Mexican Fairy Tale

Once there lived a boy in a place called San Juan. His name was Juan, his job was looking after pigs.

Juan never went to school, none of his family had ever been to school because where they lived there was no school.

One day when Juan took the pigs out to eat some garbage he heard somebody crying. The pigs started to behave in a funny way, because the voice was coming out of a ruin. The pigs tried to see inside the ruin, but weren't tall enough. Juan sat down to think. He thought: This voice makes me feel sad inside my stomach, it feels as if there was an iguana caught inside jumping around trying to escape. I know that this feeling is really the little voice crying in the ruin, I am afraid, the pigs are afraid. However I want to know, so I shall go to the village and see if Don Pedro will lend me his ladder so I can climb over the wall and see who is making such a sad sound.

Off he went to see Don Pedro. He said: "Will you please lend me your ladder?"

Don Pedro said: "No. What for?"

Juan said to himself: I had better invent something, because if I tell him about the voice he might hurt it.

So out loud he said: "Well a long way off behind the Pyramid of the Moon there is a tall fruit tree where there are a lot of big yellow mangoes growing. These mangoes are so fat that they look like gas balloons. The juice they drip is like honey *but* they grow so high up on the tree that it would be impossible to pick them without a tall ladder."

Don Pedro kept looking at Juan and Juan knew he was greedy and lazy so he just stood and looked at his feet. At last Don Pedro said: "All right, you may borrow the ladder but you must bring me twelve of the fattest mangoes to sell in the market. If you do not return by the evening with the mangoes and the ladder I will thrash you so hard you will swell up as big as the mangoes and you will be *black* and *blue*. So take the ladder and come back quickly."

Don Pedro went back into his house to have lunch and he thought: Mangoes growing up here in the mountains seems very peculiar.

So he sat down and screamed at his wife: *"Bring me little meats and tortillas. All women are fools."*

Don Pedro's family were afraid of him. Don Pedro was terrified of his boss, somebody called Licenciado Gómez, who wore neckties and dark glasses and lived in the town and owned a black motorcar.

During this time Juan was pulling and dragging the long ladder. It was hard work. When Juan arrived at the ruin he fainted with fatigue.

All was quiet, except for the faint grunting of the pigs and the dry sound of a lizard running past.

The sun was beginning to sink when Juan woke up suddenly shouting: *"Ai."* Something was looking down at him, something green, blue, and rusty, glittering like a big myrtle sucker. This bird carried a small bowl of water. Her voice was thin, sweet, and strange. She said: "I am the little granddaughter of the *Great God Mother* who lives in the Pyramid of Venus and I bring you a bowl of life water because you carried the ladder so far to see me when you heard me inside your stomach. This is the right place to listen, in the Stomach."

However

Juan was terrified so he kept on shrieking: "*Ai. Ai. Ai. Ai. Mamá.*"

The bird threw the water in Juan's face. A few drops went inside his mouth. He got up feeling better and stood looking at the bird with joy and delight. He was afraid no longer.

All the while her wings moved like an electric fan, so fast that Juan could see through them. She was a bird, a girl, a wind.

The pigs had all fainted by now with utmost fright.

Juan said: "These pigs do nothing but eat and sleep and make more pigs. Then we kill them and make them into little meats which we eat inside tortillas. Sometimes we get very sick from them, especially if they have been dead for a long time."

"You do not understand pigs," said the bird, whirling. "Pigs have an angel." Whereupon she whistled like an express train and a small cactus plant rose out of the earth and slid into the bowl which the bird had left at her feet.

She said: "Piu, Piu, Little Servant, cut yourself into bits and feed yourself to the pigs so they become inspired with Pig Angel."

The cactus called Piu cut himself into little round bits with a knife so sharp and fast that it was impossible to behold.

The morsels of Piu leapt into the mouths of the unconscious pigs, whereupon the pigs disintegrated into little meats roasting in their own heat.

The smell of delicious roasting pork brought drops of saliva into Juan's mouth. Laughing like a drainpipe the bird took out a telescope and a pair of pincers, picked up the morsels of pig meat, and set them in her small bowl. "Angels must be devoured," she said, turning from green to blue. Lowering her voice to the dark caves under the earth she called: "Black Mole,

Black Mole, Come out and Make the Sauce because Juan is going to eat the Angel, he is hungry and has not eaten since daybreak."

The new moon appeared.

With a heaving and steaming of the earth, Black Mole poked his starred snout out of the ground; then came flat hands and fur, sleek and clean out of so much earth.

"I am blind," he said, "but I wear a star from the firmament on my nose."

Now the bird whirled so fast she turned into a rainbow and Juan saw her pour herself into the Pyramid of the Moon in a curve of all colours. He didn't care because the smell of roasting pigs made food his only desire.

Mole took out all sorts of chiles from the pouch he wore. He took two big stones and ground up the chiles and seeds into pulp, then spat on them and poured them into the bowl with the cooking pig meat.

"I am blind," said Mole, "but I can lead you through the labyrinth."

The red ants then came out of the ground carrying grains of corn. Every ant wore a bracelet of green jade on each of her slim legs. A great heap of corn was soon ground up. Mole made tortillas with his flat hands.

All was ready for the feast. Even Saint John's Day had never seen anything so rich.

"Now eat," said Mole.

Juan dipped his tortilla into the bowl and ate until he was gorged with food. "I never had so much to eat, never," he kept saying. His stomach looked like a swollen melon.

All the while Mole stood by saying nothing, but taking stock of all that happened with his nose.

When Juan had finished the last scrap of the fifth pig Mole began to laugh. Juan was so full of food he could not move. He could only stare at Mole and wonder what was so funny.

Mole wore a scabbard under his fur. Quickly he drew out a sharp sword and, swish and shriek, cut up Juan into small pieces just like Piu had sliced himself up to feed the pigs.

The head and hands and feet and guts of young Juan jumped about shrieking. Mole took Juan's head tenderly in his big hands and said: "Do not be afraid, Juan, this is only a first death, and you will be alive again soon."

Whereupon he stuck the head on the thorn of a maguey and dived into the hard ground as if it were water.

All was quiet now. The thin new moon was high above the pyramids.

MARÍA

The well was far off. María returned to the hut with a bucket of water. The water kept sloshing over the side of the bucket. Don Pedro, María's father, was shouting: "I shall beat that hairless puppy Juanito. He stole my ladder. I know mangoes don't grow around here. I shall thrash him till he begs for mercy. I shall thrash you all. *Why isn't my dinner ready?*"

Don Pedro yelled again: "She has not come back with the water? I shall beat her. I shall twist her neck like a chicken. You are a no-good woman, your children are no good. *I am master here. I command. I shall kill that thief.*"

María was afraid. She had stopped to listen behind a large maguey. Don Pedro was drunk. She thought: He's beating my mother. A thin yellow cat dashed past in terror. The cat is also afraid, if I go back he will beat me, perhaps he will kill me like a chicken.

Quietly María set down the pail of water and walked north towards the Pyramid of the Moon.

It was night. María was afraid, but she was more afraid of her father, Don Pedro. María tried to remember a prayer to the Virgin of Guadalupe, but every time she began *Ave Maria*, something laughed.

A puff of dust arose on the path a few metres ahead. Out of the dust walked a small dog. It was hairless, with a speckled grey skin like a hen.

The dog walked up to her and they looked at each other. There was something distinctive and dignified about the animal. María understood that the dog was an ally. She thought: This dog is an ancient.

The dog turned north, and María followed. They walked and sometimes ran till they came to the ruin and María was face to face with Juan's decapitated head.

María's heart leapt. Grief struck her and she shed a tear which was hard as a stone and fell heavily to the earth. She picked up the tear and placed it in the mouth of Juan's head.

"Speak," said María, who was now old and full of wisdom. He spoke, saying: "My body is strewn around like a broken necklace. Pick it up and sew it together again. My head is lonely without my hands and my feet. All these are lonely without the rest of my poor body, chopped up like meat stew."

María picked a thorn off the top of a maguey, made thread out of the sinews of the leaf, and told the maguey: "Pardon me for taking your needle, pardon me for threading the needle with your body, pardon me for love, pardon me for I am what I am, and I do not know what this means."

All this time Juan's head was weeping and wailing and complaining: "Ai, Ai, Ai. My poor self, poor me, my poor body. Hurry up, María, and sew me together. Hurry, for if the sun rises and Earth turns away from the firmament I shall never be whole again. Hurry, María, hurry. Ai, Ai, Ai."

María was busy now and the dog kept fetching pieces of the body and she sewed them together with neat stitches. Now she sewed on the head, and the only thing lacking was the heart. María had made a little door in Juan's breast to put it inside.

"Dog, Dog, where is Juan's heart?" The heart was on top of the wall of the ruin. Juan and María set up Don Pedro's ladder and Juan started to climb, but María said: "Stop, Juan. You cannot reach your own heart, you must let me climb up and get it. Stop."

But Juan refused to listen and kept on climbing. Just as he was reaching out to get hold of his heart, which was still beating, a black vulture swooped out of the air, snatched the heart in its claws, and flew off towards the Pyramid of the Moon. Juan gave a shriek and fell off the ladder; however

María had sewn his body together so well that he was not really hurt.

But Juan had lost his heart.

"My heart. There it was, beating alone on the wall, red and slippery. My beautiful heart. Ah me, ah me," he cried. "That wicked black bird has ruined me, I am lost."

"Hush now," said María. "If you make so much noise the *Nagual* may hear us, with his straw wings and crystal horns. Hush, be quiet, Juan."

The hairless dog barked twice and started to walk into a cave that had opened up like a mouth. "The Earth is alive," said María, "we must feed ourselves to the Earth to find your heart. Come, follow the Esquinclé."

They looked into the deep mouth of the Earth and were afraid. "We will use the ladder to climb down," said María. Far below they could hear the dog barking.

As they started to climb down the ladder into the dark earth the first pale light of dawn arose behind the Pyramid of the Sun. The dog barked. María climbed slowly down the ladder and Juan followed. Above them Earth closed her mouth with a smile. The smile is still there, a long crack in the hard clay.

Down below was a passage shaped like a long hollow man. Juan and María walked inside this body holding hands. They knew now that they could not return and must keep on walking. Juan was knocking on the door in his chest crying, "Oh my poor lost heart, oh my stolen heart."

His wailing ran ahead of them and disappeared. It was a message. After a while a great roar came rumbling back. They stood together, shaking. A flight of stairs with narrow slippery steps led downwards. Below they could see the Red Jaguar that lives under the pyramids. The Big Cat was frightful to behold, but there was no return. They descended the stairs trembling. The Jaguar smelled of rage. He had eaten many hearts, but this was long ago and now he wanted blood.

As they got closer, the Jaguar sharpened his claws on the rock, ready to devour the meat of two tender children.

María felt sad to die so far under the earth. She wept one

more tear, which fell into Juan's open hand. It was hard and sharp. He threw it straight at the eye of the beast and it bounced off. The Jaguar was made of stone.

They walked straight up and touched it, stroking the hard red body and obsidian eyes. They laughed and sat on its back; the stone Jaguar never moved. They played until a voice called: "María. Juan. Juan. Mari."

A flight of hummingbirds passed, rushing towards the voice.

"The Ancestor is calling us," said María, listening. "We must go back to Her."

They crawled under the belly of the stone Jaguar. Mole was standing there, tall and black, holding a silver sword in one of his big hands. In the other hand he held a rope. He bound the two children tightly together and pulled them into the presence of the Great Bird. Bird, Snake, Goddess, there She sat, all the colours of the rainbow and full of little windows with faces looking out singing the sounds of every thing alive and dead, all this like a swarming of bees, a million movements in one still body.

María and Juan stared at each other till Mole cut the rope that bound them together. They lay on the floor looking up at the Evening Star, shining through a shaft in the roof.

Mole was piling branches of scented wood on a brazier. When this was ready, the Bird Snake Mother shot a tongue of fire out of her mouth and the wood burst into flame. "María," called a million voices, "jump into the fire and take Juan by the hand, he must burn with you so you both shall be one whole person. This is love."

They jumped into the fire and ascended in smoke through the shaft in the roof to join the Evening Star. Juan-Mari, they were one whole being. They will return again to Earth, one Being called Quetzalcoatl.

Juan-Mari keep returning, so this story has no end.

Et in bellicus lunarum medicalis

"Russia Donates Team of Trained Rats. Experienced in Operating on People. Due to the Recent Strike of Doctors, the Russian Government Has Graciously Donated a Team of Rats Highly Specialized in All Types of Surgery and General Practise." The news appeared in the Great Metropolitan Newspaper.

Naturally.

And so there was a reunion of State Ministers, Doctors, Bankers, Priests, and other politicians.

It became evident that the idea made them uneasy. The famous Dr. Monopus announced: "This move cannot inspire the necessary confidence in our patients. An operation is too delicate a matter to be undertaken by rats. Moreover, it would not be hygienic." A government minister wearing an English suit stated: "Soviet rats are always sterilized before operating on a patient's body. Besides, if we don't make use of these rats, the Russian Government will be offended."

A disagreeable silence overtook one and all.

Señor Alcaparras, a powerful banker well-known for his democratic attitude, had the courage to break the silence: "Gentlemen," he said with his habitual smiling suavity, "there is no problem here. We will simply donate the rats to the President of the United States, and thus we can please everybody. The Americans, just like the Russians, are very modern."

"I don't believe it is correct to give gifts as a gift," said a priest, Father Podmore, confessor to ladies of good society. "I myself am modern and a complete atheist like all enlightened ecclesiastics, but . . . even a man as open as I am becomes perturbed by a lack of good manners."

"He's right," said the government minister. "No one wants war against the Russians and the Americans at the same time. They're armed to the teeth, as they say."

"I'm against substituting rats for human beings in the hospitals," said Dr. Monopus firmly. "Better to make an official donation of the rats to the Psychoanalytical Association."

The imposing Institute of Semi-Applied Sciences and Other Metaphorical Activities covers several square kilometres in our city and is surrounded by a lovely park with fountains that occasionally spout water. This was the place where the Great Soviet Gift would be presented. There was music, flags, French cooking enveloped in gelatin: the *enchiladas à la Bordelaise* enjoyed special favour.

The physicians themselves presented the wise Rats, amid music and speeches, to the psychoanalysts.

The Head of the Psychoanalytical Association, Dr. Siegfried Laftnalger, received the gift of the Rats in the shadow of the Monument to Semi-Applied and Metaphorical Science. This monument, recognized throughout the world as unique, consists of three heroes and a horse triumphantly penetrating a streptococcus culture.

Standing under the monument, Dr. Laftnalger received the gift with bowed head, murmuring, *"Ai Chingao,"* vowing revenge against his enemy Dr. Monopus.

ET IN BELLICUS LUNARUM MEDICALIS — 161

Following the banquet the psychoanalysts gathered at a secret place in the hills of Las Lomas to contemplate the Soviet Bequest. "I don't wish to speak against a medical colleague," said Dr. Laftnalger, "but Monopus is a goat. Now how are we to use these rats in analysis?"

"It's an insult," said Dr. Von Garza, "an open declaration of hostility and aggression, a palpable rejection."

"Transference from patient to rat will present unprecedented difficulties," said Dr. Zodiac Pérez, an ugly man who thought a lot about transference. "One cannot conceive any practical use for these animals in dealing with recalcitrant neuroses. We should not forget that patients, too, are human beings."

"Here, here!" cried several doctors who spoke good English.

"Should we charge the same rates for sessions with rats, or only half?" said Dr. Benito Wurst, who had a problem of insecurity as well as a *tic nerveux* and six children who ate a lot.

No one knew the answer. At length Dr. Laftnalger said: "Quatch!" and then, with a slight smile, added, "We'd be better off to give the rats to the gynaecologists." Some laughter followed this gloomy joke.

The quandary thickened. After various sessions in the luxurious bronze mansion on the slopes of Las Lomas—all bronze, marble, ivory, and decorated with bisons—the psychoanalysts decided to kidnap Dr. Monopus and force him to take back the rats to work in the operating theatres of hospitals. Meanwhile, the rats were eating vitamins and taking orderly exercise in an electronic corral.

In the end, it was Dr. Zodiac Pérez, disguised as a lass from Daxara, who was chosen to abduct Dr. Monopus, who was removed to a secret hiding place in the elegant basement of the Psychoanalytical Mansion. . . . He was to be kept there until he agreed to take back the rats once and for all.

As a prisoner, Dr. Monopus displayed surprising resistance to the psychological ingenuity used against him. He denied all responsibility for the rats. "Though they are adept at bookkeeping, they are not, I believe, trustworthy and have no sense of responsibility," he admitted after a triple electroshock procedure and a treatment of subliminal persuasion over several nights. "I don't want rats in the operating theatre. Period."

The prisoner's diet consisted of strawberry-flavored cornmeal gruel, without milk, and he grew thin. The fourth week of captivity was coming to an end when Dr. Laftnalger sighed and said: "There's nothing for it, we'll have to sacrifice both Monopus and the rats at the same time. We'll deposit the bodies in an anteroom of the Ministry of the Interior so that the affair will come to public attention. We'll let it be known that Monopus killed the rats and then committed suicide because he was a counterspy. Everything has a solution."

"Here, here!" cried those who spoke English. The rest feigned discreet coughs.

They thought of mixing poison into the strawberry-flavored cornmeal, which tasted bad anyway. "Let's not make him suffer too much. Let's use something quick. Quatch!"

"Here, here!"

In the meanwhile a shipment of arms was received at the border to capture the rats and send them on to the Pentagon by helicopter for military purposes. "Who knows," said an American general, "they might be sent by submarine." A civil war would have ensued, if it had not been for a fortuitous incident. In the bathroom of the basement of the Psychoanalytical Mansion the toilet got plugged up.

How?

The prisoner, Dr. Monopus, infuriated by his lack of liberty, had begun to throw all kinds of objects belonging to the analysts into the toilet bowl: watches, ties, shoes, and the complete works of Erich Fromm. It was soon obstructed. *The Art of Loving* blocked the exit from the main pipeline.

They called the plumber. Señor Jasón Malvavisco, licenced plumber, arrived with his helpers. "You'd have to use dynamite," he told Dr. Monopus, who now desired to use the facilities.

"Such a solution won't do," said the doctor. "After all, I'm locked up in here."

Señor Jasón Malvavisco was an amiable man, full of good humour, and he offered the doctor a cigarette. "Are you a professional?" he asked Monopus.

"I'm a doctor."

"Well, in a certain sense I'm a doctor, too," said Jasón. "My friends call me Doctor, inasmuch as I'm responsible for the intestinal system of the subterranean tubes of the city."

"Very interesting," said Monopus, "but I don't think that dynamiting the patient falls within the limits of professional ethics."

The plumber bowed to this logic. His own principles were well established. "In that case, there's going to be a big stink. There's no way . . ."

At this point the Soviet Rats themselves appeared on the scene, trying out a new dance step, the Paso Doble Pancreas, a new therapy based on manipulating the digestive system by eating bricks instead of meat (thus also saving money).

Jasón was well informed on the psychological customs of the rats, and he knew how to communicate with them through symptomatic idiom.

"They're ready," he finally told Dr. Monopus. "They say that to fix the toilet all they need are some pliers and a simple ladder."

The Soviet Rats disappeared quickly down the underground tubing. They never came back. They never appeared again in daylight or by the light of the moon.

The toilet, however, was unblocked.

As regards the psychoanalysts, they decided to wear uniforms of black velvet studded with buttons. Laftnalger announced: "We, too, have our dignity and our own organization. In spite of everything, psychology lives in the flesh. And without flesh we would have no patients. Thus, even a bone that talks is worth more than a rat that thinks."

Amen. . . .

> *Even though you won't believe me*
> *my story is beautiful*
> *And the serpent that sang it*
> *Sang it from out of the well.*

—Translated from the Spanish
by Anthony Kerrigan

My Flannel Knickers

Thousands of people know my flannel knickers, and though I know this may seem flirtatious, it is not. I am a saint.

The "Sainthood," I may say, was actually forced upon me. If anyone would like to avoid becoming holy, they should immediately read this entire story.

I live on an island. This island was bestowed upon me by the government when I left prison. It is not a desert island, it is a traffic island in the middle of a busy boulevard, and motors thunder past on all sides day and night.

So . . .

The flannel knickers are well known. They are hung at midday on a wire from the red green and yellow automatic lights. I wash them every day, and they have to dry in the sun.

Apart from the flannel knickers, I wear a gentleman's tweed jacket for golfing. It was given to me, and the gym shoes.

No socks. Many people recoil from my undistinguished appearance, but if they have been told about me (mainly in the Tourist's Guide), they make a pilgrimage, which is quite easy.

Now I must trace the peculiar events that brought me to this condition. Once I was a great beauty and attended all sorts of cocktail-drinking, prize-giving-and-taking, artistic demonstrations and other casually hazardous gatherings organized for the purpose of people wasting other people's time. I was always in demand and my beautiful face would hang suspended over fashionable garments, smiling continually. An ardent heart, however, beat under the fashionable costumes, and this very ardent heart was like an open tap pouring quantities of hot water over anybody who asked. This wasteful process soon took its toll on my beautiful smiling face. My teeth fell out. The original structure of the face became blurred, and then began to fall away from the bones in small, ever-increasing folds. I sat and watched the process with a mixture of slighted vanity and acute depression. I was, I thought, solidly installed in my lunar plexus, within clouds of sensitive vapour.

If I happened to smile at my face in the mirror, I could objectively observe the fact that I had only three teeth left and these were beginning to decay.

Consequently

I went to the dentist. Not only did he cure the three remaining teeth but he also presented me with a set of false teeth, cunningly mounted on a pink plastic chassis. When I had paid a sufficiently large quantity of my diminishing wealth, the teeth were mine and I took them home and put them into my mouth.

The Face seemed to regain some of its absolutely-irresistible-attraction, although the folds were of course still there. From the lunar plexus I arose like a hungry trout and was caught fast on the sharp barbed hook that hangs inside all once-very-beautiful faces.

A thin magnetic mist formed between myself, the face, and clear perception. This is what I saw in the mist. "Well,

well. I really was beginning to petrify in that old lunar plexus. This must be me, this beautiful, smiling fully toothed creature. There I was, sitting in the dark bloodstream like a mummified foetus with no love at all. Here I am, back in the rich world, where I can palpitate again, jump up and down in the nice warm swimming pool of outflowing emotion, the more bathers the merrier. I Shall Be Enriched."

All these disastrous thoughts were multiplied and reflected in the magnetic mist. I stepped in, wearing my face, now back in the old enigmatic smile which had always turned sour in the past.

No sooner trapped than done.

Smiling horribly, I returned to the jungle of faces, each ravenously trying to eat each other.

Here I might explain the process that actually takes place in this sort of jungle. Each face is provided with greater or smaller mouths, armed with different kinds of sometimes natural teeth. (Anybody over forty and toothless should be sensible enough to be quietly knitting an original new body, instead of wasting the cosmic wool.) These teeth bar the way to a gaping throat, which disgorges whatever it swallows back into the foetid atmosphere.

The bodies over which these faces are suspended serve as ballast to the faces. As a rule they are carefully covered with colours and shapes in current "Fashion." This "fashion" is a devouring idea launched by another face snapping with insatiable hunger for money and notoriety. The bodies, in constant misery and supplication, are generally ignored and only used for ambulation of the face. As I said, for ballast.

Once, however, that I bared my new teeth I realized that something had gone wrong. For after a very short period of enigmatic smiling, the smile became quite stiff and fixed, while the face slipped away from its bonish mooring, leaving me clutching desperately to a soft grey mask over a barely animated body.

The strange part of the affair now reveals itself. The jungle faces, instead of recoiling in horror from what I already knew to be a sad sight, approached me and started to beg me for something which I thought I had not got.

Puzzled, I consulted my Friend, a Greek.

He said: "They think you have woven a complete face and body and are in constant possession of excess amounts of cosmic wool. Even if this is not so, the very fact that you know about the wool makes them determined to steal it."

"I have wasted practically the entire fleece," I told him. "And if anybody steals from me now I shall die and disintegrate totally."

"Three-dimensional life," said the Greek, "is formed by attitude. Since by their attitude they expect you to have quantities of wool, you are three-dimensionally forced to 'Sainthood,' which means you must spin your body and teach the faces how to spin theirs."

The compassionate words of the Greek filled me with fear. I am a face myself. The quickest way of retiring from social Face-eating competition occurred to me when I attacked a policeman with my strong steel umbrella. I was quickly put into prison, where I spent months of health-giving meditation and compulsive exercise.

My exemplary conduct in prison moved the Head Wardress to an excess of bounty, and that is how the Government presented me with the island, after a small and distinguished ceremony in a remote corner of the Protestant Cemetery.

So here I am on the island with all sizes of mechanical artifacts whizzing by in every conceivable direction, even overhead.

Here I sit.

The Invention of Mole
A Play

CAST OF CHARACTERS

Montezuma
A Friend
The Archbishop of Canterbury
The Great Witch Tlaxcluhuichiloquitle
The Imperial Cook
Ocelots, quetzales, and servants

MONTEZUMA (*naturally in Nahuatl*): And so my esteemed sir, you were telling us that in the course of your rites the people play a relatively passive role. The role, let us say, of mere observers watching the general activities of the Priest with his artefacts. We would like to hazard a guess without wishing to be critical, that the faithful must get mortally bored.

THE ARCHBISHOP (*a bit startled*): Our Holy Mass consists in the sacred communion of all participants, including the most ordinary people, who form part of the ceremony, whether or not they be immoral, of low social origin, or forego bathing.

MONTEZUMA: But they don't *do* anything. And you yourself told us that there are no magical demonstrations of any kind. Their participation therefore would be purely theoretical?

THE ARCHBISHOP: In spiritual matters, the theoretical is reality made manifest. On the other hand, every time the public does participate actively in the ceremonies, then discord, disputes, and confusion arise. The activity, as such, is reserved for the clergy.

MONTEZUMA: So, then, the people watch the same ceremony over and over again, without miracles, magic, sacrifices, or dances! Such a religion is bound to stagnate completely in a few centuries!

THE ARCHBISHOP: The Holy Church is founded on the Rock of Eternity and the very gates of Hell shall not prevail against Her. The universal nature of the Church will allow Her eventually to absorb all of humanity.

MONTEZUMA: If what you say is true, I am happy to think that by then I will no longer be among the living. A humanity feeding on theories and speculations relating to eternity will have turned into a mechanism for suicide. Our own anguish is something more vital, our desires, our passions, our deep thirst for marvels must be satiated. Otherwise we'd all turn into phantoms, or into something worse, empty ideas.

THE INVENTION OF MOLE, A PLAY — 171

THE FRIEND (*who until now has been busy knitting an incredibly long and tubular sweater destined for Quetzalcoatl*): Really, I do believe it's time for the Archbishop to begin his ablutions. Supper has been announced for nine o'clock and your guest, King Pederast of Texcoco, must meet those new adolescent boys brought up from the coast. You musn't forget that the king is going to give you a giant armadillo in exchange for three boys.

MONTEZUMA: Heavens, yes! That animal is a fascinating sight. Its scales pure gold, with a patina, and its claws as long as ocote branches. I must acquire it for my zoo in Cuernavaca.

THE ARCHBISHOP: Supper at nine, with guests coming? Don't, please, go to any bother for my sake, I beg you. My stomach is a bit upset from all the condiments and spices you use. I'll be happy to have a boiled turkey, and, if possible, a few of those delightful corn cakes. And perhaps a cup of that delightful drink which you call chocolate, I believe.

THE FRIEND (*ignoring the Archbishop*): The Imperial Cook has prescribed a vigourous scouring with pumice stone and hay, followed by an immersion in fiery pulque for three hours.

MONTEZUMA: You know well enough that we never interfere in kitchen matters. They can prepare him as they like.

THE ARCHBISHOP (*gaily*): I don't think I'll drink any pulque, much less bathe in it. I got a little drunk the last time I tried it, and I don't think it's good for my liver.

MONTEZUMA: A liver which is adversely affected is big and fat. Ablutions in pulque can be quite satisfying, you'll see, though the scouring with pumice may not prove so nice. Nevertheless, it is absolutely essential that your skin retain no trace of the odour of vestments and no scent of perspiration. Such odours would only mar the gastronomic symphony.

THE ARCHBISHOP: Oh, is there going to be a musical accompaniment? It sounds like a most joyous evening. For the moment, though, I think I'll forego the scrubbing and simply change my undershirt. A bath at this time of year would do my bronchial system no good.

MONTEZUMA: I'm afraid your usual regime and your traditional way of life will have to be modified even if ever so slightly. Please understand: the monarch of Texcoco possesses a most refined palate, extremely so, and is terribly demanding as regards the aroma of sauces. The slightest hint of the odour of sweat alters his spiritual appreciation of life for months.

THE ARCHBISHOP: I trust you will not consider me obtuse if I confess that I cannot follow your reasoning very closely. . . .

THE FRIEND: Really, it's quite simple. You will forgive my frankness if I tell you that you people, you whites, are so lax in ritual bathing that your flesh, even after repeated immersion in spices and pulque, is far too coarse for good eating. But, as regards you personally, we have decided to adopt certain hygienic measures beforehand, while you are still alive. And therein lies the difference, for we expect that the lard you'll lose will do away with the indelicacy of taste and the lack of proper savour to your flesh.

THE ARCHBISHOP (*turning as pale and grey as a roast hog*): What are you trying to tell me, monstrous pagans?

MONTEZUMA: My dear sir, don't get yourself worked up, and don't lose your sense of humour. None of us is going to live forever.

THE ARCHBISHOP: This is quite inconceivable! Do you mean to say that you plan to assassinate me and, in fact . . . devour me?

THE FRIEND: Now *devour* is the least appropriate word to use when speaking of the delicate palates of the Great King of Texcoco and of His Majesty, the Emperor of Mexico, and of their taste in meats. You will simply be assimilated, *absorbed* by these royal princes, once you are soaked in the most exquisite sauces, everything done with utmost dignity and aristocratic manners. At all times the conversation will shine with humour, ingenuity, and culture. Of course you yourself will no longer be in a state to participate.

THE ARCHBISHOP: Don't you realize the abomination, the great sin you will be perpetrating in assassinating one of the holy servants of the Lord!

MONTEZUMA: All sorcerers know how to perform miracles and they endure great periods of fasting to do so. All you do is eat and sleep, and talk and talk. Why should we believe that you are a real sorcerer? Do you fast? Do you flagellate yourself? Can you work miracles, even one, one tiny one?

THE ARCHBISHOP: Only God can work miracles!

MONTEZUMA: My good sir, you are completely wrong if you think that God is the only one able to bring forth miracles. Even a novice priest must be a competent prophet before being accepted as an apprentice to the Pyramids.

THE ARCHBISHOP: Those are no miracles, you scoundrel! What you pagans do is the work of the Devil, black magic. . . .

THE FRIEND (*as he continues knitting*): Call it what you like: black magic, or dealings with the Devil, it's still more interesting than your cataract of words, theories, and more words. Besides, who can tell the colour of magic, when it's sometimes more complicated and richer than any prism?

THE ARCHBISHOP (*beginning to howl*): I don't believe a word of any of this, I don't believe a single one of your witches can produce any magic, black or blue! . . .

MONTEZUMA: Well, if that's your attitude, there's nothing for us to do except to call on our Third Great Priestess, Tlaxcluhuichiloquitle, a wizard at magical demonstrations and displays. After all, we must maintain our reputation when we record these events in our Codex.

(The Friend lights some incense and runs around the victim thrice, calling out):
> *Tlax tlax caki Tlaxcluhui chi lo quitle*
> *Woman of the wilderness*
> *Refuses to accede to your alien practises*
> *Unwritten Codex, we beseech you come near*
> *Do us the favour, come forth and appear*

(The witch Tlaxcluhuichiloquitle slides out from under the Archbishop's cassock and sets about preparing certain artefacts with professional skill).

MONTEZUMA: Do us the honour, O Tlaxcluhuichiloquitle, Third Great Priestess of Imperial Mexico! A single favour, one manifestation to calm the nerves of the Archbishop before the Imperial Cook prepares him for supper.

(The witch does not speak: she cackles rapidly like an excited chicken. But her movements are slow. Sud-

denly, a multitude of ocelots and quetzal birds appear from under the ecclesiastical cassock and engage in mortal combat. They begin to kill each other off, and turn into banana peels and piles of fluff, respectively. She disappears, and only her cackling is heard.)

FRIEND: The banana peels leave me cold. I'm disillusioned. I expect she must be saving her vibrations for later on tonight.

(The Imperial Cook appears with a great earthen casserole fit for an Archbishop. He is accompanied by a variety of servants. He has the air and extraordinary good humour of a dentist about to extract a deeply rooted wisdom tooth.)

THE COOK *(rubbing his hands)*: Well, well, well. And how are we feeling today? It will all be over in a couple of hours, and you won't feel a thing, absolutely and relatively nothing. . . .

CURTAIN on the increasingly piercing shrieks of the prelate.

—Translated from the Spanish
by Anthony Kerrigan

The Happy Corpse Story

White girl dappled mare
the stags and the ferns in the wood.
Tuft of black hair caught on a thorn
She went by so fast
Now she is gone.

The young man, dressed in purple and gold with a blond wig and carrying a jukebox, threw a tantrum and fell on the mossy knoll in a passionate fit of weeping.

"She never returned," he cried.

"Sentimentality is a form of fatigue," said the Happy Corpse, greyish, swinging to and fro on the gnarled elm, like a wasps' nest.

"Nevertheless," shrieked the youth, "I must seek her, because I am in love."

The Happy Corpse laughed. "You mean your secret thread

THE HAPPY CORPSE STORY

got wound around a galloping damsel. The thinness of it being pulled is a sinful waste and woeful want."

The young man's wig fell off, showing a skull covered with black bristles.

"However," continued the Happy Corpse, "if you catch hold of me and ride on my back, I may help you to find this woman."

"Whoop!" yelped the youth and grabbed at the corpse, which fell into ashes and appeared on the other side of a brandleberry bush.

"Not so fast."

Around and around the brandleberry bush they ran, and as the young man got nearer and nearer the corpse got thicker and thicker, till the youth leapt on its back; whereupon the Happy Corpse stamped its foot and away they ran.

Thorns grabbed at the pair as they hurried through the wood. Great Scot, a nasty black-and-white terrier, ran constantly at the corpse's heels, snapping. This mangy creature lurked the haunts where Happy Corpses abide, since one can hardly say live in this case. The dog smelled as bad as the corpse; it was practically impossible to tell one from the other. They just looked different.

Being full of holes and dents, the corpse could talk out of any part of its body. "Now," said the corpse through the back of its head, "I shall tell you a story." The youth heaved a groan like a death rattle. He felt too preoccupied to listen. Nevertheless the story began. Think of listening to a story told straight into your face out of a hole in the back of the head with bad breath: surely this must have troubled the delicate sensibility of the young man. However, what can't be cured must be endured.

"The story," said the Happy Corpse, "is all about my father." As they unravelled themselves from the tendrils of some poison ivy, the story continued: "My father was a man so utterly and exactly like everybody else that he was forced to wear a large badge on his coat in case he was mistaken for anybody. Any body, if you see what I mean. He was obliged to make constant efforts to make himself present to the attention of others. This was very tiring, and he never slept, because of the constant banquets, bazaars, meetings, symposiums, discussions, board meetings, race meetings, and simple meatings where meat was eaten. He could never stay in one place for more than a minute at a time because if he did not appear to be constantly busy he was afraid somebody might think he was not urgently needed elsewhere. So he never got to know anybody. It is quite impossible to be truly busy and actually ever be with anybody because business means that wherever you are you are leaving immediately for some other place. Relatively young, the poor man turned himself into a human wreckage."

A thing like a great black rag flew past heavily, saying, "Hands up, Infidel."

"What was that?" asked the youth, alarmed. The Happy Corpse smiled through the hole in its head. "That was Dick Turpin, once a Highwayman, always a ghost. He is going to the Fantomat."

"The Fantomat?"

"Yes, the Fantomat is an automatic Fantomator. There are a lot of them, chainwise, as we get nearer and nearer to Hell."

Terrified by now, the youth became blue around the lips and was too alarmed to reply.

"As I was saying about my father," continued the Corpse, "he eventually became an executive for a firm. This meant that he actually executed persons with showers of legal documents proving that they owed him quantities of money which they did not have. 'Firm' actually means the manufacture of useless objects which people are foolish enough to buy. The firmer the firm the more senseless talk is needed to prevent anyone noticing the unsafe structure of the business. Sometimes these Firms actually sell nothing at all for a lot of money, like 'Life Insurance,' a pretense that it is a soothing and useful event to have a violent and painful death."

"What happened to your father?" asked the youth, mostly

to listen to his own voice for comfort during the increasing horror of the journey. Now the woods kept fluctuating with apparitions: beasts, garbage cans overflowing with decomposed entities, leaves chasing each other chaotically, so that no shape was ever constant; grass behaving like animated spaghetti, and a number of nameless vacuums, causing events that were always unhappy or catastrophic.

"My father died of a heart attack during a telephone conversation, and then of course he went to Hell. Now he is in Telephone Hell, where everyone has these apparatuses constantly glued to their lips or ears. This causes great anguish. My father will be with his Telephone for nine hundred and ninety-nine billion aeons before he gets rid of it. Afterwards he might even become a saint. Before actually maturing into a real Entity, everybody goes to Hell first, and if they are not too careful, afterwards they must begin all over again."

"You mean that your father is actually in Hell?" asked the youth. "And why do you never mention your mother?"

Here the Corpse almost paused. The trees were scarcer, so that a stretch of desert was visible in the distance.

"My mother committed suicide from boredom. My father was so busy that she had nobody to talk to. So she ate and ate and then shut herself into the refrigerator and half froze and half suffocated to death. She also went to Hell, but in the refrigerator, eating constantly. I composed a poem to her memory. It goes like this:

> *When Father's Face was hard to bear*
> *Mother got into the Frigidaire,*
> *Father, said I, I'm so unhappé*
> *Mother is completely frappé.*

Tears were now streaming down the face of the young man. "The whole story is quite dreadful. And really much worse, because my own poor mother also committed suicide. She shot herself with a machine gun."

The Happy Corpse stopped suddenly, throwing the youth

to the ground, saying: "You silly boy, do you suppose I don't know that? I am your mother. How would I ever have carried you so near to Hell had I been another, a stranger?"

"Mummy?" said the youth, trembling violently. "Forgive me."

"You always used to eat strawberry-jam sandwiches for tea."

They were both lost for a moment in memories of the strawberry-jam sandwiches. After a while the Happy Corpse said: "Now you had better return, since you forgot the white girl on the dappled horse, as those on their way to Hell forget.

"Now you must remember, and in order to remember you must return again, alone."

So that the boy should find his way back, she tied his leg to Great Scot the terrier with a long black hair. Off they went, and one can only hope they found their way back. The Happy Corpse dissolved into ashes and, laughing heartily, returned to the tree.

How to Start a Pharmaceuticals Business

I picked the site for the picnic with trepidation. The occasion was a solemn one for me because of the distinguished quality of my guests: the well-known noble of the highest Mexican society, Lord Popocatepetl, and his closest friend, the Viscount Federal District. I had devoted great thought to choosing the most adequate place to enjoy the company of these two gentlemen and, given the high price of even vulgar restaurants, I finally decided to invite them to a beautiful old cemetery close to the ruins of the Latin American Tower.

Once the monarchy had been well established in Mexico, King Chapultepec von Smith the Second (son of Atzcapotzalco Guggenheim) promulgated the law definitely prohibiting all instruments of speech transmission of a nonanimal nature (whether radios, telephones, televisions, walkie-talkies, microphones, etc. etc.). Our civilization thereupon rapidly advanced toward a Golden Age in which pleasurable silence has made every street a garden and every home a centre for peaceful, if not always intellectual, thought.

It is now customary for the most distinguished members of society to hold picnics in the very centre of the city. Games like chess, snakes and ladders, and ludo have become peaceful national pastimes. It is said that in the old days the masses killed bulls for pleasure. It is not known how they did this exactly, but it can be assumed that they used firearms or some such artefacts in common use in those dark and barbarous times.

Ever since the edict issued by the Black King of the North, New York the First, an edict titled the Law of De-Electrification of the Americas, it has been unclear how those powerful electrical forces were once used, forces we now make use of only in our rituals.

But I see that I am wandering from my story. It was on a hazy day in the month of May that I made my way to the Saint George Light and Power Cemetery in my modest one-mule sled, loaded with my choice foods: not only tins of Norwegian enchiladas from Japan, but six bottles of the rare old Indian drink called cocacola, bottled at the source.

The cemetery was shrouded in a veil of mystery in the early-morning light: its closely packed tombstones gleamed white on the side the rains washed them, black on their shady side. In the middle of this spiderweb of narrow alleys was a tavern, the Fat Swallow, to which those visiting this city of the dead repaired for the comfort of strong drink. The place had apparently been some sort of church in the old days at the end of the Christian Era: that is, a place where melancholy rites were celebrated and believers gathered to hear discourses from a priest while they contemplated their God (now dead), a poor man nailed in an awful way to a wooden construction and languishing in apparent agony. An interesting example of the psychology of our ancestors, that they should have adored such a sinister image!

Seeking a site for our picnic, I made my way slowly to a comparatively open space where two men were digging a hole.

They told me they were unearthing the remains of the distinguished Lady Haughty Corner, who had only recently died in the course of her studies of the customs of the underground "Home Office," or Ministry of the Interior. Her widely known thesis, *Prayers of the Twentieth Century*, deals with the mystifying discoveries made by archaeologists when they opened up the famous Home Office Building.

"This cemetery is for the exclusive use of ladies," said the taller of the two diggers. They asked if I would lie down in the hole to help measure its size.

The humid ground was not as inhospitable as might be supposed. I even felt a certain languor and sleepiness as I made myself comfortable in Lady Haughty Corner's grave. The men went about taking their measurements with great care. When their work was done they helped me out and, as I was taking my leave of them, I discerned my two guests approaching through the mist: Lord Popocatepetl and the Viscount Federal District.

I picked up my basket and went to encounter my distinguished friends. We soon found a tranquil spot. Lord Popocatepetl recounted the latest developments of his rheumatism. "Ever since the beginning of the year, on account of the humidity, the lower half of my spine had been prey to spasms. I've consulted Dr. Major-Magician, who assured me aches and pains are purely psychological, and advised me to wear pants lined with monkey skin, tanned in pulque. So far I've felt no relief."

"Quack!" responded Federal District. "Rheumatism is caused by disturbances in the equinox. The grey fluids flow with sephilococcus."

"There are such things as antirheumatoid collars, you know," I said. "I've been using one only recently, the very best. Of my own manufacture, by the way. They cost only two fermented cheeses. Manufacturer's price, for you."

As we chatted in this manner a man wearing a white suit approached us. He hesitated a moment before addressing me: "Señora Carrington?"

"Yes," I answered, somewhat surprised that a stranger should know who I was. The man handed me a packet some ten inches by thirty in size. "It's the National Lottery prize. You won it with the number XXXccc. I congratulate you, Señora Carrington."

After thanking him, I opened the packet carefully. He disappeared into the shadows with a little bird's laugh, which I did not like.

We soon discovered that the packet contained an India rubber casket, fit for a very small child.

"What practical use this prize may serve escapes me," said Federal District. Popocatepetl, however, examined it carefully through his lorgnette and announced: "It could serve very well as a table for our picnic lunch." True enough: it would be a good idea to keep our picnic off the humid ground of the cemetery.

While we ate, however, we became more and more conscious of a disagreeable odour emanating from the diminutive casket. We had scarcely finished eating when my companions tendered their excuses and made off, leaving me with the picnic leftovers and the India rubber casket. On the outskirts of our sad savage town, I was overcome by a feeling of profound melancholy, though I fought it off by stuffing a large amount of jasmine essence up my nose. Fear kept me from opening my prize packet. I simply went on staring at it for a long time. I felt an uncertainty and a degree of anxiety that seemed to emanate from the ancient graves of the cemetery itself. It was as if the anguish was not properly mine, but something from out of that distant twentieth century of dread repute.

I don't know how long I was prey to these sensations. But suddenly I heard again the same tiny bird's laugh and, looking around, I could make out the white silhouette of the person who'd handed me the India rubber casket. His face was so shrouded in haze I couldn't make out his features, but his voice sounded right beside my ear: "Go ahead and open it. Why hold back?"

With no will of their own, my hands lifted the rubber

cover embellished with lily-of-the-valley designs—only to find another box made of that ancient substance that once used to be called plastic. I would have liked to desist in my task, but continued to obey the voice of the white individual and with a dexterity of their own, my hands succeeded in opening the rose-coloured box. What I saw caused me to stare with a mixture of wonder and fear. It was a human corpse more or less the size of a toothbrush. The homunculus boasted an enormous moustache. It was marvellously preserved, probably by some method known once to the inhabitants of the Amazon jungle. I realized that this little body had been larger in real life, but still not as large as the average man today. My eyes were drawn to an inscription on the inner side of the cover: "Joseph Stalin. A.D. 1948. Received on the occasion of her birthday by Queen Elizabeth the Second of England, who sent it as a Christmas present to Dwight Eisenhower, USA, who sent it to the National Museum of Mexico in commemoration of Saint Light and Power, canonized in 1958 by the Vatican. *Quia Nobis Solis Artem per nos solo investigatam tradimus et non aliis.*" Had this doll perhaps been a contemporary of Saint Rasputin, a noble at the court of the Tsar of Russia? With growing excitement I examined the letters of the inscription preceding the name of that Eisenhower. Another Russian perhaps? Doubtless the letters USA had been correctly translated by Haughty Corner in her thesis as "United Self-Annihilation." Just as USSR stood for (according to the same authority) "United Solo Sepulchre Regression." Perhaps this is a phrase from the ritual of the Catholic Church or something of the sort? I could not understand the Latin phrase very well, of course, but I surmised that it had something to do with the desiccated mannikin. Who knows but that he might have been a dwarf who served as court fool?

While these romantic notions were passing through my mind, the man in white approached closer and said: "Nowadays all initiates are aware of the dark ages when the world was empty and could not count on the gods. Divine spirits manifested themselves on earth only after the unmentionable catastrophe filled the entire planet with horror. This relic from those ill-fated times possesses medicinal value too. Ground into a powder with a few drops of marigold oil, and some royal poinciana seeds, it yields a valuable salve for the treatment of Depression No. 20. It is also useful in certain exercises of light levitation. We all know that Western medicine includes a branch of benign poisons, good for curing certain pathological conditions."

He proceeded to pluck one of the long hairs from the moustache of the mannikin and place it delicately in my mouth. I noted a sardine taste that made me shiver: twentieth-century druggists promoted odd practises. I suddenly felt invaded as if by a divine light that whispered: "Aspirin was like this." I fainted.

When I came to the man in white had disappeared, and I was left with the homunculus of the Tsar in the India rubber casket.

It's scarcely necessary to add that the tiny mannikin allowed me to found what today is the leading pharmaceutical establishment in the entire city. Naturally imitations and falsifications abound, but the authentic "Apostalin" is one of the country's leading exports. It is useful in the treatment of

Whooping cough
Syphilis
Grippe
Childbearing
and other convulsions.

Though not exactly rich, I enjoy ease and tranquillity, everything I need, and whatever is required for an agreeable and distinguished life.

—Translated from the Spanish
by Anthony Kerrigan

My Mother Is a Cow

Our family is modest, my mother is a cow. Or rather, my mother is a cow-faced fan. Who is she? And does she also live behind her fan-self? A face before a face before a . . . who am I to say? We ask, here, who are you? She laughs, but receives offerings of a kind. We call her Holy One if we know her. But we are very few.

Our small sanctuaries are empty, containing only my Mother's horned face. Each of us gives what we have to offer. The offerings are returned to human beings as small truths, great truths, medium truths, or quite often as lies and fibs. It all depends on what we do with them. The offerings in the first place are quite devious: tears and honey, shrieks and tobacco, burning resin, chocolate, white nights.

Red ochre, whitewash, and soot.

My purpose, however, is to tell how I went to question her and what she replied. This is what happened.

For years I have been a prisoner of the people of the set

now called the Watchers. These great hypnotists have no idols, their magic is powerful and their appetite insatiable. They thrive on misery, but have great delicacy in choosing their victims. They evoke compassion but have none themselves. They possess unlimited knowledge but have no understanding, and this gives them the power of absolute, concentrated hate.

And so,

When I was captured they called me Sin. They had forgotten that Sin was the name of a Goddess they had murdered.

Sometimes I remembered, sometimes I forgot. I suffered intensely.

This suffering produced a particular sort of food for them, which I mistook for a vitamin. I thought that if I gave enough they would stop picking at my lunar plexus and be satisfied, and perhaps richer?

This of course was not so. I became progressively sicker.

I called my Mother's horned image and asked if she wished my death, and if not, to provide a cure.

She said her disused sanctuary should be consecrated again, but the doors should be closed, the new entrance spiral. Spiral, she said, like the umbilical ladder out of the human body; this, she added, is very holy. As long as the doors are closed you will be safe and I shall not leave you, she said.

I did exactly what I had been told. The Watchers allowed the consecration after I paid six gallons of salted blood.

A sailor from Ulysses' ship, who had been a hero, was also a captive of the Watchers. They had made him a chartered accountant, but his memory was unimpaired. He remembered how my aunt had turned him into a pig for a joke, how her daughters the Sirens had wanted to make love to him because the dolphins seemed impotent compared to the beautiful sailor. He was still angry, although wars, at that time, were close enough to nature for enemies to love each other. So we became friends under the hungry observation of the Watchers. This sailor remembered our small, empty sanctuaries from the past. Never, never open the doors, he said, or you will be in danger. He had my welfare in mind.

His own small sanctuary was hermetically sealed, but the price had very nearly cost him his life; I had paid only six gallons of salted blood.

This is just how things stood when a certain combination of stars produced events where the presence of the Gods became directly discernible to certain human beings: those who took part in the dance, and others.

I took part and got bitten in the stomach by a man-eating shark disguised as Harlequin.

Every mistake we make in these dances must be turned into a question, otherwise they are fatal to our human condition.

The sailor who was watching the dance from the bar was horrified at my clumsy gavort and told me that at least my leg would get broken. He refused to join the dance. It had happened all too often, he said. I believed he was ashamed for me, since from the very first he had seen the Harlequin as a shark.

I could only tell him it was not a real shark. I don't know if the sailor understood me as I kept leaving the gavorting herd to tell him the following: that the ways of my horned mother were strange. Since she had chosen to make me dance again, I could not do otherwise. "The more ignorant we are the closer we participate. But I have asked questions before, and so I know I am dancing."

The sailor said: "Leave now, or you will probably break your neck."

I went on dancing in my grotesque disguise, but not before I told him: "I am lonely and miserable but I am wearing my last skin. Since you are almost face to face with the Gods do not abandon me." In human language, this is called love.

Then I danced again on my burning feet, which became heavier and heavier until I was prancing like a cart horse on bleeding stumps.

Then I made a wrong turn in the dance and the Watchers

dressed in executioner purple stepped quietly into the whirling mob and put me in solitary confinement on a diet of putrefied shark meat.

After I made my false step I presented myself to the Horned Goddess. Her sanctuary was desecrated, the doors wide open, the floor covered with shark droppings, the hallows strewn around in chaos.

My misery was so bitter that I was unable to handle the sacred broom. I stayed all night in the sanctuary, crying bitterly and imploring the presence of my Mother, who had withdrawn.

Here I sit, Holy One, in all my abandoned misery. Let me disintegrate in this most horrible suffering.

Still the Goddess was absent.

I cried and threatened and pleaded and tried to dash my brains out on the wall. Only at sunrise did I remember that I had asked no question. So I washed my hideously decomposed face and presented myself once more before the Horned Image.

Why am I human? I asked.

Now the Goddess has no mouth, no tongue, no vocal cords. Her presence defies description but is absolute. Therefore I must pretend the following communication was in human speech.

This was her reply: To be one human creature is to be a legion of mannequins. These mannequins can become animated according to the choice of the individual creature. He or she may have as many mannequins as they please. When the creature steps into the mannequin he immediately believes it to be real and alive and as long as he believes this he is trapped inside the dead image, which moves in ever-increasing circles away from Great Nature. Every individual gives names to his mannequins and nearly all these names begin with "I am" and are followed by a long stream of lies.

I asked: What is the use of these mannequins, Holy One?

The Goddess said: Human beings could never communicate with each other if there were no mannequins, they could only unite in lovemaking or fighting in their bodies of flesh, blood, and bone. Through the mannequins they can talk to each other, hypnotize each other, dominate each other, and in fact indulge in all the titillating activities, including suffering, happiness, esthetic enjoyment, self-importance, politics and football, etc.

And I asked her: What is suffering?

And she replied: Suffering is the death or disintegration of one or more of these mannequins. However, the more dead mannequins a creature leaves behind, the nearer she or he comes to leaving the human condition forever. The only trouble is that when a being is obliged to abandon the invented presence of a disoccupied mannequin, he or she is quite often busy again building bigger and better mannequins to live in.

Then all mannequins are vampires?

The Goddess said: Mannequins are like the Great Cabalistic Pentagon called Death impregnated with life, which whirls eternally through the twelve houses.

How can I leave the circle, Holy One?

When you die, you step out of the circle.

How can I step out of the circle with no feet? I asked. The Goddess was pleased with such a malicious question, and her laughter was like rain on the roof of my head. You must knit yourself a body with spider yarn, she said.

Of course I had realized this long ago, but had been woefully wasting my yarn on more and more mannequins.

So bit by bit I pulled back the strands and now as I sit, I am spinning again, as the Greek sailor predicted.

Here I sit in the ziggurat, knowing that I danced because that was the only way of killing another mannequin whose name was "I am still rather attractive and I will die if I don't get some human love. Everybody needs to be loved no matter how old they are. Besides, if I dance fast enough I might even become liberated from the Watchers."

The Horned Goddess, contrary to all expectation, arose again with the sun.

But why am I human, Holy One? What have I done to deserve this?

Human means written in flesh, the word is pain and pain and pain again—

Who was The Witch of Nazareth?

A Hieroglyph written in Blood which makes sense if the story starts with the Crucifixion and is read progressively backwards—The Christ-man was stripped of his father on the cross.

Then there is no learning?

There is none. Understanding is only that which is written in living, primary matter. The primary shadowless beings are letters that make words you can't read. Their condition is constant suffering because they're naked and skinless. Their bloodstream is without defence.

Who are they?

Those who no longer pretend to know who they are.

Judith

Characters:
Judith, a widow whose weeds are a garden of crêpe.
Issachar, her great bearded father.
Gibeon, a chair and a castrated ram.
Esrom, pretending to the hand of Judith.
Barbaroth, a scorpion.

Scene: The alcove tent or boudoir of Issachar, faint through the dense smoke of a stove upon which a pot is boiling. A dust storm rages in the desert; it is now dusk. Judith is singing to a skin instrument. She is invisible; only Esrom and Gibeon the chair can be seen. Esrom is very pale, and Gibeon looks dead.

JUDITH'S VOICE To Shiloh put a moonless night that my love comes home again,

> O faceless sweet and singing bird, I know not if
> your voice be heard
> In my heart or in the night or in my night's
> heart darkest own.
> Sweet and faithless bird, fly home.

ESROM Judith, I am here.

(A pause.)

JUDITH Esrom?

ESROM Esrom.

(Judith appears, veiled.)

ESROM Judith, I have returned, I could not wait . . .

JUDITH A week too early. I have decided nothing yet. You promised you would stay away till the next new moon and the sky is still empty of her; besides you know why you went.

ESROM *(Making a snatch at Judith and missing by inches.)* Judith, I have come to take you home and marry you.

JUDITH Yes, that is what you said before you left.

ESROM Judith, I need you, I will give you the sons Salmon never gave you; you will be happy queen of my house, and I have your father's consent.

JUDITH Queen of your house, Esrom? And my father's consent? And Salmon still warm under those stones?

ESROM No longer warm.

JUDITH My father does not wish me to leave him, and if he gave his consent it was merely to quiet your persistence. In the great kindness of his heart he took pity on you. My father knows that I will not and cannot leave him, an old man alone with his chair.

ESROM You dream, Judith. Your father is old indeed, but eternally in his prime and quite strong enough to take seven young wives and get them all with child.

JUDITH You are tricked by his great beard and bull roaring. I will not leave him feeble and lonely with you as my master.

ESROM You do not love me, Judith.

JUDITH I love you well enough.

ESROM Not well enough.

JUDITH — 195

JUDITH Who am I to say "I love"? If Love in a cycle takes me along for a while, then must I say "I love"? Who is that?

ESROM Those are wild words, they have no meaning.

JUDITH And even less after we had been bedded for a year.

(*There is a commotion outside, and roaring.*)

ESROM (*awed*) Your father in clouds of dust; he comes like the desert.

JUDITH Yes, roaring and toothless. I will get his soup.

(*She retires and Issachar lurches in, bringing dust and wind. Shaking his great beard and heavy head.*)

ISSACHAR What, boy, back again so soon?

(*He claps Esrom heartily on the back, knocking him over the stove.*)

ESROM (*recovering his upright position*) Sir, I have returned, but Judith says too soon.

ISSACHAR Ha, too soon? Never too soon, my son, to take a wife?

ESROM Your daughter will not decide to return with me.

ISSACHAR (*sits heavily on Gibeon, who groans.*) Since when do decisions lie within the powers of women? I gave her to you three weeks ago and you went dawdling after wild geese where nothing grows; she would have gone well enough had you taken her then.

ESROM She would have me cross the river first to see what lay over there.

ISSACHAR (*a roaring which may come from within him but seems to come from under the seat.*) Did you cross the river?

ESROM (*afraid*) The boatman would not take me across so I stayed and gambled at the blind man's inn these three weeks.

ISSACHAR In my youth I would have struck you dead for doubting my word. Now, however, I merely call you a fool and repeat, by the seven hundred and seventh whisker on the right side of my beard, that beyond the river there is nothing, you hear, nothing whatever but bones, the bones of those who have crossed to their eternal death.

ESROM I hear you, Sir, and will never doubt again, but I desired your daughter and I would have pleased her so she would marry me.

ISSACHAR You fool, who ever got a woman by pleasing her? Take her and begone, and you owe me more than the three hundred head of fat sheep to which we agreed with wine in the stone cup. For indeed you owe me the right to breathe this dust-polluted air. When I suck the fat off the tails of your sheep, know that they will rest in the last male belly of this circle for many generations to come, for sheep became fish and fish crowing women with beards with salt water flowing out of them. Beware of the she-goat for, sotted with milk as you are when I am gone, remember me at least in your testicles.

ESROM Father, what terrible prophecy is this? God help me, my knees knock. What is that?

(*groaning and knocking from Gibeon the chair and a subterranean rumbling from some deep cave inside the earth.*)

ISSACHAR That is the rumbling and grumbling from my mighty paunch calling for its dinner. One belch of mine and you, soft and hairless maggot, would be blown across the river, and not for the asking of a woman.

ESROM Order your daughter to follow me and she will obey, Sir. Help me, I do implore you.

ISSACHAR (*with demonic laughter issuing from beneath his buttocks*) Rape her tonight, you fool, and carry her off.

ESROM Your guards would kill me if I entered the camp after midnight.

ISSACHAR Then hide yourself here, and when I have drunk wine and sleep you creep out and take her by force. Later you can tell her you put a sleeping draught in my wine. For this you can send me your three sisters with the sheep.

ESROM And all virgins.

(*He hides behind some hangings.*)

ISSACHAR Judith daughter, Judith slut, bring my supper.

(*enter Judith with soup and wine.*)

JUDITH You sent Esrom away, Father?

ISSACHAR He has gone. Sing to me.

JUDITH 197

(*Judith takes the skin instrument and sings:*)

JUDITH To Shiloh put this moonless night that my love comes home again,
> O faceless sweet and singing bird, I know not if your voice be heard
> In my heart or in the night or in my own heart's darkest night,
> Your voice perhaps mine own.
> Barbed eagle once when star we shared,
> Where right was left and left was right,
> Your blood ran in me, mine in yours,
> Then rocked upon the timeless curve
> Claimed by outer darkness, love,
> Apart we ran a sport of any wind
> And helpless hoped those winds would drive us home again.
> Luckless faceless bird, your voice I heard,
> Bend your fallow wings, return.

(*deep groaning from the chair, Gibeon.*)

GIBEON I am helpless, trapped, this weight is breaking my old wood.

JUDITH Who spoke?

ISSACHAR That was no more than the creaking of my old bones.

GIBEON Your father lies — hear me, Judith.

JUDITH Who spoke then, Father? That was not your voice.

ISSACHAR Each of my bones has a voice of its own, they creak. Fetch more wine.

(*She retires, looking anxiously over her shoulder.*)

GIBEON Issachar, you are a cunning old fox, but your time has come.

ISSACHAR Quiet or I will burn you for firewood.

GIBEON That you never will. I cannot move, but here I stay, Issachar, long after you have stunk and crumbled and mouldered into the sand. Prisoner that I am, a time will come when indeed my wood will turn to fire; that I find an honourable change. And when I burn, Issachar, my heart will run free like a roaring lion, you will indeed be ten. No, Issachar, you at least know better than to warm your soup with my fire.

ISSACHAR Horrible voice from a lump of dead wood. If at least you were a living tree, I could believe you to be some ghost. And what if I hacked you into splinters, would your voice be quiet?

GIBEON You know who I am, Issachar.

ISSACHAR How can I be rid of that voice already jeering at my corpse?

(*He rises and hunts around till he finds an axe, which he swings menacingly at the chair.*)

GIBEON Hit hard and straight, Issachar, free me, set me free.

ISSACHAR You lie, dead monster. Inanimate horror, if I split you apart your croaking would go with you.

GIBEON Well try then, Issachar, why do you wait? There are worms enough crawling inside me to sing a fine dirge over my splinters.

ISSACHAR Misery, where has this generation fallen that Issachar should be mocked by a chair?

(*Judith returns, carrying a jar of wine.*)

JUDITH Father, who was here? I heard you speak.

ISSACHAR You heard your own weak dreams, give me my cup.

(*He drinks deeply.*)

JUDITH I heard the dust and the wind rushing through the camp, but I heard a voice that was not yours. A voice I know, but long forgotten.

ISSACHAR (*goes and lies down on a low bed in the shadows; he is faintly visible through the dense smoke.*) Your rank widowness, your lonely bed, is making you mad. Black barren, childless and haunted with voices like a deserted cavern gnawed with rats. Is my name to die with a barren madwoman?

GIBEON What strange voices leak through all men's sleep and day's half. Night can prick a pointed ear at things unheard when we rub and chaff and chatter in her bright companion day.

JUDITH What again? I must be raving — there is no one here but

JUDITH

my father, who sleeps already drunk and snoring.

(*horrible guttural snoring from Issachar*)

GIBEON And when the griffon clacks her shining beak she answers, who am I? From whence do I come? And do I go, but where? She raves, but griffon's talk is raving, and if she drops some feathers to pick out a path to spiral tower, turn back, she raves, for here lies madness. Turn back — your right is to one half of the apple, but what is right and what is left, for who shall eat the other half?

JUDITH O my blood! From what hidden place in your sticky stream comes this voice? Now I am twisted with passion, now lust, now hunger, now terror, what is my name?

ESROM (*voice from behind the hangings*) Judith.

JUDITH No longer that, we are legion and cannot fit into a name.

ESROM Judith. (*emerges from behind the curtain*) Come to me.

JUDITH (*screams*) Now visions, I am falling into a hundred shapes and even yours.

ESROM Now I have waited long enough, will you come with me in love and peace?

(*He keeps creeping towards her.*)

JUDITH Thick and heavy, yet I do believe another fragile shape invading my staggering mind. Get gone.

ESROM Judith, do you love me? Come.

JUDITH No. Get gone.

ESROM I will have you anyhow or leave you dead. (*He grabs her arm but she wrenches free, leaving her shawl behind, and rushes into another part of the tent. Esrom follows, panting libidinously, knocking over objects on his way. They are both lost from sight and a presumable rape takes place, accompanied with bloodcurdling screams.*)

ISSACHAR (*rising heavily from the low bed*) If there was a soft place in me for pity, it would turn raw. But I am Issachar, the Man. Issachar, Issachar Knows Best for All and I will live in my daughter's sons and they will turn back and say Issachar, the Man!

(*enter Esrom, looking considerably dishevelled, he points a trembling finger at Issachar*)

ESROM It is done, and your daughter is the tomb of my manhood, for I will never look on a woman again without seeing her writhing face of hate, and her screams erase all other sounds from my ears. If I had never been born your tyranny would never have possessed me, and I, unnamed and free, would never have squeaked and twitched on a pin called Issachar.

ISSACHAR You weak-bellied thing that calls itself a man, you should still be creeping under the mud, for you do not yet belong upright on two legs; you should have six and ten joints to each, like the nerveless grubs that eke without thought under stagnant water.

(*Judith appears behind them, dressed like a dead queen of Ur. Subterranean bull roaring.*)

JUDITH Time is the cavern stables will render the roaring bulls who paid enough blood into the belly of this planet, and they will charge out of the deepest place beneath and carry the tide of the past before them into nothing. Golden calf, now turn and toss them on your horns which, greater now as the crescent moon, are rising again into time.

ESROM She raves and is mad. I cannot bear such a weight. Now indeed I will cross the river, miserable fish drowned in its own water. Yes, I will return to the mud which formed me into guilty meat.

(*He lurches out of sight, presumably to drown himself.*)

ISSACHAR I, Issachar, my Word is Law. Go with that man and bear his children, or my name will be lost.

JUDITH So that is what you wish? (*She picks up the hatchet and chops off his head. She commits a ritual dance carrying the bloody head by the hair.*)

GIBEON The Ram and the Fish abluted out of time with fire. Judith, I am their funeral pyre.

JUDITH Yes, voice. Only yours now to command.

(*Knocking and roaring from beneath, steadily increasing in volume. Judith places her father's head on the seat of the chair and lights a taper at the stove with which she sets fire to the hair of Issachar's head. A great burst of flame.*)

GIBEON Hark, time, I come.
(*A great roaring now, almost at the surface of the earth. Crackling of the fire and a sudden storm. Heavy rainfall.*)
JUDITH I am Silence and Gradiva's walk,
    I am the darkness of the Nile,
    I, the Sphinx's smile.
    I, hyena's love-shriek on a moonless night.
    The gold in honey and I, the breath of lions
    Slaughtered by Samson, time was.
    I, the jewel in Serpent's eye,
    And I who curdle the nightjar's cry,
    I ripple on the rising hairs of fear,
    Yet I, the single bitter tear
    Shed by Mother Isis on Osiris's bier.
(*Scorpio steps out of Gibeon's ashes.*)
SCORPIO Judith, I am your horse, now free again to lash heaven into froth with my jewelled and poisonous tail. Ride as one with Scorpio, we are centaur, griffon, Sphinx. With my sharp claws I'll rip a road through all the mealy angels of the firmament.
JUDITH My own true love, complete I'll ride at peace in the roaring heavens. I sprouting from your back, one beast, no longer mutilate.
SCORPIO Across the river the boat has come.
(*the shadow of a boat*)
JUDITH Lead on, our time too has come.
(*darkness; the howling of jackals*)

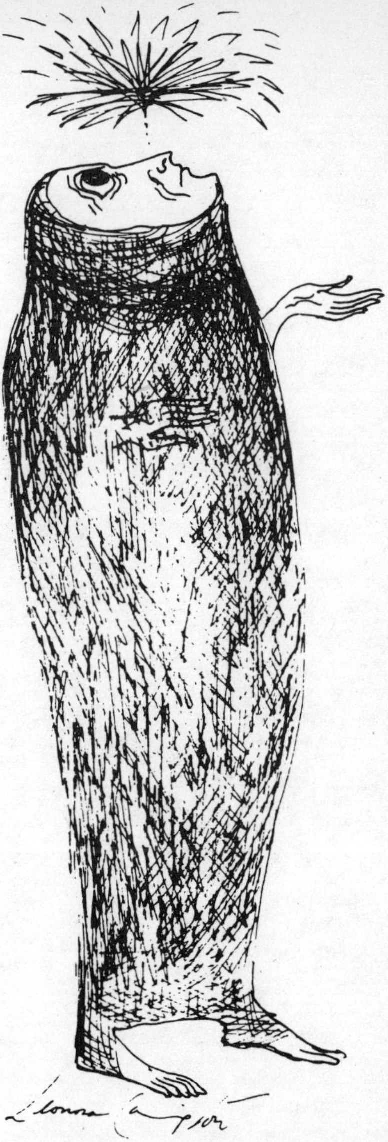

A Note on the Texts

The preceding tales were written over a period of some thirty years, and only some were composed with a view towards publication. For this volume the author reviewed and in some cases revised English-language and English-translation texts, and she prepared the shorter version of *The Stone Door* included here. Details of composition and publication are as follows:

"As They Rode Along the Edge." Written between 1937 and 1940, in French. First published as *"Quand Ils passait"* in the volume *Pigeon, Vole*, edited by Jacqueline Chenieux. Editions Le Temps Qu'il Fait, Cognac, France, 1986.

"The Skeleton's Holiday." Written in 1938 or 1939, in French, as part of a collaborative novel, *L'Homme qui a perdu son squelette* (*The Man Who Lost His Skeleton*), with Hans Arp, Marcel Duchamp, Paul Éluard, Max Ernst, Georges Hugnet, and Gisèle Prassinos. First published in *Plastique*, nos. 4–5, 1939.

"Pigeon, Fly!" Written between 1937 and 1940, in French. First published as *"Pigeon, Vole"* in *Pigeon, Vole*.

"The Three Hunters." Written between 1937 and 1940, in French. Previously unpublished.

"Monsieur Cyril de Guindre." Written between 1937 and 1940, in French. First published in *Pigeon, Vole*.

"The Sisters." Written in 1939, in French, as *"Les Soeurs."* First published in English translation in the journal *View*, nos. 11–12, New York, 1942. First French publication in *La Débutante*, Éditions Flammarion, Paris, 1978.

"Cast Down by Sadness." Written between 1937 and 1940, in French. First published in *Les Cahiers du double*, nos. 3–4, 1979.

"White Rabbits." Written in 1941, in New York. First published in *View*, nos. 9–10, New York, 1941–42.

"Waiting." Written in 1941, in New York. First published in the journal *VVV*, no. 1, New York, 1942.

"The Seventh Horse." Written in 1941, in New York. First published in *VVV*, nos. 2–3, New York, 1943.

The Stone Door. Written in the 1940s, in Mexico City. First published as *La Porte de pierre*, translated into French and edited by Henri Parisot. Éditions Flammarion, 1976. The completed, original English manuscript, reviewed by the author, from which this version derives, was published in 1977 by St. Martin's Press, New York.

"The Neutral Man." Written in the early 1950s, in Mexico City, in French, as *"L'Homme neutre."* First published in the review *Le Surréalisme, même*, no. 2, Paris, 1957.

"A Mexican Fairy Tale." Written in the 1970s, in Mexico City. First published in part, in French translation, in *Le Nouveau Commerce*, nos. 30–31, 1975.

"Et in bellicus lunarum medicalis." Written in Mexico City in the early 1960s, in Spanish. First published in the review *Snob*.

"My Flannel Knickers." Written in the 1950s in Mexico City. Previously unpublished.

"The Invention of Mole." Written in the early 1960s, in

A NOTE ON THE TEXTS

Mexico City, in Spanish, as *"La invención del mole."* First published in the review *Snob*.

"The Happy Corpse Story." Written in 1971, in Mexico City, in English. First published in French translation as *"Histoire de l'heureux fantôme"* in *Le Nouveau Commerce*, nos. 30–31, 1975.

"How to Start a Pharmaceuticals Business." Written in the early 1960s, in Mexico City, in Spanish, as *"De como funde una industria o el sarcófago de hule."* First published in the review *Snob*.

"My Mother Is a Cow." Written in the mid-1950s, in Mexico City. Previously unpublished.

"Judith." Written for Leonora Cardiff in Mexico City in 1961. Previously unpublished.

VIRAGO MODERN CLASSICS

The first Virago Modern Classic, *Frost in May* by Antonia White, was published in 1978. It launched a list dedicated to the celebration of women writers and to the rediscovery and reprinting of their works. Its aim was, and is, to demonstrate the existence of a female tradition in fiction which is both enriching and enjoyable. The Leavisite notion of the 'Great Tradition', and the narrow, academic definition of a 'classic', has meant the neglect of a large number of interesting secondary works of fiction. In calling the series 'Modern Classics' we do not necessarily mean 'great' — although this is often the case. Published with new critical and biographical introductions, books are chosen for many reasons: sometimes for their importance in literary history; sometimes because they illuminate particular aspects of womens' lives, both personal and public. They may be classics of comedy or storytelling; their interest can be historical, feminist, political or literary.

Initially the Virago Modern Classics concentrated on English novels and short stories published in the early decades of this century. As the series has grown it has broadened to include works of fiction from different centuries, different countries, cultures and literary traditions. In 1984 the Victorian Classics were launched; there are separate lists of Irish, Scottish, European, American, Australian and other English speaking countries; there are books written by Black women, by Catholic and Jewish women, and a few relevant novels by men. There is, too, a companion series of Non-Fiction Classics constituting biography, autobiography, travel, journalism, essays, poetry, letters and diaries.

By the end of 1989 over 300 titles will have been published in these two series, many of which have been suggested by our readers.

Also by Leonora Carrington

THE HOUSE OF FEAR:
Notes from Down Below

Introduction by Marina Warner

The book opens with the 1937 story, "The House of Fear", the summons to a voyage of initiations that Carrington would accomplish dramatically in both her life and art as she fled her Ango-Irish upbringing to elope with Max Ernst to Paris. It continues with five of her finest stories and a novella, the tale of a triangular love affair, "Little Francis", published for the first time in its original English. The volume concludes with "Down Below", Carrington's harrowing account of her descent into madness following Ernst's incarceration in a concentration camp during the Second World War. It is one of the most remarkable of all literary representations of the experience of madness.

Published with photographs of Carrington, her friends, lovers and family, with collages by Ernst and paintings by the author, *The House of Fear* is a classic of Surrealist literature, for "the landscape she travels remains a place enchanted" — Marina Warner

"Romantic heroines, beautiful and terrible . . . come back to life in women like Leonora Carrington" — *Octavio Paz*

Also of interest

EVERYTHING IS NICE:
The Collected Stories

by Jane Bowles
New Introduction by Paul Bowles

With her idiosyncratic combination of high style, comic acuity and disquieting strangeness, Jane Bowles captures those slips between the lines — the silences, alienations and uncomfortable juxtapositions — which comprise the dislocations of life. An awkward widow and her shy neighbour fall in love via silence and anger; an American traveller, caught in the shabby exoticism of a Guatemalan town, has an affair with his landlady; a small girl drills imaginary troops, but finds she can no longer command them when she makes friends with a young boy; and an Algerian woman carrying a porcupine in a basket insists that a European woman accompany her to a non-existent wedding. These and other tales create an atmosphere of surreal tragi-comedy, where the ordinary is bizarre and the grotesque is everyday.

"One of the finest modern writers of fiction in any language" — *John Ashbery, New York Times Book Review*

Jane Bowles (1917–1973) produced a small but remarkable body of work: a novel, *Two Serious Ladies,* the play *In the Summerhouse,* and the laconic, distinctive stories published here, including six fictional pieces discovered after her death, and three stories which have never before appeared in print.